I WAS A TEENAGE
WEREDEER

C.T. PHIPPS
&
MICHAEL SUTTKUS

I was a teenage weredeer. Specifically, I ceased to be a teenager as of eight o'clock that morning. I was an adult, eighteen years of age. I couldn't legally drink but I could vote and… Hmm, actually, that was pretty much it. I graduated from Bright Falls High School a year ago due to skipping my freshman year and started taking community college courses a month before.

So my birthday was less of a rite of passage than it might have been. Mind you, I was glad none of my family was making a big deal out of my birthday. Being a shifter meant you went through a lot of rites of passage, especially in my family. Your first change, your first antlers (thankfully, I didn't get those), when your Gift comes (mine was reading objects), and that thing that involved a sweat lodge I'm not looking forward to.

I was Jane, Jane Doe. Which, yes, was probably the least imaginative name you could come up for a girl you expected to be a weredeer. Then again, my father's name was John, and my mother's name was Judy. I had a sister named Jeanine and a brother named Jeremy. So, really, I should be grateful I lucked out and got the name most identified with anonymous female murder victims. Yes, could you tell I was bitter?

CHAPTER ONE

I was a teenage weredeer. Specifically, I ceased to be a teenager as of eight o'clock that morning. I was an adult, eighteen years of age. I couldn't legally drink but I could vote and... Hmm, actually, that was pretty much it. I graduated from Bright Falls High School a year ago due to skipping my freshman year and started taking community college courses a month before.

So my birthday was less of a rite of passage than it might have been. Mind you, I was glad none of my family was making a big deal out of my birthday. Being a shifter meant you went through a lot of rites of passage, especially in my family. Your first change, your first antlers (thankfully, I didn't get those), when your Gift comes (mine was reading objects), and that thing that involved a sweat lodge I'm not looking forward to.

I was Jane, Jane Doe. Which, yes, was probably the least imaginative name you could come up for a girl you expected to be a weredeer. Then again, my father's name was John, and my mother's name was Judy. I had a sister named Jeanine and a brother named Jeremy. So, really, I should be grateful I lucked out and got the name most identified with anonymous female murder victims. Yes, could you tell I was bitter?

I was busing tables at my mother's diner, the Deerlightful. It was a groan-worthy pun but far from the only one I'd had to deal with from my family. Most weredeer seemed to find them fascinating. My cousins owned the Deerly Beloved wedding supply, my uncle the Stag Party strip club, and my brother planned on opening a funeral home called the Deerly Departed. He was just dumb enough to believe this would fly.

The Deerlightful was a 1950s-style diner that fits in well with the fact Bright Falls was stuck in said decade. Well, aside from most of the townsfolk moving out and drugs replacing lumber as the primary source of employment. It was two in the afternoon, so the lunch crowd had left. It meant I had a chance to think in between busing tables.

Jeanine was cheerfully taking the order of two flannel-wearing lumberjacks at the end of the room as the song "Bad Moon Rising" by Creedence Clearwater Revival played in the background. My dad had thought it clever to make just about everything moon-related in our music selection. Other shifters in the town—and there were a lot— seemed to find it cute, so maybe there was something to it, but aside from this song and "Blue Moon" by Elvis, I wasn't a fan.

Jeanine was pretty much my opposite in appearance, being a tall and curvaceous curly-auburn-haired girl who resembled the weredeer ideal of beauty. I was thin, an A cup, and had flat black hair that I kept in a bowl cut. The fact that the Deerlightful's yellow uniforms were made for women quite a bit more, uh, well, *ample* didn't help my job. I'd said my mother shouldn't try to make her own daughters into Hooters waitresses, but she'd said I'd fill in. Not what you wanted to hear when you were seventeen.

Oh well, it was money for college and getting out of this one-Starbucks town. My dad pronounced it Star Bucks. Ugh. Hefting a bus box full of plates, I grumbled about the fact I could be writing my great American novel instead. It was a mystery-romance about my heroine caught between two handsome suitors in the unsettled seventeenth-century frontier. Alas, it was presently more *Twilight* than *Catcher in the Rye.* You could take the teenage weredeer out of the forest, but you couldn't take the forest out of the teenage weredeer.

"If at first you don't succeed, give up and decide to sell real estate," I grumbled aloud.

Jeanine called over to me. "Oh, Jane, would you do me a solid and take the rest of my shift? Brad and I are going on a date and I need to get ready."

I stared over at her and wondered if my older sister was actually just going to dump all of her work on me. Oh, right, of course she was. "Do I get your share of the tips?"

Jeanine frowned. "You know it is hard living away from Mom and Dad."

No, I didn't, because I couldn't afford to. "Sure, Sis, I will gleefully do even more work so you can mack with your incredibly rich boyfriend."

"Super!" Jeanine said, waving at me, then walked through the doors to the kitchen.

I stared at her then followed. "Clearly, sarcasm is not my strong point."

The Deerlightful kitchen was a single large room with a walk-in fridge, bathroom on the other side of the room, office for my mother, and a series of fridges as well as stoves. There was a calendar and bulletin board to my right, listing all the various messages my mother tended to get for her other job as the town shaman.

Jeanine was already skipping out the backdoor and I didn't have a chance to correct her misassumption about my volunteering to cover for her. I guess I was stuck with it. I looked for my mother, but didn't see anyone but Dad and Jeremy. Judy ran the Deerlightful while my father cooked. They were also weredeer or Cervid (I thought was a secret name for our kind until discovering it just meant "deer" in Latin) who'd married at eighteen in an arranged union. Both seemed cool with it and genuinely seemed to love each other.

Thankfully, John didn't seem too eager to follow in late Grandpa Jacob's plan to keep the bloodline pure and hadn't talked to me about any of that. John, a tall, broad-shouldered man with a brown mullet, was presently grilling three burgers while singing "Achy Breaky Heart". I swear, I could hear him call it 'Hart' in his inflection.

"And yet you do sarcasm so well," my brother, Jeremy, said from my side. He was currently doing a fresh load of plates in the sink.

Jeremy was more like me than my sister in that he was thin with short, dark hair. Jeremy was wearing a white apron over blue jeans and a House Baratheon t-shirt. He had a pained look on his face that never seemed to go away which had started when he hadn't made the Change by eighteen. That was two years ago, and given that I'd made it by fourteen, it was pretty clear he was never going to be a weredeer and was just an ordinary human. Personally, I didn't see the big deal, as it meant he didn't have to do the family runs every full moon, but I could tell it bothered the hell out of him.

"Yeah, you know me," I said, putting the bus box by the sink. "I'm always trying to bring a little dry hipster sarcasm to our lives."

Jeremy half smiled. "You realize being a hipster is a bad thing, right?"

"It is?" I asked.

"Yes." Jeremy nodded, sharing his sage wisdom of being two years older. Putting his arm over my shoulder, he said, "I'm afraid you have yet to realize you are not a sage source of post-modern ironic wisdom."

"I'm pretty sure those words don't actually mean anything when strung together," I said, smiling and hugging him back.

"It means that I, too, am studying Mr. Jameson's philosophy course," Jeremy said, referencing our shared desire to go to college and escape Bright Falls. The chances of either of us escaping my small Michigan hometown were pretty slim, though. In 2008, the vampires had done all the world's supernaturals a "favor" by coming out and revealing themselves to the world, which had resulted in all the others getting revealed in short order. While there were plenty of people who hated the undead for being blood-drinking parasites and almost, to the man, sociopaths, shifters actually got the worst of it.

Of forty-eight states—Michigan and Vermont exempted—if you were shot by someone then all they had to do was prove you were a shifter for it to be justified as self-defense. Also, it was entirely legal to discriminate against shifters in the marketplace, so if I ever were to leave town then my options were to go to Vermont or Canada, and that felt like a lateral move at best.

My cousin, Jill (God, what was it with the J names?), had moved to the newly revitalized Detroit, but that meant she was in the power of the vampires. Plus, she was a stripper and while that was her choice, it wasn't a career path I wanted or was equipped for. I was going to try to find somewhere other than the shifter capital of Michigan to live, but that was going to take more than the education provided by Bright Falls Community and Technical.

"Well, I suppose I should be grateful for the work," I said, muttering under my breath. "It nicely avoids my parents having to pay for my college. Keep it all in the family. Specifically the money."

"Hey, maybe she'll marry Brad and then his family will eat her and we'll collect a big insurance payout," Jeremy said cheerfully.

I chuckled. "Yeah, I don't think so. We can't afford the insurance and the O'Henry family owns the insurance company."

The O'Henry family was one of the twelve shifter clans in the town, and by far the most powerful. They were actually powerful on a national level, with lobbyists in Washington working on shapeshifter rights (badly) and rich enough to own a senator or two. The fact that they chose to live in Bright Falls to lord over the few thousand shifters here rather than someplace nice told me everything I needed to know about them.

"It's a dog-eat-dog world with them," Jeremy said.

"Hey, some of them are nice," I said, thinking about my friend Emma. "I mean, there's Lucien, the town drug dealer, Sheriff Clara, who hates me, and…uh, nope, can't think of any others."

"Victoria is hot," Jeremy said.

"Ugh," I said, thinking about her and trying not to let my blood boil. "Talk about a woman needing a silver bullet."

Victoria O'Henry was my own personal *Mean Girl* archnemesis and one of the chief reasons I was glad to have graduated from high school. She was a year older than me and one of the worst people I'd ever met. Werewolves were pack hunters and she'd assembled a little gang of her cousins around her to rule the school. The fact that her Gift had turned out to be able to learn people's deepest, darkest secrets had made her the terror of Bright Falls as a whole. The fact I'd been best friends with her sister Emma growing up made her desire to ruin my life doubly strange, but I guess Victoria didn't want her sister crossing the predator/prey divide. Now Brad and Jeanine were seeing each other, which meant we might become sisters-in-law. Yikes.

"You shouldn't say that sort of thing," John said, turning his head to look at us. "The O'Henrys are like royalty."

I rolled my eyes. "Dad, it's the twenty-first century. No one actually takes the whole royalty thing seriously anymore."

"We do in this house," John said, his voice low. "If they're not royals then we're not shamans."

That was another thing about shifter culture that annoyed the hell out of me. Every one of the twelve clans had a specific role assigned to them. The werewolves were the rulers, the weredeer were the shamans, the werebears were the guards, and so on. It was like any other caste system in that the modern world had left it behind, but there were shifters, like my dad, who took it way too seriously.

"Mom's a shaman, you're a short-order cook," Jeremy said, saying more than he probably should have.

Dad stood still for a second and I thought he was going to blow up. "You just keep doing your job, son, and focus on what making a connection with your true self."

That was even worse because John was the only member of the family who still thought Jeremy had a chance of changing. I understood why Dad wanted it to be so: he was the one who believed most in the Old Ways, the old religion, and it was a stinging cut to know he didn't have enough of a Gift to be a priest. But to sire a human? Someone without any Gift at all? That was bad. Made worse because I knew Dad loved Jeremy best. It sucked, but it was true.

"That's it," Jeremy said, pulling off his apron. "I'm gone. You can find someone else to do your damn dishes."

"Jeremy—" Dad started to say before noticing the hamburgers were burning. "Dammit!"

I sighed and watched Jeremy walk away before looking to Dad. "Please tell me you don't expect me to do the dishes."

"I'll do them," John said, sighing as he started over the burgers again, tossing the burned ones into the trash. "I mean what I said about talking smack about the royals, though. They're dangerous."

I blinked and sighed. "What, is Victoria going to have my head cut off?"

John turned around and crossed his arms. "That's not so farfetched an idea. You've grown up in a time when the supernatural was public. In my day, though, they had the power of life and death over their subjects."

"Which is creepy," I said, looking out to the restaurant beyond and seeing if we had any new customers. Thankfully, we didn't. It was a slow Thursday. "In any case, I've hated on Victoria for years and she hasn't had my head cut off yet."

"Yet," John said. "The royals still have all their old authority. They don't use it often, but most of the other clans respect it."

"Dad…"

"Just cut it out with the silver-bullet threats. Please."

Seeing my dad was serious, I sighed and nodded my head before going to get a pad to take orders. That was when I heard thunder outside and my ears perked up. There was something in the air that made me uncomfortable and I couldn't quite put it into words. Closing my eyes, I saw a storm coming and felt a terrible *thing* was coming. I'd only had that kind of impression of the future a few times, one of which had been right before the vampires had revealed themselves and the subsequent violence.

All weredeer had the Sight, just varying degrees of it, with Dad having the ability to sense absolutely nothing more than his next dinner while my mother was able to see things years in the future as well as talk to the animals like Doctor Doolittle. I was somewhere in the middle and could pick up impressions from objects as well as get visions of the future on occasion. Knowing something bad was going to happen didn't give me a way to stop it, though, and my stomach turned a bit.

Should I tell my father? Tell him what—I have a bad feeling about this? My mother? Maybe. "Dad, where's Mom?"

"Off," John said.

"Off?" I asked.

"Off," He repeated. "Shaman things."

"Oh joy," I said, knowing that meant she could be anywhere from the middle of the woods to selling scented candles at a party.

I went back to work instead.

As Jeanine's and my shift finally came to an end, I was pretty tired on my feet and debated going out back to change so I could regain my energy. A rainstorm had already been going for the better part of an hour, though, so I didn't want to. You'd think being part-wild animal I wouldn't mind getting wet, but it turned out weredeer really resented thunderstorms.

Heading to punch my time card—weird with a mostly family business—I watched the backdoor open up and my soaked best friend run through the door. Emma O'Henry was about six inches taller than me and gorgeous in the same way my sister was, except with bright-crimson-red hair.

Emma was wearing a pair of cut-off jean shorts and an open flannel shirt over a House Stark shirt my brother had given her. A little silver locket was hanging around her neck in the shape of a wolf. I, personally, had never seen the need to advertise my animal type to the world. I was about to greet her warmly when I noticed she looked horrified. Her makeup was smeared and her eyes teary.

I blinked. "What's wrong?"

My father looked over at us. "Are you okay, Emma?"

Emma grabbed me in a hug. "It's terrible. I came here right away."

"Eh?" I said, wondering why I was the crisis person all of a sudden before remembering my earlier bad feeling. "What's happened?"

"My sister has been murdered. They're looking at your brother."

Okay.

Crap.

CHAPTER TWO

I took a moment to process what she was saying. "What?"

My father looked like he was about to explode before his cellphone rang and he checked it. Picking it up, he started talking. "Judy? Yes, I just heard from Emma. I'll be right down to the station."

"The sheriff's office?" I asked stupidly. I was too gobsmacked by the news to react.

"Can you close down the store?" John asked and didn't wait for my reaction before grabbing his keys and jacket then heading out the door.

"Uh…" I started to say, then took a deep breath.

Emma gave me another hug. "This is awful."

I pushed her away. "Oh hell no, you don't get to say your family is accusing my brother of murder and then give me hugs. This isn't a dented car."

"Victoria is dead!" Emma said, looking about ready to burst into tears again and I felt like crap for pushing her away.

It took a second to orient my brain and process the information that had flooded it in the past few seconds. My brother was many things, but he wasn't a killer. Hell, he'd probably have trouble taking me in a fight, and not just because weredeer were surprisingly strong even in human form. He was a weird introverted goth kid who hung around with a bunch of losers while talking shit about the royals and, oh my god, I just explained why he was a suspect. No, it couldn't be that easy, could it?

"I'm sorry," I said, giving Emma a hug and patting her on the back as I tried to muster up any sort of sympathy for Victoria O'Henry. All I could think about was the time she'd blabbed to the entire school how

Lisa Marsh of the abstinence league was actually a lesbian, causing her to try to overdose on pills. Thankfully, she'd gotten the help she needed and her parents had done a one-eighty on being bigoted assholes.

Emma pulled away, sniffing. "Listen, I know you didn't always get along—"

"No, it's cool," I said, pushing down my feelings. "Victoria was a human being and a shifter. Also, your family. But you have to understand, I'm not worried about that right now. Why do they think Jeremy killed her?"

He only had a job because our parents owned the place, but that was far from the kind of person who would kill somebody. I mean, yeah, he wore a lot of black and had a bad attitude, but that was a red herring in mystery fiction. I mean, he barely knew Victoria, right? She was my archnemesis rather than his.

Emma grabbed a couple of napkins off the countertop then wiped off her face. "He was the one who found the body and they were seeing each other."

Mind blown.

I blinked. "Jeremy was seeing *Victoria*?"

"Yeah," Emma said, looking down at the ground. "For a few months now. I was looking for the right time to tell you."

"How about never," I muttered.

Emma frowned.

"Sorry!" I said. "Still letting all of this sink in."

Both my siblings had a major love for the O'Henrys, it seemed. Then again, Emma was my bestie, so maybe there was a weird predator-and-prey thing going on.

"They were keeping it secret," Emma said, her voice changing in pitch as if she couldn't quite manage her emotions. "Father doesn't approve of inter-clan relationships. He just barely tolerated Brad and Jeanine's because he was still negotiating a proper marriage for him."

Ouch. Well, that was going to put a crimp on my sister's plans for becoming Mrs. O'Henry. Marcus O'Henry owned Bright Falls and nothing happened in the city without his say-so, even marriages between shapeshifters. Wait, what was I talking about? I needed to focus on what was important. "Why did you come to me, though?"

If it was just because we were friends and she needed my help, I would be there for her. Still, I needed to get the diner shut down and join my father down at the sheriff's office. Clara O'Henry was going to throw the book at my brother. She was the "hanging judge" of the town, even if she wasn't a judge, and worse, she'd just found out her niece had been killed. If I were her, I'd want to strangle the first person who looked guilty.

"I came to you because you know things," Emma said, taking a deep breath.

"Know things?" I repeated. "Oh, you mean my Gift?"

"Yes!" Emma said. "You can figure out anything. I once saw you deduce who was cheating on whom at the homecoming dance just by looking at everyone's pictures with their date."

That had actually just been guesswork. Though, admittedly, I had turned out to be right with everyone. "You want me to use my psychometry? To what, solve Victoria's murder?"

"I know your brother would never hurt anyone, especially Victoria! I was hoping you'd help me solve her murder so we can make sure her soul rests in peace."

"Her ghost," I said, stunned by her request. "I'm not a police officer, Emma. I pick up things like spitting in my coffee and money troubles. I don't know anything about solving real-life crimes."

Psychic and magical examinations of evidence were inadmissible in court due to the fact they still hadn't worked out a way to separate the frauds from the real deal with most supernaturals. Vampires and werewolves turning into animals were easy to regulate, you could see that, but things like my Gift weren't one hundred percent accurate.

For example, I'd seen myself dating Bobby Horne because I'd desperately wanted to. My vision "felt" right and it had turned out the only thing he'd wanted from me was sex in the backseat of his car. Not my finest hour as a soothsayer. Not even hiding his five hundred-dollar leather jacket in the woods had made me feel better.

Emma gave me a wide-eyed puppy stare. "Please."

"Okay," I said, taking a deep breath. "Wait, you really want me to read her corpse or something?"

"Or her car keys or something," Emma said, shrugging. "Isn't that what you do?"

Technically, Emma was correct, but that wasn't something I'd ever relied upon in order to solve a murder. I could pick up impressions of objects and the emotions of those who last held them, but I didn't want to feel whatever psycho had killed Victoria.

Still, my brother was in trouble. "I'll do it."

"Super," Emma said, hugging me for a third time.

I hugged her back. "It'll be all right. I promise."

I didn't have any platitudes or sympathy to give her. I was supposed to be a shaman-in-training for the Cervid clan, but I didn't know much about the afterlife, souls, or how to counsel people. If my mother was here, she would have not only described the Underwood but named each and every ancestor that would come to greet Victoria.

I'd never been particularly religious and the whole concept was a bit beyond me. I believed in gods, ghosts, and spirits because my family did—not because I had any real attachment to them. My brother had called me a meh-theist. I preferred 'part-time spiritual.'

Emma pulled away and looked guilty for a second. "I'm sorry about your brother too."

"Nothing permanent has happened to him," I said, looking at the door. "I hope. Will you help me shut this place down?"

"Sure," Emma said, taking a deep breath.

I bit my lip, trying to figure out how to ask my next question. "I hate to ask this, but do you know anything about when this all happened?"

"Not much," Emma said, thankfully not taking offense. "She was found in Bright Falls Woods a few hours ago."

"Why the hell would they think my brother was involved?" I said, looking at her. "I mean, aside from the fact he was carrying on with Victoria?"

I managed to just barely suppress a horribly mean remark: *Which goes to show he has no taste.* I still hadn't quite adjusted to the fact Victoria

12

was dead and never coming back. I'd hated her, but I didn't want her dead. Hell, I didn't want anyone dead, save maybe those jackasses in Washington who called for shifters to be banned from human schools and registered like sex offenders. Those were the moderates too.

"He's the one who found the body," Emma said, taking a deep breath. "Also, she died last night, at a time when he didn't have an alibi."

I tried to think about what my brother was doing for most of the night and realized I had no idea. He was two years older than me and barely spent any time at home anymore. Most of the time he slept over at friends' houses or stayed at the family cabin. It was frustrating, as I would have lied for him in an instant. Weird that I felt good about realizing that. It made me know I valued my family to the point of criminal behavior.

"Damn," I said, hoping the sheriff didn't have anything more.

Emma looked guilty. "I'm sorry, I couldn't find out more, but Clara didn't even talk to me. She was too busy riding herd on my grandfather and aunts. Aunt Alice is preparing a press statement so it doesn't reflect on the family."

"What about your parents?" I asked. They were both lawyers whose only clients were the O'Henry family. Sort of like the mob.

"Dad is in Washington," Emma said, frowning. "He didn't take the news well when he heard it, and he assaulted someone in wolfman form. They're currently holding him in prison. Thankfully, Washington D.C. isn't a varmint state, and he's offered the cops a lot of money to let him go. He should be back tomorrow."

"Go bribery," I said, sympathetic. "What about your mom?"

"Rebecca took a bunch of pills and is sleeping off a bottle of gin," Emma said, scrunching up her nose. "She'll let grandfather handle the investigation and funeral."

Yikes.

Emma and I came from fundamentally different families. Not just because I was from the middle class and she was the kind of girl who would carry around a dog in a purse if not for the fact it was probably a relative. Her family just didn't operate the same way mine did. There was some care and love in Emma's family, but on a very real level, they were strangers. I was honestly glad Victoria had someone to stick up for her post-mortem.

"Yeah, well," I said, looking at the kitchen. "Let's get to work."

It took longer than I wanted to get everyone out of the Deerlightful and shut everything down, especially those people who weren't going to get their meals but we did it. Honestly, I hated the fact I was being treated this way by my family. I wanted to be there with Jeremy too, in part so I could find out what the hell he was thinking dating Victoria, but only after we'd cleared his name and found the real culprits.

Heading out the backdoor to the parking lot, I looked at the remaining cars in the lot and saw two. The first was a bright-red Ferrari that was a couple of years old but Emma still thought it wasn't an impressive graduation Gift. The second was the Millennium Falcon, which was what I called my old busted-up green 2001 Hummer. I'd gotten the Falcon as a hand-me-down when poor old Grandpa Jacob had died. Well, not so poor, as the Old Buck had been ninety-seven but looking sixty-five. He'd died because his heart had given out during an intimate situation I'd really rather not have known about.

"Let's take your car!" Emma said cheerfully.

I stared at her. "You're serious?"

"It's awesome!" Emma said, clapping her hands like a little girl. "You know, because it's safe and all. Because if a car hit it, that other car would be trashed."

I stared at her. "It gets about a mile to the gallon and I only drive it between here, school, and home. Everything else I walk or take the bus. You, by contrast, drive a Ferrari. If it's about driving, I totally wouldn't mind doing so."

"It's so different from the kind of car my family drives! It's roomy!"

"It's different because it's twenty years old!" I snapped.

"Please!" Emma's sad-puppy face was irresistible.

"Okay, fine, we can take my car." I sighed. There was something weird about the way Emma seemed to see things I owned (because I couldn't afford better) as inherently cooler than things that her money could buy.

"Thanks," Emma said, frowning. "I don't like driving around in mine today."

"Why?"

"It was Victoria's Sweet Sixteen present before Dad got it replaced because she wanted a white one."

Sometimes there were no words. I was about to get into the driver's seat when I heard a voice nearby. "Hey, Jane, wait a minute."

I grimaced and looked over to see a lanky, gray-hoodie-wearing nineteen-year-old with pale skin and raven-black hair. He wasn't bad looking, but there was something about Rudy Stone that made me uncomfortable. He was my brother's best friend and someone I'd thought was just a human being until his sister had spontaneously developed the power to be a wereraven.

"I'm kind of busy now, Rudy," I said, not at all happy to have him present.

Everyone had that friend of their siblings they felt was a bad influence or just bothered them. In Rudy's case, it was because the guy was an enormous creep. In addition to being addicted to drugs that seemed a good deal harder than pot, I once caught him trying to plant a camera in the girls' locker room. Jeremy hadn't believed me and it had led to our only serious fight. It was hard enough to believe he'd be interested in Victoria, but I just flat out did not understand his friendship with Rudy.

"Is it true Jeremy killed Victoria?" Rudy said, walking up.

"No, he's innocent," I said, glaring at him. "As you should know."

"If he did kill her, it was justified," Rudy said, smiling. "Victoria was a bitch."

Emma growled and walked toward him. "You piece of—"

I grabbed her by the arm. "He isn't worth it, Emma."

"You should smile more, Jane," Rudy said. "You might finally get a boyfriend if you did."

I stared at him. "Are you literally every douchebag cliché rolled into one?"

"It's a bad moon," Rudy said, pointing to me then Emma. "A very bad moon. You need to watch yourself."

Rudy then turned around and walked away, raising his hoodie and sticking his hands in his pockets.

"What the hell was that?" I asked.

Emma shrugged. "Drugs, maybe?"

"I'll never understand the appeal," I said, sighing.

Emma looked guilty. "Let's just get to the sheriff's office."

CHAPTER THREE

The Millennium Falcon managed to make it to the sheriff's office, a one-story brown building in the middle of town that looked like a post office. I'd been here a couple of times before due to my stupid brother's antics as well as the fact my father had once been busted for drinking too much at the Fourth of July party then scaring off some tourists with his antlers. Totes embarrassing. I think I'm using "totes" right. There's not really a cool crowd in Bright Falls for me to learn from.

"Do you really think we're going to be able to get access to Victoria's body?" I asked, less than pleased at the idea of touching the body of someone who'd died. I wasn't even sure it would work despite the fact a body was an object rather than a person.

"Of course," Emma said cheerfully as she hung her head out the window and let her tongue hang out.

"That's weird," I said, pulling into a parking space in the lot beside the building. "You're a wolf, not a dog."

"Not much of a difference," Emma said calmly. "In my wolf form, I can talk to them too. I can also understand coyotes."

"Where did you meet a coyote?" I asked. They existed in Michigan but I'd never seen one.

"Out west," Emma said, pulling her head back in. "Grandpa took us to a big mesa for some sort of werewolf spiritual retreat thing. It was also a place he wanted to make arrangements for marriages and establish the inheritance line for our clan."

"Right," I said, sighing. "I'm sorry, I'm not a big fan of this shifter stuff. Still, are you okay? I mean, your sister just died, so if you need time—"

"I'm trying not to think about it," Emma said, her expression changing instantly. "I'm thinking about everything from *Star Wars* to boys to girl stuff. Anything to get my mind off of this. I can't think about it until we know who killed her; then I can let it become real."

I blinked, unsure of how to react. "Right, I understand."

Emma looked out the window. "I hope not. I mean, I loved my sister, but I don't know how to feel about this."

"Huh?" I asked, surprised.

Emma looked guilty. "Nothing. It's nothing. Honest."

"Come on," I said, reaching over to touch her arm. "It's me. You know you can tell me anything."

Emma flinched when I touched her. Something she'd never done before. "Sorry, it's just, Victoria and I had a complicated relationship."

"Well, that's sisters for you."

"She tried to drown me when I was nine," Emma said.

My eyes widened. Drowning was the worst way to die. I still had nightmares about what happened to my cousin Jill. And at the hands of family, too? "Wait, wouldn't she have been, like, ten?"

"Victoria was always an overachiever. She called me a fake werewolf and an impure stain on the bloodline." Emma looked down. "Victoria later claimed she was just joking but it felt awfully real at the time. There was also the time she set fire to my dollhouse with all my dolls in it. One time, Brad even caught her with a silver letter opener. That was when she got sent to boarding school for two years. They only brought her back when she developed the ability to change. She was a late bloomer like your brother."

I remembered Bright Falls High School had been a lot more peaceful for those two years. It had allowed me to concentrate on my studies and not have to deal with everyone complaining about all the hell she was raising.

"I think my brother is a no-bloomer but that's not his fault," I said, taking a deep breath. "So you've got mixed feelings about her death and feel guilty about it?"

"Yeah," Emma said, frowning. "I mean, I shouldn't but I do. It was especially bad this past year when she got into a bad crowd. I mean, badder than the cocaine-snorting bitches—I can say that because they're my cousins—that were her girl posse."

"That crowd include my brother?" I asked, realizing what she was implying.

Emma made a little whimpering noise. "I mean, surely you knew something?"

"I am not my brother's keeper," I said, unbuckling my seatbelt and stepping out of my ratty old car. "I knew he was hanging around with a bunch of losers, but I thought it was just your typical stoner crowd. What did you hear? I mean, contrary to what certain politicians say, cocaine is significantly worse than pot."

Emma looked down then looked out the window again before unbuckling her seatbelt. "It was Brad who told me to stay away from Victoria and your brother. That they were doing stuff my grandfather had to cover up."

"Like drugs?" I asked, wondering how much her grandfather really was against inter-shifter relationships if he was covering it up.

"Like dealing them," Emma said. "Rudy is where Vicki and the posse got their drugs. Your brother was involved."

Holy crap.

"That's a factor you could have brought up earlier," I said, taking a deep breath. "My brother the drug dealer."

"You didn't know?" Emma asked.

"Of course I didn't know!" I said, shocked. "Jesus, Danu, and Herne. I am so going to kick his ass after we prove he's innocent and solve your sister's murder."

Emma smiled and gave me her 'mentally wagging my tail' look. "Thank you, again. I don't have my head on straight through all of this, but Victoria didn't deserve to die. She was a good person at heart, right?"

"Yeah," I said. "Bitchiness doesn't equal Joffrey."

"Who?"

"You obviously didn't spend too much time with my brother."

The two of us proceeded to the sheriff's office entrance and entered to find an argument brewing I didn't want any part of. It wasn't a particularly interesting-looking building on the inside, either, with bullet-proof glass separating from some desks, some doors, and a big sheriff's star on the back wall. Standing in front of the star were Marcus O'Henry, Clara O'Henry, and a handsome man dressed like an FBI agent off of TV.

Marcus O'Henry was a silver-haired, bronze-skinned man who was in his seventies but could pass as a man in his fifties due to the regenerative power of shifter blood. He was wearing a red suit and pin-stripe purple pants that were a crime against fashion, but I also noticed the cane in his hand with a silver wolf's head. I remembered him beating his son, Christopher, with it during one of the Moon Gatherings. Scared the hell out of me. While my father was conservative, he didn't rule his family with an iron fist the way Marcus did.

Clara O'Henry was a woman in her early thirties and the baby of Emma's three aunts. Clara had short red hair, freckles, and a well-muscled but lithe frame that still caught a lot of attention around town. At least from the humans. Clara was wearing a brown sheriff's uniform with blue jeans and standing her ground with her father.

Clara was the least attractive of her siblings. That meant she only looked like a supporting player in a soap opera than the lead. Mythology was full of ugly-ass monsters and beautiful female ones and that, unfortunately, seemed to be true in real life. Shifter men came in big and beefy while the women were sultry, buxom, and curvy, with rare exceptions like myself.

The handsome man looked to be in his mid-twenties rather than the older type you'd expect as an FBI agent, but I saw the little badge on his front. It reminded me of that NBC show with the ridiculously beautiful cast. He was tall, black haired, and had a broad grin. I thought he might be partially Asian like Keanu Reeves or Dean Cain, but it was difficult to tell and just a guess on my part.

"I want that monster locked up," Marcus snapped, his voice having more than a little werewolf growl to it. "No, worse, I want him turned over. We should settle this the old way."

"We're a civilized people now," Clara said, not the least probably because there was an FBI agent beside us. "We follow the law of the United States now."

"He murdered my girl!" Marcus shouted. "A royal of the red-wolf lineage!"

"That and a dollar will get you a soda," Clara said. "The law must be respected. Do you not think I want to see Victoria avenged? She's my niece!"

"If I may speak up," the FBI agent said. "I don't think it is Mr. Doe who is responsible for the murder and I would like to conduct my own investigation without tribal interference."

"Tribal!?" Clara snapped, turning to him. "Listen, you damn spook—"

"Oh, I'm sorry," the man said, spreading out his hands. "Is that not the right word? Please, I only want to help."

"Um—" I started to say, raising a finger to interject.

"You!" Marcus turned around and pointed at me. "You and your family have been nothing but a plague on mine!"

"Hi, Grandpa!" Emma said, waving.

Marcus stared at her, looked half ready to shift right there, then looked back at Clara before storming off past us.

"Well, that could have gone better," the FBI agent said, clasping his hands together.

"You think!?" Clara said, sighing. "Hi, Emma. Hi, Jane."

"Hi," I said, unsure how to proceed. "I really don't think my brother is a murderer."

"I have to investigate all possibilities," Clara said, her voice low. "Either way, your family is with your brother in the back. If you'll excuse me, I have to go handle some things. Like an insane old wolf who is threatening all sorts of things."

21

Clara walked past me through the front doors, presumably to go speak with her dad.

"Nice to meet you," the FBI agent said. "I'm Special Agent Alexander Timmons, Supernatural Affairs Division. It's like the Department of Supernatural Security, but not incredibly racist."

"Is it?" I said, having been brought up to have a healthy fear of anyone with a badge. "Because I'm pretty sure it's legal to shoot me as vermin in most states."

"Yes," Alex said. "It's an appalling situation that I support the federal government interceding upon. Everyone has a right to a fair trial, due process, and protection from violence."

"Except vampires. They're all evil," Emma said, completely oblivious to the hypocrisy. "Also, fairies. Demons too. Oh and rakshasa!"

Alex chuckled. "In any case, your brother isn't responsible for the late Ms. O'Henry's death."

"Duh, I knew that. My brother couldn't kill time. I remember when I killed a squirrel and brought it back. He threw up." Emma elbowed me as I realized this was actually important. "Wait, how do you know that?"

"While astral projecting, I saw a vision of the Archangel Gabriel who bore the face of my dead mother. That was, of course, just one of the many spirits that assume human form from the expectations of the viewer. This spirit told me the individual responsible for the murders I'm investigating is actually a werewolf. Also, that I should beware the color fuchsia."

I stared at him. "Bulls—"

Alex interrupted me. "I'm considered unconventional due to the fact I'm a practicing theurgist and wizard. A little Hermetic spiritualism, some ki-enhanced martial arts, a dash of Daoist sorcery, and a cherry of postmodern will-working. However, in this case, the answers are very difficult to come by and I suspect this case will be more difficult than most."

"Uh-huh," I said. "Listen—"

"You're a psychic," Alex said. "A powerful one. Your mother recommended you be allowed to examine the body."

"My mother?" I asked. "Wouldn't she?"

"Marcus O'Henry has refused access to the body," Alex said. "However, should I leave the door open, I think it'd be in your best interest to walk through."

I blinked. "Wait, you want an eighteen-year-old random stranger to interfere in your investigation?"

Alex patted me on the shoulder, smiling a winning smile. "Absolutely."

He then gestured down the hall to the last door on the right then walked to join Clara and Marcus outside.

After he left, I looked behind me. "What the hell was that?"

"Well, that was easy," Emma said cheerfully.

"Did you arrange this?" I asked, looking at her.

"No!" Emma said, frowning. "I came right to you after I heard!"

I stared at her. "The FBI is allowing me to look at a corpse of someone I…uh, was friends with. That's normal. Also, why is there an FBI agent here already? There's only been one murder and it was a couple of hours ago."

"They found the body three hours ago."

"Ah," I said, wondering why she was correcting me on specifics. "The FBI doesn't get involved in local crimes until they're part of larger cases. Television told me that."

"He said God told him to," Emma said, as if it was the most natural response in the world. "Isn't that enough?"

"Uh, no," I said, staring at her. "Even if I believed in the Christian God, which I'm not sure I do, I don't think that's how it works. Otherwise, angels would have fallen down and told us who Jack the Ripper was."

"The Lord works in mysterious—"

"Don't, please," I said, raising my hand. "This is already weird enough for me."

Emma frowned and I remembered her sister was lying in the morgue just a dozen yards away. It was hard to remember that.

Victoria's death just didn't seem quite real yet. I had to wrap my head around that.

"Whatever the case, I'm going to go in there now. Could you serve as a lookout?"

"For whom?" Emma asked, frowning. "We have permission."

"I don't think we have permission-permission," I corrected her. "Agent Cooper isn't playing with a full deck even if he is telling the truth. If human mages are anything like shifter ones, he may be operating at an entirely different level. You've never met Uncle Jorge. He lives most of the year as a stag and claims he has regular sex with the moon."

"Timmons," Emma said.

"What?"

"Timmons, not Cooper," Emma said.

"It's a reference to *Twin Peaks*," I said, sighing. "Something I just realized you've never seen. Okay, will you just do that for me? If one of us gets trouble, it should be me."

"I want to see my sister," Emma said, her voice low. "Please."

I closed my eyes. "Okay, sure. I'm sorry."

I headed into the morgue and was surprised it wasn't colder. There was a single room with the right wall covered in a dozen slots for bodies while a pair of tables sat in the middle of the chamber. There was a body bag on one of them that caused me to suck in my breath, as I knew it was Victoria. There was just something in the air that felt like her presence, bitchy and judgmental but also fully confident of her own invincibility. I admired that about her. Now she was never going to be able to judge anyone else again.

That made me sad.

"I'm sorry," I said, walking in the room and shutting the wooden door behind us. There was no medical examiner in sight and I was extremely glad of that, since what we were doing wouldn't look right if we were caught. *No, Officer, the sister of the victim and sister of the primary suspect were just trying to get psychic vibes off of the body. We weren't trying to tamper with evidence or anything.*

Crap. Maybe we shouldn't be here.

"Is that her, you think?" Emma asked, locking the door behind us. That wasn't a good thing, because there wasn't another exit.

"Yeah," I said, sucking in my breath. "Time to do my magic."

That was when one of the morgue slots opened up and a tray slid out with a fully dressed body on it.

A body that sat up.

I screamed.

Chapter Four

Emma covered my mouth, muffling my scream. It put to lie any idea I was going to be handling this investigation better than her. Thank Danu this room had thick walls.

Looking up to the man who had been laying on the morgue tray, I saw he was wearing a white lab coat and had pale white skin with shining black hair. He was gorgeous, with movie-star sculpted good looks and perfect white teeth. There were things "off" about him, though, that set my inner animal to the 'flight' rather than 'drool' response. His fingernails were unnaturally long and sharp like claws, while his canines were extended ever-so-slightly. His gaze was also lacking the kind of warm inflection the living possessed. He wasn't breathing and just sat there, unnaturally still, like a statue.

A vampire.

The creature before me then raised one hand. "Howdy, folks! Sorry about that. I bet I gave you a real fright."

He was trying for a rural Michigan accent and failing miserably.

Emma let go of her hand over my mouth then grinned, clearly as terrified as I was but handling it better.

"Hi," Emma said.

I took a deep breath. "Are you the coroner?"

"Yes," the man said, extending out his raised hand to shake mine. "Gerald Pasteur. Did you know you don't have to be a doctor to be a medical examiner? I am, though. It's just that not many people in the town want to be treated by a vampire."

This was surreal. I didn't even know there was a vampire in Bright Falls, let alone one who worked for the sheriff's office. Werewolves and vampires had a complicated relationship. Unlike what *Underworld* taught, they weren't innate enemies and even had some sort of connection.

Vampire children—they could have those with humans—often spontaneously became shifters. Sometimes dead werewolves rose as vampires. In Bright Falls, though, vampires were considered a plague on the town and any shifter who served them was considered to have demeaned themselves.

"Uh, right," I said, looking around the room. "Why were you sleeping in the morgue?"

Gerald shrugged. "I sometimes sleep here during the day when I'm working late. I decided to get a fresh start while the sun was still up today."

Wow, he was way too cheerful for his job. "Ah, then you don't know."

Gerald looked over to the body bag on the table. "Oh, someone died, I take it?"

"My sister," Emma said, her voice low. "Victoria. She was murdered."

Gerald reacted to Victoria's name as if he'd been shot, his eyes widening then becoming almost human for a moment. He raised a hand toward the body bag then took a single breath. A gesture all the more noticeable since he didn't breathe at all. "I see."

"Did you know my sister?" Emma asked.

"Yes," Gerald said, frowning. "I did. She was a beautiful ball of sunshine in a town covered in darkness, secrets, and lies."

For a moment, I look at the vampire and imagined him as the horrible monster who murdered Victoria. Were they having an affair? Had he killed her? It was in that moment I realized I was being horribly racist. Treating him the same way shifters were treated across the country. "So you haven't had time to examine the body yet?"

"No," Gerald said, walking over to the body bag. "But I promise I will find out who was responsible for her death."

"Right," I said, knowing this was now extra awkward. "Listen, could you—"

"Does this have anything to do with the other murders?" Gerald asked. "That FBI agent who burned with true faith and witchcraft said murders were coming, but I didn't believe him. Clara didn't believe him. Dammit."

I stared at him. "There have been more murders?"

"You have to let her touch the body!" Emma suddenly piped.

"What?" Gerald said, now probably thinking we're a pair of crazy people.

"I have psychic powers," I said a little too quickly. "I can read objects. I'm like…a…well, psychic."

Gerald raised an eyebrow at me. "Really?"

"It's a weredeer thing," I said, taking a deep breath and puffing it out. "I mean, Emma is family."

"Yes, I give permission for her to uh…read my sister's corpse," Emma said. "Something I can totally do."

Gerald looked at her then me. "Okay."

I blinked. "Okay?"

"Oh, that was easy!" Emma piped in. "Again."

"Okay," Gerald said, nodding. "We're all here to try and solve a murder."

"Yes!" Emma said, raising her fist for an entirely inappropriate fist-bump.

"What is wrong with this town?" I muttered under my breath and reluctantly returned Emma's fist bump. "Seriously, this is not natural behavior from law enforcement."

"If you read me," Gerald said.

"Wait, what?" I asked, suddenly drawn back to the vampire.

"Well, I'm not going to just let you tamper with evidence," Gerald said, extending his hand again. "However, if you can prove to me you actually have psychic powers, then I have no reason to deny you access to the body."

"Except all the many, many good reasons," I said, uncomfortable.

"Jane!" Emma said.

"Sorry," I said, grimacing. "It's just, uh, I've never tried to read a vampire before. Is it even possible, reading a vampire? I mean, you're people and not objects."

"We qualify as dead," Gerald said, his voice low. "Assuming your power is psychometry."

"What?" Emma said.

"Object-reading," I said. "My cousin Juniper has the ability to take photos with her mind and send them to the nearest camera. Thoughtography is what it's called. Which, given that everyone has cellphones, is like the most useless power ever."

Gerald shook his head. "Oh no, I knew a vampire who had telepyrosis powers. What Stephen King called pyrokinesis."

"That seems pretty damn useful," I said. "You know, if you're psycho."

"Vampires are burned by flame and scared to death of it," Gerald said. "It means he can't use his own power...well, couldn't. He burned to death last month."

"Yeesh," I said, grimacing. "I mean, sorry. That must have been hard."

"Not really," Gerald said, still holding out his hand. "He was one of the witnesses who banished me from New Detroit. I mean, I like maple syrup and trees as much as the next vampire, which is to say not at all, but this isn't exactly where I was meant to be."

Banished? This just got weirder and weirder. I wondered if he'd meant to tell me this much. "Okay, I'll read you. Just promise not to kill me if I find out any deep, dark vampire secrets."

"Oh, not in the sheriff's station!" Gerald said, cheerfully.

I stared at him, not taking his hand.

"Joke," Gerald said, helpfully.

"Right," I said, taking his hand and trying to read it. "Real funny."

I was almost immediately overwhelmed by visions of blood, fear, and terror. I saw a younger Gerald Pasteur in the '80s getting grabbed by a beautiful woman who drained him dry then locked him up with his family to feed on them. All because Gerald hadn't been able to save the vampire's lover from an overdose. I saw him wandering in the fringes of society, trying to save more lives than he took as he struggled with his hunger. I saw him banished for some crime I couldn't see in his soul, the shame too great, only to end up working here.

I tried to focus on the image of Victoria in his mind, but I could feel him resisting. In the end, that resistance actually made it easier to think of her. I saw the beautiful golden-haired werewolf, wearing her signature blue jacket over an elegant silk blouse and white dress. She was one of the most beautiful women I'd ever seen in a town of incredibly beautiful women. Gerald had agreed and Victoria had been willing to allow him to drink her blood in exchange for samples of his. Also, other things.

"Ugh," I pulled away, disgusted. "Jesus, you were giving her vampire blood for sex?"

"What the fuck!" Emma said, horrified.

Gerald looked down. "I'm sorry. I truly am. I thought…I thought we had a connection."

"Getting high?" I snapped. "Maybe you did it!"

"I didn't!" Gerald said, holding out his hand. "Go ahead and read it."

"I don't want to touch you!" I said, about ready to turn him in. Certainly this looked better for my brother since we now had a vampire suspect. Then I realized I was willing to use racism and felt ashamed.

"Disgusting undead—" Emma started to speak, standing between Gerald and her sister's corpse.

I grabbed his hand. "Just shut up and don't try to hide anything from me."

Gerald didn't resist and I got the rest of what I was looking for. This wasn't like reading an object; he could steer the conversation and the power of the vision. Nevertheless, I felt what I felt and soon caught a vision that told me everything I needed to know.

Their last meeting.

Victoria was standing in this very room, her arms crossed and all the warmth gone from her demeanor. She was wearing a beret and a red dress and stockings that were an eclectic fashion choice for Bright Falls. "What?"

"We shouldn't see each other anymore," Gerald said, his voice low and filled with guilt.

"We're having sex," Victoria said, her voice sounding a lot more contemptuous than Gerald had ever mentioned. "That's not 'seeing each other'."

"Nevertheless, it's wrong," Gerald said. "I apologize for doing what I did."

Victoria snorted. "You did what I wanted you to. However, if you don't want this anymore then that's your business. Plenty more where you came from."

Victoria gestured down to her body as if she was displaying a new car. Wow, it was wrong to think of her that way, but she really was a she-wolf in more than just the literal sense.

"I also can't give you any more blood," Gerald said, his voice soft and cold.

"The hell you can't!" Victoria said, walking up to him. "I have customers."

"You said that was for your mother to help with her depression!" Gerald said back.

"And you believed me!" Victoria said, shaking her head. "Do not get all morally judgmental with me, leech!"

Wow, that was the equivalent of the n-word for vampires.

"You need to get out," Gerald said, his voice low and cold. "Clearly, I misjudged you."

"Oh boo-hoo, the vampire lonely for attention who doesn't want to use his powers or hurt people. Stop being such a walking cliché," Victoria said, getting up in his face and displaying some fang. "I'm not leaving without what I came for, though."

I felt Gerald's attraction for Victoria, something really weird and off-putting, but also his disappointment. He really had thought they'd shared something and I just wanted to roll my eyes at that. There was something else, though. It was more than physical attraction—a persistent need to obey.

"No," Gerald said.

That was when Victoria pulled out a little cloth doll wearing a Doctor Barbie white medical coat with hair nailed to it. Victoria took a little wooden toothpick and then jabbed it into the chest of the doll. Gerald crumpled to his knees as I felt the immense pain he did, followed by paralysis. Victoria then put the doll to one side, grabbed three syringes, and stuck them into Gerald's neck to take as much blood as she could sell. Leaving him "staked" for the rest of the night.

I pulled away. "Okay, that just comes off as motive."

"What did you see?" Emma asked, her voice rising as her eyes turned a predatory yellow with claws extending from her hands.

"I'd never hurt her," Gerald said.

Surprisingly, in that moment I knew he was right. Not because he loved Victoria, though, but because I'd sensed just how sad and lonely the vampire's life was. "No, you wouldn't. Because of the vampire who created you. She forced you to hurt people and you'd never hurt anyone willingly. You might have done it involuntarily, though."

Gerald looked like he'd been hit with a car. He then sank his shoulders and took a deep breath. "You're right. That's part of the reason why I was banished. I never wanted anyone to have control over my mind again, and that's not an option among vampires."

I remembered something from his memories: helping another vampire escape from her creator. He was going to use her as a slave to satisfy his needs. Gerald had staked the other vampire and sent him on a one-way ticket to Dubai in a wooden crate. So I guess Gerald wasn't just a teenager-loving creeper.

"Also," Gerald said, "where was Victoria murdered?"

"Across town in Darkwater Preserve," Emma said. "Which...oh, right, vampire. You couldn't be out in the sunny woods."

Damn, didn't I feel stupid.

"You're still way too close to this," I said, shaking my head. "Also, what you did was against the law."

"I never touched her until she was eighteen and I was merely twenty-three when I was changed," Gerald said. "But you're right."

I wasn't sure it mattered if vampires looked twenty-three when they were actually in their fifties. Then again, I'd always found all of those vampire romance novels creepy. I didn't think two-hundred-year-old guys were hooking up with girls like Victoria and me for conversation.

Emma growled at me. "So are we killing him or not?"

"Killing him? Goddess, no!" I said, trying to think of something to say other than 'Down, girl.' "He's not a murderer. Well, sort of. He's just…he's not Victoria's killer. Gerald, you still need to tell everything you know to Sheriff O'Henry or Agent Timmons or both. My brother is not going down for this and I'm pretty sure you'll be the next suspect."

"Thank you," Gerald said, puffing up a bit. "That's kind of you, considering."

"It's not kind," I said, taking a deep breath. "It's me wanting to actually find my friend's sister's killer."

Wow, that didn't sound sympathetic at all.

I tried to figure what else to say then shook my head. "Now open up the body bag and let me see if I can find out who really killed Victoria O'Henry."

"I understand," Gerald said, walking over to the tray.

I looked at Emma. "Did you know your sister was a witch?"

Emma's eyes returned to normal as did her fingernails. "What?"

"Yeah, full-on Voodoo doll stuff. Enough to make a vampire into her own personal pin cushion."

Emma looked as stunned as I felt. "No. That kind of magic would get her killed."

"Wait, what?"

Emma nodded. "Grandpa Marcus has decreed any study of witchcraft in the family is punishable by death."

That was when Gerald finished unzipping the body bag and I got my first glimpse of Victoria's corpse.

I almost threw up.

33

Chapter Five

I'd seen dead things before in the woods on runs with my family. I'd been to shifter funerals before, too, that involved the bodies being burned on pyres throughout the night while all of the clans attended. Sort of like they did Qui Gon in *The Phantom Menace* despite the fact that Jedi were supposed to disappear after death.

This, however, was something different. Victoria's face and shoulders were perfect—so perfect that she looked like she might sit up like Gerald had. However, there would be no resurrection for the queen of Bright Falls High.

Her heart had been torn out.

I wasn't speaking metaphorically, either. There was a big honking hole in the right side of her chest. I'd read enough murder mysteries to know the heart wasn't that easily penetrated. My father had made me take self-defense classes that told me a wooden stake wouldn't easily get through a vampire's heart (wow, we were racist in this town) but it was easy for a shifter to shove a claw in if they were the right kind of predator.

That only narrowed it to five hundred or so suspects.

Great.

"Oh, Vicki!" Emma said, sounding on the verge of tears.

"I'm sorry," Gerald said.

"You shut up!" Emma said, switching her emotions like a traffic light.

"Well, now we know my brother didn't do it," I said, looking around. "He's a human being. He couldn't have done this. Why are they even arresting him? Is this a frame-up job?"

"No," Gerald said, pointing to the wound. "This was done with a serrated knife. It's not a natural attack at all, but was meant to look like one. I should—"

"Uh," I interrupted, realizing he was probably going to go into full medical-examiner mode. A job he was really disqualified for given his relationship to Victoria. I intended to tell Clara and Agent Timmons everything I knew as soon as they were nearby, but I wanted to get a read off of Victoria first.

Maybe Gerald hadn't killed her, but he probably knew things that could lead to the real killer and I didn't want him deciding it'd be better to cover up any of his involvement. What was weird was that, being inside his head, I didn't think of him as an evil man despite all the horrible stuff he'd been forced to do as a vampire. But good people didn't seduce teenagers half their age nor allow their blood to be sold as drugs.

I wasn't a connoisseur of controlled substances like my brother claimed to be, though I was the Moon Goddess if he'd tried anything harder than Ecstasy, but I knew vampire blood could be sold for five hundred dollars a hit to the people stupid and rich enough to try it. It made you stronger, smarter, faster, and feel like God if HBO's *Vice* was telling the truth about it. I doubted Victoria could have sold it for that much around here but it was strange to imagine she'd needed much money. Her family already owned the town, after all. So why become a drug dealer? And where had she learned magic? You couldn't learn it off the internet. Believe me, I'd tried.

"You should step away from the body and let her do her work," Emma said, stepping between Gerald and the body.

"Right," Gerald said, moving to the other side of the room. "You may not believe this, but I want to see her murder solved too."

"You're right, I don't," Emma said.

I walked over to the body and stared at Victoria's cold, still form. "Okay, here goes nothing."

I wasn't exactly scared, but I wasn't looking forward to reading the body either. Reading Gerald had been a pretty heavy experience and he wasn't someone who'd been stabbed to death before being eviscerated. Oh hell, I *was* afraid of going through whatever Victoria had experienced, even second hand.

"You can do it," Emma said. "This is for Victoria."

That really wasn't helping matters.

"Right, for Victoria," I said, grabbing the dead woman's hand and trying to read her.

A moment passed.

Nada.

"Jane?" Emma asked.

"Gimme a second," I said, trying harder to get something off her body. Usually I could pick up impressions off objects that had even a little contact with humans. I could get a vibe of what the factory operator had thought about his job when he packaged a doll if I tried hard enough. Here? Nothing. It was like Victoria was empty of anything resembling a psychic connection to her previous life.

"What's wrong?" Emma asked, her voice low.

I let go of Victoria's hand. "There's nothing to read. It's like she's been wiped clean of anything psychic mojo-ey. Okay, bad choice of words, but it's beyond that. There's nothing there."

I was reminded of *Mortal Kombat*, of all things. I used to play the game religiously on the old arcade machine at the pizzeria. One of the ways the main villain could kill someone in that game was to steal their soul. While I wasn't going to bring that up with Emma, it felt almost like that here. Whatever had been Victoria was gone from her body with no trace left behind.

"Dammit," Emma said, looking down. "It's all for nothing then."

"I wouldn't say that," I said, stepping away from her body. "We've found some clues."

Perhaps realizing he was the biggest clue we'd found, Gerald went to the table and picked up a box on the shelf underneath the table Victoria's body rested on. He then dumped out the contents on the second table beside him. A bunch of plastic bags containing items were inside.

"Maybe these can help," Gerald said.

"Her personal effects?" I asked.

"Yes," Gerald said. "At least, I presume so."

"Right," I said, remembering he'd just woken up.

There wasn't actually all that much to read. There was her blood-stained clothes, some condoms, a pack of cigarettes, crystalized vampire blood, some cash, credit cards, the doll I'd seen in my vision with Gerald, a purse, and a plain gold ring with Arabic writing on the side. The last drew my attention and I reached over to hold the bag. I didn't expect to be able to feel anything through the plastic, but no sooner did my hand touch it than I received a powerful vision.

I saw Victoria once more, this time wearing a black leather skirt, black bikini top, fishnets, a midnight-colored wig, and stiletto heels. She was really rocking the goth-club-girl look and I admired her ability to pull it off even if it seemed like she was the party's entertainment more than a guest. Victoria was holding the ring in her hand and putting it on her ring finger, as if she was trying on an engagement ring.

The room around her was wooden with calendars of girls on the walls and some kind of office. The song, "Lucretia, My Reflection" by The Sisters of Mercy was playing in the background and I could smell cigarette smoke in the air. My vision eventually expanded to see Lucien Lyons sitting on top of a wooden desk with a cold expression on his face.

Lucien Lyons was beautiful. Not the first word you usually associated with the town's biggest criminal. Whereas most shifter men looked like Vikings, he was slim and pretty with silver hair as well as abs a fitness model would have been proud of. I didn't have trouble making out the latter because he wasn't wearing a shirt along with his blue jeans.

Lucien also had a number of tattoos on his body with an ankh over his right pec and a sword across his belly being the most prominent. He was about twenty-five and had been my sister's crush when she'd been a freshman. You know, before he'd somehow ended up taking over organized crime in the city. Actually, that might have made him more attractive knowing my sister's tastes.

No lie, I also saw the appeal.

"Are you sure this ring will increase my ability to do magic?" Victoria asked, looking it up and down.

"You can try it out if you want but I don't sell damaged goods," Lucien said, his voice low and gruff but still somehow soft. "Unlike some people."

"People should watch what they're buying," Victoria said, shrugging. "Why is it my problem if some of it is cut?"

"It reflects on me," Lucien said softly. "There are very nasty people out there who don't like it when their dealer crosses them."

"Like you?" Victoria said, walking up to him with far more sway to her hips than necessary.

Lucien pushed her back with one finger on her right shoulder. "Like me. Besides, don't you have a boyfriend?"

Victoria snorted. "Which one?"

Oh, that bitch. I can't believe my brother was hooked up with her. I took another look at her outfit and how she wore it.

Okay, yeah I could.

"Our business is concluded," Lucien said, gesturing to the door. "Fair warning, if you want to disguise yourself, then maybe next time don't wear something that attracts everyone's attention."

"Maybe I was just going for one person's."

"Take a hint," Lucien said.

"I want the knife," Victoria said.

Lucien lifted up a Bowie knife blade with serrated edges and a handle that looked like it had been carved from bone then polished. "This knife? The one you tried to order from my supplier behind my back?"

"Yes," Victoria said, almost hissing. "The sacrificial knife."

"I told you, you weren't getting it," Lucien said, stabbing it into his desk. "I don't deal in blood magic."

"Then maybe you aren't the big bad you pretend to be," Victoria said. "Maybe you're just another poseur."

Lucien then hurled it at the wall beside her head, stabbing her wig into the door.

Victoria actually blinked.

He then walked up to her, took the knife, and then pushed her out the door into some sort of combination of bar and rave. I recognized it from descriptions, as there weren't many nightclubs here in town.

The Lyons' Den.

That was when the vision ended.

"I think I've found the murder weapon," I said, clutching the ring. "It belongs to Lucien Lyons."

"The drug dealer?" Emma said.

"The club owner?" Gerald said.

"Yeah," I said, putting the ring down.

I was about to examine the other objects when the door was unlocked behind us.

"Oh crud," I muttered, realizing how this was going to look.

Moments later, Clara, Marcus, and Agent Timmons were entering into the room with more shouting occurring as a result.

"What the hell is she doing here? Get the hell away from my granddaughter's body!" Marcus shouted at the top of his lungs.

"Gerald, why the hell are they here? Emma, step away!"

"Ah, delightful! Did you find anything?" Agent Timmons said, clasping his hands together.

Clara immediately spun around. "What?"

"My purpose is to prevent these murders from—" Agent Timmons didn't get a chance to respond more.

Marcus O'Henry shifted into the 'war' form all shapeshifters possessed. The half-man, half-wolf that had first appeared in *An American Werewolf in London* but all shifters possessed a variant of. It was a form most shifters used to kill, since our instincts were at their most feral but the human mind was also present.

He launched himself at Agent Timmons, regardless of the consequences to the community and himself.

Only to be sent flying through the air and against the ground by some sort of bizarre judo throw that caused the FBI agent's hands to glow while doing it. Clara immediately drew her gun and aimed it at Agent Timmons, then her father, then lowered it, clearly stunned by the development.

Agent Timmons cracked his knuckles. "Technically, that qualifies as assaulting a federal officer but because of your father's emotional distress I'm willing to let it slide. If he attempts to interfere or obstruct my investigation again, I will press charges."

"What the hell was that?" Clara said, putting away her gun and going over to her father's moaning form as he shifted back to human form.

"Venusian Aikido," Agent Timmons said. "I learned it from an avatar of a Hindu warrior god taking the form of the Third Doctor. I had just imbibed numerous hallucinogenic drugs and gone through a marathon session of the classic *Doctor Who* series on Netflix. It gave me a substantial boost to my already-enhanced abilities gained from studying the immortal Bruce Lee's works, but only when I fight for justice."

Everyone in the room stared at him.

Myself included.

"You were saying, Jane?" Agent Timmons said.

"Uh, right, Agent—"

"Alex, please."

I took a deep breath and gave him an abridged version of everything that had happened in the last hour. It surprised me how easily the words flew from my mouth. Clara looked furious at Gerald when the subject of him sleeping with Victoria came up.

"You slimy piece of trash," Clara snarled. "She was a girl!"

"Actually, I believe he may have been operating under a love spell," Agent Timmons, Alex, said, walking over to the doll in the plastic container. Opening it up, he smelled it. "This is a specific kind of sympathetic magic. Rosemary and cycle blood are classic tools for controlling a potential lover's mind."

"Eww," every woman in the room said simultaneously.

Alex zipped up the bag. "In any case, I don't believe Dr. Pasteur was in his right mind when he preyed on Ms. O'Henry. Be that as it may, his diminished capacity doesn't mean he should be involved in this case and I'll be asking the FBI to send over our own coroner."

Gerald looked horrified and I didn't blame him. I couldn't imagine what it would be like to be involved with someone, even someone I shouldn't have been with, only to find out someone had been messing with my mind.

"That slut," Marcus said, hissing on the ground and holding his stomach. "Baring her throat for a dead man. Disgusting. And a witch too? I'm glad she's de—*ow!*"

Clara grabbed hold of his wrist tightly. "Oh, sorry, Father, it looks like it's broken. It'll take a few hours to heal."

Marcus glared at her but didn't say anything else.

Emma, however, looked crestfallen as her grandfather's reaction hit her hard. "We have to find who did this."

"And the other murders, yes," Alex said, zipping up Victoria's body bag.

"Wait," I said, taking a deep breath. It occurred to me I'd been paying so much attention to Victoria's death I'd missed something important. "*What* other murders?"

CHAPTER SIX

Alex paused a second, as if it surprised him I didn't know what the hell he was talking about. "Ah, my apologies, the first two victims in the case. Courtney Anne Waters, selkie, nineteen, her throat cut and left arm removed. Thomas M. Hart, werestag, forty-five, stabbed and right arm removed. Both showed signs of having been killed by the same individual who murdered Ms. O'Henry."

"And you still arrested my brother!?" I said, turning to Clara and Marcus on the ground. "You think he's a damn serial killer?!"

This was insane.

"Your brother used to date Courtney Anne Waters," Clara said softly and firmly. "She was a member of his drug-dealing pack. Thomas M. Hart was also involved in their criminal business."

"He is *not* a killer," I snapped at her. *I* was more likely to kill someone than Jeremy. Not that I was going to say that to the sheriff.

"He knows something," Clara said, narrowing her eyes. "I can smell the guilt."

Oh great. That was Clara's Gift. "So you're going to charge him on the basis of his smell."

Clara kept her eyes on me. "Unless he gives me someone better to do so, yes. You, yourself, said Gerald didn't do it."

I almost brought up Lucien, whom I hadn't gotten around to talking about, but decided to hold my tongue. If this was the kind of quality police work I was to expect from my local law enforcement then I didn't want her blundering into the Lyons' Den and giving him a chance to dispose of the evidence. Goddess, now I was glad Emma had brought me into this.

I tried to remember Courtney Anne Waters and Thomas Hart, figuring I must have run into them sometime since there weren't that many shifters in the town. It turned out, yes, there apparently were since I couldn't place either of them. Courtney might have been one of my brother's friends he hung out with, a slightly overweight girl with purple hair, but then she might not have been. Thomas Hart, I assumed, was probably one of the Cervid clan and thus a distant relation, but I barely could name all my first cousins let alone third or fifth. If they were dead and my brother knew them, then why hadn't he brought them up? When were they killed? I needed to talk with him.

"I'll see that boy hang," Marcus said, slowly getting off the ground. "Even if I have to get that Unitarian nut job and my own kin thrown off the case. I'll call Judge Hawthorne, the governor, and Senator Rollins and—"

"Please leave, Mister O'Henry," Alex said. "I've been very patient and believe me, I am quite aware of who you know. I also know how to make you so radioactive that no politician will touch you, up to and including the local postmaster."

Marcus glared at him, held his wrist, and walked out through the door.

"Wow," Clara said, watching him leave. "I have never seen my father back down. It almost makes me not want to throw you out a window."

"I'm inclined to believe this is a hate crime rather than something motivated by more personal reasons," Alex said, turning around. "I think it is something that is related to whatever your brother was up to, Ms. Doe—"

"Jane, please," I said, automatically then blushed. I didn't know why I did but I just did. Maybe my emotions were still screwed up from reading Gerald.

"Jane," Alex said, continuing. There was something calm and soothing about his voice. It made everything seem okay despite the utter lunacy of recent events. "So I do think we should keep him in our custody but for his own protection as well as interrogation. After all, it is people in his circle who are being targeted. He might be in danger as well. I promise you he will be released within twenty-four hours unless startling evidence of his guilt shows up."

"You don't get to make that call," Clara said, staring at him. "This is my case and my family."

I almost snapped that she was going after my family but kept my mouth shut. Clara wasn't a bad person, but her niece was dead and there was a madman running around her town. That would have put me off my game as well. Hell, I'd broken into the medical examiner's office and was ready to withhold evidence. I was just getting started. I'd do anything to protect my brother, drug dealer or not.

"Ms. O'Henry, remember when I said you could remain in charge of this investigation?" Alex asked, turning back to Clara.

"Yeah."

"I lied," Alex said firmly with the merest hint of reproach. "You may remain on as a subordinate."

Clara sighed in defeat. "Hell, I'd do the same thing with everyone having their fingers in this pie. This whole town seems to have a relationship with Victoria."

I walked up beside Emma and squeezed her hand. "Yeah, well, I'm sure you'll find another lead soon."

Emma shot me a glance of surprise, stunned I wasn't going to throw Lucien under the bus. However, all I knew was that he had been Victoria's drug connection and she'd bought some magical items from him. The sacrificial knife, as Victoria had called it, was the key to all of this and if I could get it from Lucien then it would be the clue needed to save my brother. I mean, yeah, I sounded like a teen murder-mystery star but it was a plan that made sense.

At least to me.

"Yeah, sure," Emma said.

Gerald didn't respond, looking instead like he was about to be sick. I didn't know if vampires could vomit, but he certainly looked like it. I felt awful for him, mind control was one of the worst things you could do to a person, but it meant he wasn't bringing up Lucien either. I had to think of my brother first. Still, I hoped he'd get some counseling for what happened. Human law hadn't caught up with magic in terms of what was legal and not, but what she'd done was unforgivable among supernaturals.

"Can I speak with my brother?" I asked.

"Yes," Alex said. "However, if I can borrow you for my investigation, I'd appreciate your help. Inadmissible or not, the abilities you possess could lead us to the real killer and potentially save others."

"Do you need me now?" I asked, really wanting to get after Lucien.

"No, but probably later tonight."

He pulled out his cellphone and I gave him my number as I found myself looking at him and thinking about him. He was extremely good looking; now that I got a chance to look at him up close, there wasn't that much of an age difference between us. I mean, he was what, twenty-five? Okay, seven years, but that wasn't that bad.

Was it?

In my mind I saw myself as a deputy, working to solve crimes here in Bright Falls well into my twenty-fifth year. Agent Timmons and I were together, kissing, with some sort of relationship going on. I shook that thought away, unsure if it was a vision of the future or just my overactive imagination. I didn't want to be a deputy. I wanted to be a writer.

"Yeah, I'll give you my number," I said, mumbling it before heading toward the door. "Good luck."

I felt slightly sick at myself for fantasizing about the cute young FBI agent when Emma's sister's body was just a few feet away and my brother was still a suspect in her murder. Forcing that thought away, I walked to the door where Emma was holding it.

As soon as I passed through the door, Emma shut it before grabbing my arm. "What the hell was that?"

Emma's eyes were yellow and she had the same expression she'd had on earlier when she'd threatened Doctor Pasteur. Her strength pressed down right beneath my elbow and hurt like hell. I'd never seen her that angry at me before.

"Which part?" I asked, trying not to grimace. I wasn't afraid of my best friend. Maybe I should have been, but I wasn't.

"The part where you didn't tell them about Lucien," Emma said, lowering her voice practically to a hiss. "I need you here, Jane."

I closed my eyes. "We need to do this ourselves. We need to go to Lucien and make sure we get him to tell us what he knows."

Emma blinked rapidly. "Like on TV?"

"Yes, except I can read objects," I said, shrugging. "It won't be that difficult to find out what he knows."

Actually, it sounded extraordinarily difficult, but I wasn't about to tell her. Also, I didn't exactly want to tell her I was afraid her racist old grandpa and aunt were going to set up my brother.

"Are you sure?" Emma said, letting go of my arm. "I mean, I trust you and everything, but this is a big thing you're asking."

I looked at her. "Would you believe I had a vision about it?"

"Yeah, sure."

Damn, now I felt awful for lying to her. "Well, I did. This is how it has to go."

Emma frowned and looked at my arm then her hand. My arm was starting to bruise, but, being a shapeshifter, it would probably heal in about an hour. "I'm sorry. I shouldn't have grabbed you."

"It's okay," I said, shrugging. "You're a wolf, I'm a deer. It's in your blood."

"That's racist!" Emma said.

"What's racist?" my father asked, causing me to jump.

I turned to look at my mother, Judy, and John standing beside a handcuffed orange-jumpsuit-wearing Jeremy. My mother was a short, dark haired, copper-skinned woman who was about middle-of-the-road for werewomen. Which, in her case, made her look like an Odawa model and I felt inadequate even next to my own mom. She was wearing a black wool sweater with a pentacle over a burning heart necklace that reflected her weird Christian-Wiccan mish-mash faith that was apparently something she'd been brought up with. She also had a long dress that was covered in a forest pattern I found vaguely unsettling.

"Hi," I said, taking a deep breath. "If I'm arrested in the next twenty-four hours for interfering in a police investigation, please don't blame me. Blame Jeanine somehow."

John narrowed his eyes. "Jane, what are you up to?"

"What she has to do," Judy said, coming to my rescue. "Trust her and the spirits will reward us."

"Oh, yeah, great," John muttered. "I really would rather trust my son to confess whatever the hell he's hiding."

"I'm not hiding anything!" Jeremy said, obviously lying to my trained sister eyes. He wasn't acting like a killer, though. "My girlfriend just died. I'm upset!"

Emma looked between my parents. "Uh, why aren't you in the interrogation room?"

"Oh, I asked if we could take him to see Agent Timmons," Judy said. "He agreed and is currently re-evaluating his life."

My mom's Gift was the fact she could make almost anything seem reasonable. She didn't use it on us; otherwise I would have studied much harder, but it was something you really couldn't fight against because she was naturally persuasive.

"I'm not saying anything," Jeremy said, his voice hard even in the face of Mom's voice. "Everything will be fine."

I wanted to grab my brother and throttle him. This was serious and he was acting like a spoiled brat. "Jeremy, were you dealing drugs?"

Jeremy looked at Emma accusingly only for her to look away.

"Stay out of this, Jane," Jeremy said. "This is only going to get you hurt."

I wanted to smack him so hard right then. "People are dead, Jeremy! Not just Victoria but someone named Courtney Waters and another guy named Jonathan Hart. This is some serious…stuff."

Yeah, I didn't swear in front of my parents.

Sue me.

"Courtney's dead?" Jeremy asked, looking paler than usual. "Jesus."

"Now will you talk?" John said, looking down at him.

He didn't answer.

"Mom, could I have a word with you?" I asked, realizing I wasn't going to get anything out of my stupid brother.

"Of course," Judy said, taking me to a corner of the hall. "What is it, dear?"

I gave her a really compressed version of the past hour then looked at her. "Why did you tell Agent Timmons I could help him? This entire thing is crazy, with Emma just asking me to look into this and now a member of the FBI wants me to help!"

"It was your destiny," Judy said, a beatific smile on her face.

I stared at her like she'd grown a second head. "Seriously? You're using the same line Darth Vader used on Luke?"

"Destiny is a bit older a concept than *Star Wars*," Judy said, sighing. It was her disappointed-mom tone. "Which you'd know if you'd agree to be my apprentice. However, it's like having a map to the many pathways through the Great Woods. You can see where they go and try to choose the best one, though only the greatest seers can tell exactly how the paths lead. All of them end up in the same place, of course."

The Great Woods were one of the many spirit realms my mother believed in and probably Agent Timmons too, if his earlier claims about astral projection were real. I didn't have any reason to doubt they existed but I'd never seen any hard evidence either. The astral plane was like outer space in that regard—something I trusted was real but was unlikely to ever visit. Supposedly, my ancestors included shamans who could visit the Great Woods physically around here but that knowledge was lost. Now they were just a metaphor about traveling through life.

"Of course?" I said, confused as hell as to what my mother was talking about. "Destiny ending up at the same place being—"

"Death," Judy said a little too cheerfully. "But hopefully not for many years to come."

Now I wasn't sure who was irritating me more, my mom or my brother. "But why this path?"

"It's the only path where your brother doesn't die in the next few days. Probably."

My mouth hung open. "When...what...when were you going to tell us this?"

"Dinner," Judy said. "I find some hot soup and veggies help bad news go down well."

After that, I decided not to ask any more questions. It was clear everyone in this town was insane except me.

My mom smiled. "Oh, no, my dear, we're all mad here. You too."

I narrowed my eyes. "What have I said about reading my mind?"

My mom gave me a hug. "I know this is going to be hard on you, honey. I wish I could say I've seen it work out, but there are powerful forces at work. Things that are clouding my vision and I can't see objectively when it comes to my babies. Something dark inhabits this town and I think we have to remove it."

"We?" I asked, hugging her back.

"You and me. You and Agent Timmons. You and Emma. I can't say much more."

"Can't or won't?"

"Can't as in don't know," Judy said. "I wish I was as omniscient as my grandmother. However, she died utterly insane and babbling about the vampires revealing themselves. That was in 1977, so I shouldn't complain too much."

I pulled away. "I understand. None of this makes any sense, but I'll do my best to see Jeremy freed."

"So will I."

"I've got a lead—" I started to say.

"Follow it," Judy said, cutting me off. "Put your trust in the spirits and they will see you through."

"The spirits help those who help themselves," I said. "Probably because I haven't seen much help from them lately."

"Haven't you?" Judy said, chuckling.

I started to walk toward my dad and hoped he wasn't about to get into more trouble by being around his son with no guards.

My mom had one more thing to say. "Jane, it's about Victoria's body. You mentioned you didn't get anything from it?"

"Yeah?"

"Blood sacrifices, the oldest and darkest magic, drain every bit of life and magic out of bodies. They have nothing left inside of them. Not even souls. A person who sacrifices a shifter, let alone three, will have almost unimaginable magical power."

Great.

That was all I needed.

CHAPTER SEVEN

I was too freaked out to drive after my talk with my mother. Instead, Emma took the wheel of the Millennium Falcon and I sat in the passenger's seat I leaned my head against the side of the window while the rest of the town passed by. My mind was abuzz with the possibilities her parting words had left me with.

Human sacrifice? In this day and age? I mean, I knew shifters had done it in the olden times, but I thought those were things abandoned centuries ago. Then again, supernaturals tended to lag a few hundred years behind the times. Vampires still existed under a feudal structure with its own court system and brutal punishments to anyone who stepped out of line. It wasn't until my dad's time that arranged marriages weren't mandatory and the clan lord as well as wolf king hadn't the authority to kill anyone who looked at them cross-eyed.

No, I couldn't think of this as some sort of fucked-up shifter tradition gone wrong. This was, if Emma would pardon the racism, some sort of lone-wolf crazy-person stuff. More Ed Gein than anything to do with us. The Reveal had brought out all the crazies who lived on the edge of vampire, shifter, mage, and fae society. Hell, it was probably a human who wanted to become supernatural.

Yeah, that was the ticket. Some psycho pathetic wannabe who thought killing shifters would make him a god. Some human who was jealous of the ability to do magic and wanted to gain it through whatever means possible.

"Okay, that's just racist on my part," I muttered. "God, I really am an awful person."

"Any insights?" Emma asked, staring at the road.

"I dunno," I said, looking over at her. "Is Lucien a shifter?"

"I think so," Emma said, clearly unsure. "I mean, there's a lot of cat imagery around him."

I frowned. "That doesn't mean anything. There's not an O'Henry breed of wolf. Only Cervid make horrible puns of their name."

That wasn't strictly true, but my sister had a dream of opening a music store called the "Doe Rae Me" so there had to be something genetic about us and puns. Something I was very glad hadn't been passed down on me.

"Maybe," Emma said, frowning. "But if I was going to think of someone who would be willing to murder someone, I'd look to the town's biggest criminal. Also, if someone were going to kill someone for magical power then I'd think it was the guy who has the sacrificial dagger."

"Is that our working theory?" I asked, surprised Emma was taking the lead on this. "Local drug dealer murders weres for magic?"

"Your brother and my sister worked for him," Emma said. "Maybe he's killing his employees who've crossed him and thinks he can get more out of it by doing it in a ritualized way."

I thought about that then frowned. "Emma, how did you know my brother was dealing? Why didn't you tell me? Don't give me any of the 'I thought you knew' garbage either. You know me better than that."

Emma frowned. "I was buying Spark from him."

I opened my mouth. "Emma!"

Spark was a strictly shifter-only drug. It was a mixture of various herbs and chemicals that did nothing to humans but worked like Ecstasy on shifters in large doses while making you incredibly perceptive in smaller ones. At least, so I'd heard. Some hunters actually used verbena gathered in the light of the full moon or the more dangerous wolfsbane to cut it as a kind of poison for shifters. A typical "scare you straight" story ended with a young werewolf or weredeer dying after taking it.

"I use it to study!" Emma said, frowning. "I don't want to stay in this town forever and my grandfather controls all the money in the family."

"Isn't your dad a lawyer?" I asked.

"Yeah," Emma said. "With one client. Dad doesn't speak to me much, either. Victoria was the apple of his eye."

Ah.

"Was this before or after she tried to drown you?" I asked.

"Both," Emma said, taking a deep breath. "I should probably mention Christopher O'Henry isn't my biological dad."

I blinked. "What?"

Emma sighed. "That's the reason Grandpa Marcus hates witches and wizards so much."

"I thought that was because he got his ass handed to him by a guy one-third his size in war form," I said, still chuckling at the image.

"No," Emma said, her voice somber. "This is serious."

"You have my attention."

Emma sighed. "I don't know the exact details, but my mom explained the rough outline once I was old enough to understand. There was some kind of land deal, back when the town was prosperous, and a married couple of magic users was called on to arbitrate. The vampires were on one side and the O'Henrys were on the other."

"What happened?" I asked, wondering what this had to do with her father not being her mother's sperm donor.

"The magician sided with the vampires and Grandpa made his displeasure known by killing one," Emma said.

I blinked. "Okay. Not often I'm told about a murder, but today seems to be a day for that."

"That's how things were done before the Reveal," Emma said. "The witch used her husband's blood to curse the O'Henrys. The male line was rendered infertile and the town was cursed to lose its businesses."

I looked around to the many boarded up store fronts around us. "I'm pretty sure that's more due to the collapse of the American export industry, but what do I know about magic? Also, why just the male line?"

"Old-time magic is sexist. She was wrong, anyway. Grandpa is from the Reagan era, not the Stone Age," Emma said, grumbling.

"Greed is good," I said, chuckling as I imagined Marcus O'Henry as a Gordon Gecko-esque Wall Street executive. Honestly, it was a pretty good fit since he didn't look like that far from Michael Douglas did now.

"Not funny," Emma said. "Mom was a werewolf, though, and wanted to carry on the lineage. With Dad's permission, she went to an old boyfriend and—"

"I get it," I said, grimacing. "I take it that didn't go over very well with Grandpa Marcus."

"Not at all, but not for the reasons you'd expect," Emma said softly. "Mom was his late brother's granddaughter. Which, ick, but that's the way our family rolls."

"Like in Appalachia."

"Ha-ha," Emma said. "Like royalty."

"Go on," I said, trying to ignore the fact her parents were second cousins. Well, not in the having-children sense but yes in the married sense. Ugh. Too much information.

Emma continued. "Grandpa Marcus was only angry that our bio-dad was a human. He said that would make us less likely to become werewolves. That's why Victoria tried to drown me. She thought she was Christopher O'Henry's only 'real' daughter."

"Was she?" I asked.

"No," Emma said. "We're both children of Bart Matthews. Brad has a werewolf father from out of state. Victoria cried for a week when I turned at fourteen; she didn't turn until last year."

I actually knew Bart Matthews. He was the guy who ran the gas station and oil-change service nearby my house. He was also biracial, which probably hadn't contributed to Marcus O'Henry's high opinion of his grandchildren. I mean, biracial people were awesome and beautiful. Halle Berry and Rosario Dawson were two of the women who looked just as good as supernaturals and...okay, wow, I really was racist. I needed to see a therapist about these issues.

"Wow," I said, taking a deep breath. "That's cool. So you're part b—"

"Not the point, Jane."

"Sorry," I said, grimacing. "Liberal weredeer guilt."

Emma rolled her eyes. "Well, you see where I'm going with this."

"No, actually, I don't. I mean, this is a fascinating and kind of horrifying story you've told me about your grandfather being a murderer and all—"

"He's killed a lot more people than that weredeer woman. There used to be thirteen clans in the town."

I'd heard about that, but even my parents hadn't been willing to talk about it. There were kitsune, selkies, werebear, wereboar, werecats, werecoyotes (who were just a kind of werewolf in my opinion), werecrocs, weredeer, wererats, wereravens, werespiders (eesh!), and werewolves.

There were other kinds of shapeshifters ranging from wereowls to weresquirrels (seriously). As long as vampires kept having children with humans then it was likely there would always be new species of human-animal hybrids. The twelve clans were the only groups large enough to be called actual societies—at least in North America.

"So what is it?" I asked, trying to figure out her point.

"My sister didn't become a shifter until her junior year," Emma said, scrunching her nose. "We know she was a witch then, but what if she, somehow, used magic to become one? Courtney was a late bloomer, too, and—"

"What?" I said, stunned. "You think my sister and brother were part of a make-themselves-shifters-with-magic cult?"

Emma shrugged. "It would explain why they're into magic."

"That is dumb, incredibly dumb," I said, staring at her. "Also, it would mean my brother was actually involved in this nonsense."

Emma was silent as we pulled onto the highway.

"Don't you dare!" I snapped. "Not even for a second. Also, I can prove they weren't into that."

"How?" Emma asked.

"My brother isn't a shifter, duh," I said as if it were the most obvious thing in the world.

"Oh, right," Emma said. "Never mind then."

I crossed my arms, too furious to respond for the next five or six minutes. I ended up turning on the radio to Kansas's "Carry on my Wayward Son." It was the theme for *Supernatural* and while they'd had to seriously retool that show, I still loved it. Especially after Jared Padalecki had come out as a werebear.

Eventually, Emma said, "I'm sorry.'

"Right," I said, unable to let go of the accusation but not for the reasons I wanted to. I wanted to think it was ridiculous. "Who, exactly, was in my brother's, our siblings', drug posse? There's Victoria, this Courtney person, Jeremy, and who else?"

I knew my brother's friends. Some of them, at least, but clearly I hadn't been paying much attention to them.

"Rudy and Maria Gonzales," Emma said, sighing. "Those are the only remaining members. Do you remember those two?"

"We just met with Rudy, so, yes. Are they shifters?"

Emma took a deep breath as if she wasn't quite ready to let go of this theory. "Maria is, yeah. She turned just last month and she's twenty. Wereraven."

Okay, that was frigging insane. Was there silver nitrate in the town's water or something? That shouldn't happen.

"Rudy?" I asked.

"No," Emma said. "He's just this perverted stoner who wanted to be a raven like his father and not like his human mother."

"Ah," I said.

Try as I might, I couldn't disregard that there was something really peculiar about the timing of all this. Three shifters in a group of people who weren't expected to transform all suddenly developing the power to change. Now two of them were dead.

"It's weird," I said.

"Yeah," Emma said, her voice low. "It is."

"But if people actually knew how to make a normal person into a shifter, then it'd be on the national news."

Emma's next words haunted me. "Not if it required something bad."

I texted those names to Agent Timmons.

"Oh, so we can tell him about those?" Emma asked.

"Do you want him showing up at the Lyon's Den and tipping them off?" I asked before tapping my head. "Psychic vision, remember?"

"Right," Emma said, clearly not believing a word of it. "I'm sorry, it's just a theory."

"Why I'm not angry," I said, sighing. "Much."

The two of us didn't say anything more as we continued driving for another fifteen minutes down the highway past Bright Falls Park. It was the part of the city I loved most as the place just went on for miles and miles, full of campgrounds and scenic spots that seemed at odds with the rest of the dying town.

There was actually a massive waterfall inside the location, the one that gave the town its name but it was no longer part of the park, since the O'Henrys had somehow managed to buy the land and build their hotel over it. I always found that a crying shame since I'd often gone swimming there as a little girl, but it was fenced off from anyone but paying customers now.

Bright Falls Park was actually one of five state parks and three nature preserves we had in the area with Darkwater Preserve being the smallest. That part of the forest was sealed off from the rest of the town due to the fact it was supposedly cursed. I used to wander around it with my cousins all the time as a kid but had stopped when, well, the accident with Jill had occurred.

"Do you know what the thirteenth clan was?" I asked, more for lack of anything better to do than a desire to talk about minutiae. I was still troubled by how much sense Emma's theory about it being some sort of weird shifter-wannabe cult made. Mostly because it was along the lines I'd been thinking.

Just without my brother.

"I have no clue," Emma said. "I wasn't exactly allowed into the secret family meetings where my grandpa determined were future. That was all before the Reveal."

Yeah, that was the end of werewolves like Marcus O'Henry's dictatorships over the shifter race. The revelation to humanity meant we were subject to the same laws as everyone else. Theoretically. The vampires had been able to negotiate from a far better position because, well, they were rich and had mind-control powers. The O'Henrys were rich, but not vampire-rich. Vampire-rich was less Trump-rich and more 'bailing out the entire country' rich. I still didn't know how they'd done that.

It didn't take long to get to the Outlands. That was the part of the town built on the highway toward New Detroit. Once it had been nothing but gas stations and fast-food restaurants—and not many of those either. However, since the vampires had turned New Detroit into goth Las Vegas, it was the only part of town which was growing. Unfortunately, what it was growing into was a collection of bars, strip clubs, and small casinos. A place to bilk tourists of their cash before they arrived at the place where they were actually supposed to be bilked.

Given I couldn't drink, gamble, and wasn't interested in a side job as a stripper, I didn't spend much time in the Outlands. Really, as Emma drove into the place, it felt like I was entering into a Frank Miller comic with lots of neon as well as motorcycles. The Lyons' Den was noticeably set apart from the other buildings in the area and had a significantly classier vibe. It also had security that looked fully capable of throwing around even the hardiest of trouble makers. I recognized a couple of them as werebears of the Carbone family and they looked like they were able to throw cars without turning into nine-foot-tall grizzly bears.

The building was a two-story stone one that used to be a bank and looked like a converted mansion with tinted windows and gargoyles added for effect. The sun was only now setting but there was already a line going on around the place of mostly twenty-something girls and boys. A fuchsia neon sign of a lion pouncing on a human was above the entrance. It also had a smaller sign saying "Must be 21 or older" and "No weapons, magic, or vampires."

"That's prejudiced!" Emma said, driving past the location as I searched in vain for any way in.

I rolled my eyes. "Not really the problem. We're not getting in through the front."

"I have a fake ID, but—" Emma started to say.

That was when I looked down the street beside the Lyons' Den and saw Brad O'Henry carrying out garbage. The prince of the city was blond, beautiful, tall, and not the sort of guy you expected to see cleaning up from the back of a goth nightclub.

Interesting.

"Nope, I've got a plan," I said, smiling. "We're sneaking in."

CHAPTER EIGHT

I explained my plan to Emma as we parked almost two blocks away underneath a bridge leading back onto the highway.

"Uh-huh," Emma said, clearly not impressed. "Your plan is to get my arrogant full-blooded werewolf brother to help us into a club where we're underage and our clothes won't at all stand out. Then you want to confront the city's crime boss and get him to cough up a murder dagger he may have used to kill my sister and two other people."

"First, yes. Second, full-blooded? This isn't *Harry Potter*. You're either a werewolf or you're not. There's no Halfbloods or Mudbloods."

"Says the woman not from a family where you can trace your ancestry back to Cain. The O'Henrys can."

I stared at her. "Cain from the Bible? How would that even work? We have a fossil record and everything. He'd have to be like a million-year-old *homo erectus* or something and we'd all be related to him anyway."

Yes, I've thought way too much about that sort of thing. Blame it on the fact I have a mother who believes in a literal Great Flood and that God hangs out with the Hecate sisters. Which sounded a lot crazier before I found out Agent Timmons studied fictional martial arts with science-fiction heroes.

"I don't think it's actually an accurate family tree," Emma said. "However, he's the first werewolf."

"I thought he was the first vampire."

"This isn't a roleplaying game," Emma corrected. "Your plan is stupid."

"Do you have a better one, Penelope Purebreed?"

60

Emma stared at me then smiled. "That would totally be my cartoon name."

"Yes, it would be," I said, giggling.

It was a reminder of what our relationship was like before today. No matter happened, it would never be the same. Even if we managed to solve Victoria's murder, we'd both become part of something much bigger than the usual boys, bands, college, and video games that made up our previous conversations. Actually, it occurred to me I did most of the talking about boys.

"You don't think your brother will help?" I asked.

Emma took a deep breath and stared forward. "Honestly, I don't know. My brother and I always got along a lot better than the rest of my family."

"You mean he didn't try to drown you when you were five," I said, sarcastically. I was still trying to process that tidbit from my best friend.

"No. He always was kind to me. I think whatever crazy genes were on my mother's side weren't on his dad's."

"Well, you're not crazy."

"I'm here with you, aren't I?"

She had a point.

Emma frowned. "But it seems there were parts of my family I wasn't aware about. Like, why is my brother working blue-collar labor for the man my grandfather hates most?"

"Marcus O'Henry hates Lucien Lyons?"

"Yep," Emma said. "Lucien's a twenty-five-year-old who owns the half of the town my father doesn't."

"Not all—" I paused. "Okay, that's about right. But—no offense— aren't you rich?"

"Grandfather owns all of the family property and stock," Emma said, sighing. "He doles out money enough to keep us looking good and happy but not enough for any of us to ever leave. Everyone has to work for the family, too, in whatever position he deems fit. All of us want out of it but none of us can leave without him shutting us down. We're slaves to him because he controls the cash."

"Did Victoria want out?" I asked, trying to imagine the girl as someone struggling to free herself. Given I knew she'd tried to kill my best friend when they were both girls and had enslaved a vampire, I was having difficulty with the concept.

Emma paused. "I dunno. I think she wanted to take over, but that was never going to happen."

"Because of her human father."

"Yeah," Emma said. "Just like Brad will never be allowed to marry Jeanine."

"Does he want to?" I asked.

Emma turned to frown, anger in her eyes. "Am I my brother's keeper?"

Emma proceeded out the door and I was at a loss for words. I was finding out more things than I'd ever expected about my best friend and it occurred to me I hadn't been the best of friends to my bestie. How much had been secretly going on that I'd never bothered to ask her about? How long had she needed a confidante that I just hadn't been? I made a resolution to be a better friend to her and hoped I wasn't too late.

But it did feel like I'd missed a lot going on in my own family, let alone hers. Victoria had been a crazy magic-using rapist, her grandfather was a murderer, their family was operating under a curse, and my brother was a drug dealer involved with Victoria. Both my brother and Victoria were part of a group being targeted by a serial killer and they were all former dealers working for Lucien Lyons. Throw in the fact Victoria was apparently killed as part of a human sacrifice and I actually had a pretty good number of clues. The problem was I wasn't sure how many of these were part of the case versus just a sign of how corrupt and screwed up our small town was.

Still, I wrote them all down on my phone before getting out of the car myself. I couldn't forget any of this.

Stepping out of the Falcon, I headed over to the barbed-wire-topped chain-link fence that surrounded the back of the Lyons' Den. There was a single door in the fence leading inside but it was padlocked. Apparently, Lucien Lyons liked his security. Emma was standing at the side of the door and looking in, waiting for Brad or someone else to come out from the backdoor to the kitchen.

Interesting fact, I could actually see patterns in the graffiti on the back of the building's wall. They glowed to my eyes and showed Lucien had set out a pretty heavy set of wards to enhance the supernatural 'swerve' of the place. Aside from him, any supernaturals who entered the place with intent to harm would be severely diminished in power. I briefly wondered if my mother had set them down as she was one of the few shamans in town with the power to do it.

But that was ridiculous, right?

Seconds later, I saw Brad come out with yet another pair of garbage bags. Brad was a handsome man about twenty-three years old and had the strawberry-blond preppy haircut you'd expect from a man named Brad. Despite this, I'd never actually gotten the impression Bradley O'Henry was the kind of stuck-up jerkass I wanted him to be. He was more like Emma than Victoria but I still didn't quite trust him with my sister. He was just too good-looking, smart, and rich. He needed some dark secret to make him believable. There, I said it.

Emma whispered over to me. "How do you want to handle this."

I put my fingers in my mouth and whistled. "Yo, Brad, we need you to let us in because we're investigating your sister's death and we think your boss is responsible."

Emma flicked my ear with her finger. "What the hell, Jane!"

"Ow!" I snapped, covering my ear. "Don't you ever touch a Cervid's ear! How would you react if I flicked your nose?"

"I'd rip your spine out then feel really bad about it," Emma said, chuckling and showing not a single sign of remorse. "You can't mess with instinct like that."

"Wait, do you even know about Victoria?" I would feel really horrible if he hadn't.

Brad walked over to us and frowned, looking at us through the chain-link fence's door. "I know. I found out within minutes of Aunt Clara finding the body. Lucien gave me the day off but I wanted to get as far away from the house as I could get. I didn't want to be there when my grandfather found a homeless man or migrant worker to take the fall for it."

Ouch. "Not much faith in your Aunt Clara finding the real killer?"

Brad had a look of profound sadness on his face I'd never seen before. "I don't know why you think Lucien is responsible for my sister's murder, but if you want to point fingers then I think the best choice is Grandfather."

"You can't believe that," Emma said, her voice horrified.

"You can't?" Brad asked. "Victoria was practicing witchcraft and dating outside the clan. I'm terrified now for Jeanine and will probably have to break up with her to keep her safe. You two need to go home and stay out of this. Marcus O'Henry is a very dangerous man and you do not want to cross him."

I narrowed my eyes. "Have you told Jeanine this, yet? Because, I'm pretty sure she'd stomp a hoof-shaped hole in your head if you did."

Brad grimaced. "No, I haven't, yet. I wanted to ask her to marry her and leave this place. I was just waiting to get enough money to do it."

"Which is why you're here," I asked, trying to figure out how to convince him. Honestly, he raised a pretty good point about us being in over our heads but if Marcus was going after his own family, that just meant I had another reason to take the bastard down. Not only was he threatening my brother now, but Jeanine and I sort of liked her. Emma I'd die for, though.

"Your mom threatened to put a curse on me if I didn't get a job," Brad said, grimacing. "I don't think she trusted a werewolf could love her daughter as much as a weredeer. However, she was willing to give me a shot if I showed I was willing to live without my family's money."

"That's beautiful," Emma said. "Mrs. Doe believes in the power of love."

"Which is surprising, because Judy's kind of racist. She printed up and bound copies of the Narnia books after doing a find/replace so Aslan was a stag instead of a lion."

"I stopped liking the Narnia books when Susan went to Hell because she liked makeup," Emma said.

I looked at Emma sideways. "Really? I never read past *The Silver Chair*."

"It really happened!" Emma said.

I shook my head. "What the hell, Clive. Not cool at all."

Brad looked at us then pinched the bridge of his nose. "It's like being trapped in an episode of Buffy."

"More like *Veronica Mars* with shifters," I said, smiling. "I hear Kristen Bell's a weresloth."

Brad sighed. "I never thought I'd say this but could we get back to accusing my boss of murder? I find it less irritating than hearing you two chat on the day my sister died."

"I'm just killing time until I can figure out a way to get you to let us in," I said, grabbing the door's wire. "So why don't you just assume I gave an incredibly impressive argument and let me through."

Brad rolled his eyes. "Not a chance. Good luck, Emma, and stay safe."

"Thanks, Brad," Emma said. "You need to get away from here. At least one of us should."

"Don't help him!" I snapped at my friend.

The answer to my prayers, one of them at least, came in a most unexpected form. Specifically, it came in the form of Jeanine. She walked out the backdoor wearing an outfit which was roughly in the same league of goth sex kitten (deergirl?) which Victoria's had been. Except, looking at her boots and the fact that she was wearing a robe over it while carrying a pack of cigarettes, I realized she wasn't there as a patron but taking a break from work.

"Oh my gods," I said, horrified. "You're a stripper now!"

Jeanine did a double take at my presence. "I am not a stripper! I am a dancer!"

"That is exactly what a stripper would say!" I said, covering my mouth.

Jeanine looked ready to turn into a deer and batter down the door, which would have worked wonderfully for getting me in there. Hey, never waste a good crisis.

"Hi, Jeanine!" Emma said, waving.

"You're also smoking," I said in mock horror. "My gods, what evil has Brad led you down?"

"Could we do this on a day my sister isn't lying in the morgue?" Brad said, his voice cold and depressed.

I winced. "Sorry, it's just hard turning off my snark. I'm actually really terrified and sick about all this. I think it's a defense mechanism of some kind."

"A defense mechanism that makes people want to kill you?" Jeanine said, pulling out a cigarette before Brad glared at her and she put them away. "I'm only smoking because of your grandfather and sister."

"Don't use them as an excuse," Brad said, sighing. "Jeanine got a second job down here. We're working together to get out of Bright Falls. Also, she's not a stripper. She wears clothes. Just not a lot of them."

"Not that he would mind if I was," Jeanine said.

"I kinda would," Brad said, looking at her.

Jeanine looked at him sideways. The look said, 'we're not having this conversation in front of my kid sister' without words. "In any case, what are you even doing in this part of town? It's dangerous here."

I stared at her. "What, am I going to get mugged by the fat tourists driving to New Detroit? Maybe get assaulted by...right, Victoria's murder. I am really terrible at this."

"You just have no filter," Brad said. "I knew that from the moment I met you."

"They're trying to solve Victoria's murder and think Lucien may have been involved," Brad said, shaking his head.

Jeanine responded by doing something unexpected. She reached over to the lock on the door and waved her hand over it, causing it to open. "Come on in. I'll show you to Lucien's room and provide a distraction."

I raised an eyebrow. "What sort of distraction?"

"Get your mind out of the gutter! Danu and Jesus, what the hell is wrong with you? I thought hipster girls like you were supposed to be open-minded."

"I am not a hipster," I said, frowning as I looked down at my retro-eighties look . "At all."

Walking in, Emma followed.

"What are you doing?" Brad said, grabbing Jeanine by the arm.

Jeanine took his hand off hers. "Something is going on around here and Lucien is involved. He may be charming and maybe he helped us out, but he's also a criminal. Don't you owe it to your sister to investigate?"

Brad growled as his eyes glowed yellow. They reverted to their normal color a few seconds later. "All right. I'll help. I owe it to Vicki. She was an innocent in all this."

I exchanged a glance with Emma. Apparently, I wasn't the only sibling wearing rose-colored glasses.

Jeanine looked us both over. "Okay, we'll have to get you looking like you belong here."

Oh crud.

CHAPTER NINE

My sister's idea of what qualified as a disguise disagreed with mine tremendously. After a half-hour in the dancer's dressing room, I was dressed in a leather bustier, fishnets, and a pair of tiny ripped jean shorts. She'd covered me in white powder, mussed up my hair, and put on my fingers a set of black Lee press-on nails. Even my lipstick, actually Jeanine's, was obsidian.

Looking in a mirror, I said, "I look like Cassie Hack."

"I don't know who that is," Jeanine said, looking over my shoulder at her handiwork. "I was going for Death from *Sandman*."

"You expose your geeky roots," I said, chuckling. "You are not so far removed from the Dark Side."

Jeanine rolled her eyes.

I turned to look over at Emma, who was wearing a Lacuna Coil t-shirt and tight leather pants with a purple wig done up in a ponytail. Her mouth was open and she was drooling at the two of us like we were fresh steaks.

I narrowed my gaze. "Emma!"

Emma immediately jumped. "I wasn't looking! I mean, you look great."

"Why do you get to wear clothes that don't make you look like a vampire stripper?" I paused. "Henceforth known as a Jeanine."

Jeanine gave a tug on the back of my hair. "What was that?"

"Ow!" I said, rubbing the back of my scalp. "Sorry, vampire nightclub dancer."

"*Shapeshifter* nightclub dancer," Jeanine said. "As for why, you need to get into Lucien's office while Emma just needs to stay out of the guard's sight. The best way to do that is just to have her look like she's having fun."

"Wait, why does this look help me get into…" I trailed off. "Please don't tell me it's that."

"He has a lot of relationships with the dancers," Jeanine said, patting me on the shoulder. "Don't worry, I'll send you in when he's out on the floor meeting with the tourists. You'll just have to look like you're going to wait for him and they'll let you in. You can then look through his stuff and leave."

"This is a terrible plan and I am the queen of terrible plans," I said, taking a deep breath. "Well, maybe princess, since our mom is even worse. Also, did he ever force you—"

"No," Jeanine said, sighing. "Lucien doesn't force anyone to sleep with him."

"He's your employer," I pointed out. "He could if he wanted to."

"You'll change your mind once you meet him," Jeanine said, putting her hands on her waist. "Also, I'm seeing Brad. So I wouldn't."

That sounded way too defensive for a question I hadn't even asked. Also, I disagreed with that statement tremendously. No one was that hot that it was inconceivable no one would want to turn down an offer of sex from a position of power. Albeit, damn if he hadn't been gorgeous from what I saw in Victoria's vision. No, bad Jane. Concentrate on the fact he's probably a crazy murderer! Wait, that doesn't help. It just changes the nature of the problem.

Gah!

Jeanine put her arms on my shoulders. "It'll be okay, Jane. I believe in you."

"Because a vision told you?" I asked. "Because that's Mom's excuse."

"So you've mentioned every few seconds during this," Jeanine said, frowning. "No, because you've been a wannabe Nancy Drew since you were five. I also think this is a public place and he's less likely to hurt you here."

"That's incredibly comforting," I said, sarcastically.

"Thanks," Jeanine said, smirking. "But I want to know if Victoria was murdered by my boss too."

"And you're willing to risk your sister to do it?" Emma looked less than pleased with my sister, which surprised me.

I looked around the room to make sure no other dancers were present as a few had come in to get bottles of water or touch up their makeup while my sister helped with our disguises. No one questioned our presence and I was glad of that.

Jeanine didn't regret it. "Brad believes in Lucien. I'm not sure that's such a good idea. Besides, she'd sneak in anyway."

Emma didn't respond to that.

"What is with your boyfriend's Omerta anyway?" I asked. "That's mafia speak for code of silence, by the way."

My sister looked at my ears and frowned. "You should really get these pierced. You're eighteen, for god sakes."

"No one touches the ears," I said, covering them with both hands. "You didn't answer."

"The hell if I know," Jeanine said, sighing before removing my hands and putting on two skull-shaped clip-ons. Ear-piercings were problematic for shapeshifters unless you used silver needles and I'd never gotten around to it. "I think it's some kind of weird bro-code thing. Lucien isn't just a crime boss and club-owner. He's also a magician. I think Brad is so afraid of his grandfather, he thinks he needs someone to protect him. It's disappointing as I thought I was falling in love with an Alpha wolf but I ended up with a Beta."

"That's actually not how wolves work at all," Emma corrected her. "The 1947 test by Rudolf Schenkel misconstrued how wolves work. We're actually very social animals based on family lines. Humans are the part of us that builds hierarchies."

"Well excuse me, Penelope Purebreed," Jeanine said, staring at her then back at my reflection. "Okay, I've done as much as I can to make you look like someone Lucien would actually want to sleep with."

"I look like myself in a corset and hot pants plus all the color drained from my wardrobe. Truly you are a goddess of makeovers."

"You're also wearing makeup!" Jeanine said, waving her hairbrush. "Hell is truly freezing over."

"I wear makeup. Some, at least," I said, frowning. "Anyway, I'm not actually going to need to attract him, so it's cool."

"She's very attractive!" Emma said, frowning.

"Yeah," Jeanine said. "In a Natalie Portman in *The Professional* sort of way."

"She was fourteen in that movie," I muttered.

"I know," Jeanine said, smiling. "I'm going to watch out for you, no matter what. Just shout if you need help. I'll hear it and come running."

"You are really not reassuring me," I said, sighing, but still set on this plan.

"We're deer, we'll be fine."

"Said Bambi's mother," I said. "Noteworthy because this is the only time in my life I've ever used that reference."

"Try since last week," Emma said, shaking a fist. "I'll tear this place down if Lucien or his goons tries anything. I'll heal anything short of a silver bullet."

I exchanged a glance with Jeanine. In all likelihood, Lucien's goons probably were packing silver bullets.

Or at least plated ones.

I took a deep breath and nodded. "Well, I'm going to go break into a drug lord's office and go see if there's a murder weapon there. If there is, we'll call down the cavalry and call it a day."

"Thank you for this," Emma said, looking at me. "Truly."

Wow, I was stupid for agreeing to this. I couldn't back out now, though. Still, I needed some insurance. "Take a picture of me here and send it to the FBI guy. If I go missing, he'll know. Also, I can scare them off."

Emma and Jeanine shared a glance before doing so. I had an insurance policy now.

Sort of.

Heading out the door into the Lyons' Den, I was immediately overwhelmed by the pulse pounding tempos, sights, sounds, and smells all around me. The dressing room hadn't drowned out all of the noise, but it had certainly muted it. The interior was dark but full of people wearing rave glow-stick jewelry and neon-signs mixed with holograms.

The central room was a massive glass dance floor with artificial fog filled with lights going through it in a scintillating show of colors. The air was cool with huge fans pouring air from the balconies above. A stage was next to the room I'd emerged from and women dressed like my sister were dancing with a number of eye-catching men without shirts in front of what looked like a movie screen showing the 1931 black-and-white Dracula movie.

There was a giant bar and rooms to the side that had people sitting down and getting completely plastered. The music was a techno-beat remix of Michael Jackson's "Thriller" that included lines from various movies.

"Wow, this is way too much for a town with only partial Wi-Fi coverage," I said, taking it all in.

A guy dressed like Edward from *Twilight* with less clothes handed me a bright, glowing red drink that I took a drink of and was relieved to find was just a rum-soaked strawberry daiquiri. He then winked at me, making me uncomfortable.

A further examination told me this place was a bit more dangerous than the goth Land of Oz it looked like. I noticed all of the exits had large suit-wearing men and women who looked more like the Secret Service than bouncers. They were also armed, I could tell by the bulges in their suits and there was something about their posture that also told me they weren't human. Not shapeshifters or vampires, though, that confused me about what they could be.

"Keep an eye for security cameras," Jeanine said, coming up behind me. She then pulled out a card from her shorts. "You probably won't be able to avoid getting caught on camera in Lucien's room, but I hate this job anyway."

"Right," I said, taking it. "Are you sure?"

"Nope," Jeanine said. "But I don't like what it's doing to Brad either."

Emma came out as well and looked at the daiquiri. "Uh, should you be accepting strange drinks?"

I took another sip then paused, contemplating Emma's words. Looking at Jeanine, I asked, "Should I?"

"Security has orders to beat anyone who drugs drinks," Jeanine said. "They caught a guy last month and I don't think he made it back home."

My eyes widened. "I am torn between relief and knowing that makes this mission even more dangerous."

I handed the drink to Emma. "Where do I go?"

"There's a private elevator hidden behind that grandfather clock covered in the fake spider webs," Jeanine pointed at the prop not too far away from the bar. "Just swipe it and it'll take you up past the VIP lounge to the office level."

"What's in the VIP lounge?" I asked, more curious than anything else.

"Drugs, sex, and Lucien," Jeanine said. "Emma will go up there and text you if he leaves."

"I will?" Emma asked. "Uh, that doesn't really sound like my scene."

"I'll escort you up, Emma," Jeanine said. "Just pretend you're going to be on *America's Superhumans*."

"Oh okay," Emma said, taking a deep breath. "This is a lot different from buying drugs from your brother."

"Wait, what?" Jeanine asked.

"Bye now!" I said, immediately abandoning my friend to explain that. I headed to the grandfather clock and noticed it was an antique. It was weird with thirteen numbers and had an aura about it that made me think the object was an artifact of some kind. Magic wasn't exactly common in the world, even post-Reveal.

Universities couldn't teach the subject, as the theory was difficult for a lot of people who were otherwise able to explain quantum physics. Not because you needed to be a genius to work magic but because magic just worked for some people and not for others with seemingly no rhyme or reason. What was prayer for one Wiccan was sorcery for another, and a lot of the deep masters had very particular views of the universe that they didn't want to have subjected to the scientific method.

Money talked, though. Plenty of mid-grade and hedge mages were willing to sell the cosmic power of the universe for the almighty dollar. They were only a drop in the bucket of the millions of charlatans who now had concrete proof to back up their cold-readings or scented candles, but they had created a cottage industry of minor mystical items. I had no idea what this thing could do but it occurred to me Lucien might be one of those guys vending sorcery—and not just to Victoria.

"Oh well," I said, looking around the grandfather clock. "Open sesame. Abracadabra. Show me the elevator."

Then I noticed a keycard slot behind the grandfather clock.

I blinked. "Okay, I'm an idiot."

I slid it in the slot and the grandfather clock moved three feet forward and an elevator opened up inside. Slipping into the elevator, the doors promptly closed and I found myself in a room with no buttons. The elevator started moving before I could get used to my surroundings.

I imagined poor Emma and Jeanine in the V.I.P lounge as I passed the second floor, trying to take events as seriously as I should. I couldn't help but see Emma surrounded by celebrities and the rich guests from New Detroit hanging around her while she completely phased out. As much as Emma looked like the party-girl, the truth was she was probably the nicer of us two and I'd dragged her to the few parties we'd attended. I'd even tried to set her up at one point with Jeremy before I realized that was a curse on both of them.

Honestly, I did have faith in Jeanine's plan and I hoped I could repay her if we found out her boss was involved in Victoria's murder. I should have been scared, but something told me I wasn't in danger—yet. Honestly, I was kind of exhilarated by the prospect of breaking into a drug dealer's office to get evidence against him. It was probably all sorts of illegal, but I wasn't a cop either so any problems that happened would be something I was sure I could deal with.

Besides, I was solving a murder and that justified anything, right? At least that's what eighteen years of American television had taught me.

"I am so boned," I muttered, before jumping at the elevator making a buzzing noise before opening its doors.

I stepped out onto the third floor that consisted of railing around a square hallway with a dozen or so wooden doors. I could see the party going on down below, but the third floor still looked like the bank it had been converted from. There was a single pair of double doors on the opposite side of the balcony I was on with an Indian woman with a ponytail, hoodie, and sweatpants standing guard in front of it. She didn't look at all like the other guards, beautiful but not sexualized, and yet I could tell there was a power to her that scared me from even a hundred feet away.

Walking down the hallway, I tried to look nonchalant and whistled my way to the doors. "Uh, hi, I was given a keycard by my sister—"

Crap, that was too much information.

"I'm here for Lucien," I said, doing my best to give her the doe eyes. Which, as far as I was concerned, qualified as a superpower.

The woman was not impressed. "How old are you, girl?"

"Twenty-one," I said, lying my ass off.

The woman rolled her eyes. "Yeah, right. I don't know where you got that keycard but you're going to give it back to me and get back down to the first floor. The Boss doesn't do children."

Okay, wow, I never thought I'd be insulted by not looking sufficiently skanky. "I'm really supposed to be here. Ask your boss."

"All right, I will," the woman said, pulling out her cellphone.

Dammit!

What happened next is something I'm not entirely certain about but it amounted to me summoning up my weredeer power and punching her in the gut. I was horrified halfway through but seeing her barrel over to her knees, I brought another fist down on her head before knocking her out. I checked to make sure I didn't accidentally kill her.

"Oh Jesus, Danu, and Herne, I'm a criminal now," I said, close to hyperventilating. Checking the door and finding it unlocked, I opened it and saw Lucien's office beyond. It was the same room from my vision.

Now I *had* to find something incriminating.

CHAPTER TEN

I dragged in the body of the security guard and closed the door behind me, hoping nobody saw what I was doing. Of course, my sister had warned me about security cameras and I immediately surveyed my surroundings for some sign of them.

The interior of Lucien Lyon's office was a lot messier and more working class than the polished establishment outside. The central desk was metal and probably a decade old, the couch on the right looked like it'd seen better days, and the place had more pictures of girls than I suspect most female employees would be comfortable with.

The desk was covered with massive amounts of papers as well as a few framed pictures with their backs to me. No computer was on top of it, but a laptop case was sitting to the side. Some *Inked* and *Revolver* magazines were scattered around too, indicating the crime boss had a serious thing for tattooed metal chicks. Oh, and there was a big sliding-door closet that composed most of the left wall.

I spotted the security camera over the couch, almost invisible against the black ceiling. It hadn't turned to me yet so I ran up to it and tried to keep it from moving before accidentally breaking it with my weredeer strength. The broken stand dropped the camera down and it hung there from the cord leading back into the wall.

Oops.

"Oh yeah," I said, muttering, "this day just keeps getting better and better."

In for a penny, in for a pound, as the old saying went. Closing my eyes, I hoped no one was watching those cameras and I started looking around the office. If I was going to find something that pointed to

Lucien as Victoria's killer, then I needed to work quickly. I didn't want to end up the second Doe family member arrested today. Though it was a better alternative to being killed for breaking into a crime boss's office and riffling through his things.

"Christ, what a slob," I muttered, trying to figure out where to begin looking in this mess. "Maybe he's a wereboar."

I reached over and put my hands on Lucien's desk, closing my eyes to feel what I might from it. Seconds later, a rush of images passed through me and I immediately regretted doing so. Lucien had a LOT of sex on that desk. I now was worried how much else in this office was a gateway to psychic porn.

Shaking my head, I headed around the desk and started going through the papers on top. It was mostly bills for alcohol, party supplies, and the usual stuff. My eyes zeroed onto the fact that a lot of it was from vampire-owned companies. There was a couple of letters from the Apophis casino in New Detroit as well as someone named "Thoth" who seemed to be financing some real estate deals here. There was even a reference to something called 'were-tourism' that I assumed was the plan to make people show up at our crappy town to gawk at the shifters.

Interesting and it helped explain how Lucien had made his first million before the age of twenty-four, but it was irrelevant to the case. That was when my attention turned to the pictures on his desk. They were pictures of Lucien with what I presumed to be his family. They were all platinum-blond with gray eyes except for a woman who I presumed to be his mother. She was Japanese. I saw her features in Lucien now that I had her to compare him to. There was one other picture on his desk that caused me to do a double take.

Agent Timmons.

He and Lucien were about sixteen years old, both of them wearing goth attire as they were sitting in some sort of club that was similar to but different from the Lyons' Den. Agent Timmons wore a sour, brooding expression while Lucien was smiling and putting bunny ears up behind him.

I picked up the photo and stared at it. "Well, that's unexpected."

With that, I heard a moaning from the unconscious security guard. I went to her side and checked to see if she was armed. She was, but only with a Taser.

I grimaced. "You're going to hate me for this, I know it."

I lifted up the Taser and aimed it at her semi-conscious form. I couldn't bring myself to use it, though. I'd already attacked the woman out of the blue. What I really needed to do was finish up here. I needed to find the knife.

Putting the Taser in the back of my jeans, I headed over to the closet and slid the door open. Inside, I hit the jackpot, because it was shelf after shelf of occult bric-a-brac. There were books, knives, cups, wands, staves, card decks, powders, and more mundane items like keys. All of them vibrated with magical energy I could feel from a foot away, some more than others. There were drugs, too, mostly the kind that only affected Shifters, but a mini-fridge at the bottom I checked contained about six bags of vampire blood.

Woot.

"This is about fifteen to twenty," I said, actually having no idea how much time trafficking in black-market magical items would get him. I started searching through the knives for the one I'd seen from my vision.

There were many knives I felt had been used in murders. Indeed, that was where most of them had gained their "power" as the anger, hatred, and bloodshed had been bound for harvesting. It made me sick to touch them. I saw visions of stabbings in prisons, a woman killing her abusive husband, and even a man who got in a bar fight with a vampire. None of them had anything to do with Victoria, though, and I didn't see the one I'd seen in my vision.

Dammit.

"Are you enjoying yourself?" Lucien's voice spoke from behind me. "I confess, it takes balls to rob me."

I didn't turn around despite being terrified. "Right, open the conversation with a sexist remark. Real way of establishing your dominance."

There was a deep, throaty chuckle behind me. "What are you doing here, Jane Doe?"

Oh hell. He knew who I was.

"Uh..." I started to say then trailed off.

"Right," Lucien said.

Reluctantly turning around, I saw Lucien was standing there in a pair of blue jeans, a red jacket, and a white t-shirt that made him vaguely look like James Dean. He was over six feet tall and his hair was a stark white and he had eyes of cold steel gray. There was an aura of power to him that also caused me to take a step back as I could tell he was a shifter but didn't know what kind he was. I also felt magic from him.

Powerful magic.

Lucien was a handsome man, and I also found myself looking him up and down from a perspective as a woman too. All that feeling left me when I noticed his guard was waking up and looking extremely ticked off.

"I am going to kick her ass," the woman guard said, getting up. She then lifted her right hand and a glowing ball of water was created inside it. "Drown her, knock her about, and crush her between the waves."

"Down, Deana," Lucien said. "Jane, you've broken into my office, broke my security camera, and assaulted my employees. Do you know what's going to happen now?"

"What?" I said. "You're going to kill me?"

"No," Lucien said, pulling out his cellphone. "I'm going to call the police."

"Ha!" I snapped, pointing to the closet's contents behind me. "You can't do that with this here."

"Deana, please remove any contraband," Lucien said. "I'll escort Ms. Doe downstairs."

I grimaced then decided to go for broke. "I know you were involved in killing Victoria O'Henry! I saw you trying to sell her the sacrificial dagger that killed her! You got involved in drug dealing and now someone is killing her and her friends!"

Both Lucien and Deana stared at me.

"Are you *insane*?" Deana said.

Lucien looked down at the floor, his shoulders slumping. "So the Lodge has claimed her too."

My expression to this statement could best be summarized as a flat, *What?*

"Deana, leave us," Lucien said.

"Wait, what?" Deana said, still holding a floating ball of water over her head. "I'm just about to waterboard the whitetail."

"Go," Lucien said, staring at her.

Deana caused the ball of water to vanish into a puff of steam as the humidity in the chamber rose by about twenty percent. "I'll get to calling the police."

"Don't do anything without my permission. Understood?" Lucien said, frowning and gesturing to the door.

Deana looked between us and muttered about having severely misunderstood Lucien's type and worrying about him looting kindergartens.

"I feel like I should be offended by that," I said. "What is she, some kind of sea witch? A selkie?"

"Her mother was a sea goddess," Lucien said, as if it was the most normal thing in the world.

"Uh-huh," I said, staring at him. "What do you want to do here without any witnesses?"

Lucien frowned. "You're the only criminal here, at least in this matter. I promise you I had nothing to do with the death of Victoria."

"Your word," I said, wondering why he thought that was worth anything.

"I've killed sixteen people. Fifteen of which were trying to kill me and one rapist," Lucien said dryly. "If I killed Victoria, I'd admit it to you, but I didn't."

"Ha! I can take that to the cops and have you arrested!" I said, stunned that his defense was confessing to multiple murders.

"Your word against mine," Lucien said, clearly not impressed.

"Ha, again! I had the foresight to record this conversation on my phone!" I was lying, but the conversation had gotten away from me.

"I always carry a charm on my person that makes all recordings of me pornographic. It comes from being raised by an FBI agent and mage. Your phone has only recorded you moaning in passion as we rut on the desk. It has an alternate non-sexual setting for someone underage, but I believe you just turned eighteen, yes?"

"Eww," I said. "Wait, if I wasn't actually recording it, is it still on my phone?"

"Yes," Lucien said. "You can check it if you like."

"Ugh!" I was not covering myself in glory here. Maybe because Lucien was distractingly sexy. He was every bit as attractive to me as shapeshifter women were to men.

Lucien laughed then shook his head. "Victoria's death is not on my hands or any of the others in her gang. Indeed, as they were working for me, it's up to me to avenge them."

"Uh-huh," I said, shaking my head. "You'll forgive me if I don't buy all this honor and vengeance stuff. Did you know after *The Godfather* came out, the FBI noticed a marked change in the mafia? Wise guys who couldn't normally string two sentences together were suddenly talking about honor, duty, and respect. I don't believe in honor among thieves."

"I did know that, actually," Lucien said. "My stepfather was an FBI agent."

Okay, that was an aside that deserved some clarification. "You still aren't convincing me that you didn't have anything to do with Victoria's death. I'm also willing to tell everyone and their brother what I saw. So are all my friends and family. You can't make us all disappear and—"

While I spoke, Lucien walked over to his computer bag and pulled out the sacrificial dagger from my vision in a plastic bag. He then handed it to me. I opened it up, felt it, and got only minor vibes from its creation.

It wasn't the murder weapon.

"Oh," I said, pausing. "Well, I guess you aren't the murderer."

"No," Lucien said, sighing. "Victoria was my apprentice. I would never harm her."

He was lying. I could tell.

"She wasn't your apprentice at the end," I said, making a guess. "Not after she asked for a dagger to commit human sacrifice."

Lucien paused. "You're a lot more observant than I would have given you credit for. That can be a very dangerous quality."

I took a deep breath. "I don't buy this whole decent-crook thing, but maybe I'm willing to hear you out."

Lucien chuckled. "How very gracious of you. However would I survive your wrath otherwise?"

Okay, yeah, I was kind of screwed here. "Is Agent Timmons your brother?"

"Alex is here, huh?" Lucien said, frowning. "Well, that's going to make things complicated."

Wow, I was just guessing. "Seriously?"

"The Special Cases Division of the FBI was long ago made up of mages who dealt with the worst of the United States supernatural crimes," Lucien said, frowning. "I ended up adopted by Phillip Timmons after my family was slaughtered. The Timmons line of mages has long had contact with the shapeshifter world."

"How do they feel about your line of work?" I asked.

"They disapprove," Lucien said, softly. "I'll tell you what I know about Victoria's death but you're right, she wasn't my apprentice at the end. She became involved in black magic and the use of things better left forgotten by modern sorcerers. I should have never let her become involved in my business, particularly knowing she was an O'Henry, but I was arrogant."

"Also, she's beautiful," I said.

"I don't date children," Lucien said. "My interests were only in the fact that she was passionate about the Craft. Also, perhaps, sticking it to the O'Henry family. All shifters should be able to learn magic. Not just deer."

I stared at him. "Tell me what happened."

"Say please," Lucien said, his voice low and oh-so-sexy.

Wait, dammit, focus!

"Please," I said.

Lucien nodded. "Two years ago, Victoria came to me with an offer. The High Shaman of the Cervid had already rejected her as an apprentice. That meant she had to learn magic from either a human or me. I'm the only non-deer sorcerer in town, or at least I was back then. There've been some more since then."

"What was her offer?" I asked, noting the High Shaman was my mother.

"The secret to making humans into shapeshifters."

My eyes widened. "That's impossible. We would have—"

"There's one way," Lucien said, taking the knife from my hands. "With the right rites and a sufficient source of power, it's possible to create a skin of an animal and bestow the power of a shapeshifter on someone. It's called skindancing."

"That's a myth," I said, having heard of it. "A Native American legend."

"So are deer women," Lucien said, shrugging. "It's not an unknown Gift. It's just a mostly lost one. The requirements for it are antithetical to modern values."

My blood ran cold. "You mean you have to commit a human sacrifice to do it."

"Usually," Lucien said, sighing. "Victoria claimed to have found a way around it by seeking the spirits in the woods. The Lodge in Bright Falls is a place where many powerful spirits could be entreated to get around normal magical laws. The tale she wove was an impressive one of wandering in the woods one day until finding the spirit of the wolf who blessed her."

I shook my head. "And you believed her?"

"They're real," Lucien said. "The Spirits of the Lodge may not communicate with the shapeshifters of this land much anymore, but they're blessed with powers beyond our reckoning. Victoria offered to share what she'd learned for what I did."

"My brother and his group weren't just drug dealers, were they?" I asked. "They were a magical study group. They wanted to become shapeshifters."

Lucien nodded. "It was a possibility to change the balance of power in the United States. To make shifters able to stand up against the vampires. Humans will also be less inclined to hate us if they can become like us."

"With, what, you as their king?" I asked, stunned by the implications.

"Just of Bright Falls," Lucien said. "My price would be Marcus O'Henry's head."

"Why?" I suspected I knew.

"He killed my family." Lucien's voice was a low growl.

"You were part of the thirteenth clan," I said. "The Lyons."

"The Lyons were my mother's clan," Lucien said. "I am a dragon."

CHAPTER ELEVEN

I listened to Lucien's proclamation that he was the last of the thirteenth clan. That he was a dragon. Then I burst out laughing. Not just a little laugh, either, but a complete belly laugh that I couldn't stop. It went on for almost fifteen seconds. Not even the fact that I was trapped in the office of a crime lord with him kept me from finding it ridiculous.

Lucien's expression remained even. "You'll forgive me if I don't find this to be a laughing matter."

"Dragons aren't real!" I said, staring at him. "Certainly, weredragons aren't real! I mean, I would have heard of them."

He stared at her. "Are dragons really that much more difficult to believe in than werewolves and vampires?"

"Yes!" I said, unhesitatingly. "Because I've met werewolves and vampires. They are real. Dragons are—"

Lucien's eyes began to glow, then his mouth with an infernal light. He proceeded to turn his head to one side and breathed out a torrent of flame that caused his desk to catch fire. It burned in a fiery blaze as the office smoke detector went off.

Lucien walked past me to the closet and pulled out a fire extinguisher before blowing the blaze out while I stood there, dumbfounded.

My eyes widened. "Um, okay. You can breathe fire."

"Yes," Lucien said, simply.

"Huh," I said, blown away by this new revelation about the world I lived in.

"If it's any consolation, we're not that different from other shifters. We're werecrocodiles and only those of my line have the power to breathe fire. Some of us could also grow to great lengths and heights. It's just that stories of both abilities grew exaggerated over time."

I shook my head. "Listen, this is amazing. Really, it is, but it doesn't explain how Victoria went from being your apprentice to getting murdered."

"Tenacious," Lucien said, picking up the picture of him and Agent Timmons off the floor where it had fallen. "Victoria wanted more than just to master magic. She wanted power and wanted it quickly. Victoria also started teaching her abilities to her friends, your brother included, which I had forbidden. Then she said it was possible to perform a genuine miracle. Something we could use to make the entire world believe the shifters were creatures of God rather than monsters."

"This is starting to sound like crap again," I said.

"She said she could raise the dead," Lucien said, not improving my opinion of his information. "It just required the sacrificial dagger."

"Raise the dead," I said, taking a deep breath. "Is that possible?"

"No," Lucien said. "But the spirits in the Lodge may have said otherwise. The *Manitou* includes both good and bad spirits. Very often depending on what side of their wrath you are."

Manitou was the Algonquian name for the life force of the universe and the spirits that inhabited this life force. In truth, there wasn't that much of a difference between spirits in North America, Japan, or anywhere else in the universe. I didn't know what this Lodge was, but I guessed it was the place the previous generations of Bright Falls had used to visit the Great Woods. It was hard to believe Victoria had somehow made herself a priestess of ancient animist gods, but the entirety of this case was one weird revelation after another.

"You turned her down for it," I said, thinking back to my vision. "Not very forcibly, though."

"I was tempted," Lucien said. "I have people I'd like back myself."

"We all do," I said, thinking of three people I'd lost. "But I bet it's easier for a murderer."

Lucien didn't respond.

"So who is responsible?" I said, finally ready to crack the case.

"I have not the slightest idea," Lucien said. "Sorry."

"Oh come on!" I said, frustrated.

Lucien stretched out his arms as if in surrender. "If you're actually looking for a mundane killer behind these murders, then I think you're looking in the wrong direction. Victoria found something out in the woods and it made increasing demands of her. Demands that ultimately destroyed her and those who invoked it."

I took a deep breath. "So let me get this straight: you think the crimes were committed by the Devil."

"Or something as close to it as to not make a difference, yes," Lucien said, shrugging. "Is that so hard to believe?"

"Yes!" I snapped at him. "Yes, it is! It is more ridiculous than Agent Timmons learning a fictional martial art from *Doctor Who*."

"It's the Doctor, not Doctor Who. *Doctor Who* is the show." Lucien paused. "And no, my foster brother is completely insane. It's just an insanity reality finds infectious."

"I prefer differently rational," Agent Alex Timmons said from the doorway, causing me to jump backwards and even Lucien do to do a double take. He was standing next to Deana, who was at his side muttering as Alex held by her by the arm.

"Nice of you to drop in while you're in town," Lucien said dryly. "I would have preferred for you to call ahead, but clearly you're here to greet your beloved sibling."

"I might have made time to visit if not for the fact I'm trying to solve the murder of a girl connected to you," Alex said, his voice not having any of its usual amusement. "I had to request this assignment personally."

"Isn't that a conflict of interest?" Lucien asked.

Alex narrowed his eyes. "The director of the FBI is an appointee of the new administration. He doesn't care about threats to shifters. I do."

Ouch.

"He got past everyone and I can't move," Deana said, looking over at Lucien. "I used to be better at this."

"Don't worry about it," Lucien said, not even looking in her direction. "I'm sure you'll get a chance to wash away your sins."

"Ha-ha," Deana said. "No puns in front of the whitetail. We might be here all day."

"Weredeer do not need to do puns!" I snapped. "That is a vicious lie!"

"Right," Alex said. "Your text to me said you were hoofing it here. You also added that you were going to lick Lucien's organization and any injuries you'd suffer would just be grazes."

"That was an accident!" I said, horrified at what I texted when not paying attention. "I have no idea how that happened."

"Deer puns?" Lucien said. "I'm not a fawn of them."

"Your sister and companion are down in the back lot," Alex said, thankfully getting us away from our present topic. "Sheriff O'Henry is down there as well. If you don't mind, Lucien, and even if you do, I'll be escorting Ms. Doe down there."

"She broke in," Deana said. "Assaulted me."

"And he's a criminal!" I snapped, pointing at the closet behind me. "Look at all the…"

I trailed off as I noticed that the closet appeared empty. All of the shelves looked like they contained nothing, let alone a bunch of magic and drugs.

Lucien smiled.

How the hell had he pulled that off? Was it an illusion? "Dammit."

"We'll be going now," Alex said.

"The Lodge is the real danger here," Lucien said, staring at him. "You know it and I know it."

Alex didn't answer but let go of Deana's arm.

I stared at him. "I'm not coming with you until I get this resolved."

"Now can I waterboard her?" Deana asked.

"I've told you all I know," Lucien said, his voice soft. "Now leave."

I glared at him and debated going after Deana before I realized I had probably gotten everything I was going to get out of this trip. I didn't like Lucien. He'd turned my brother into a drug dealer and was neck-deep in all of this. Still, I had to admit he'd been remarkably cooperative to an amateur detective who'd broken several laws in the process of trying to prove he was a murderer.

"All right," I said, walking to Alex. I wondered how much trouble I was in for all of this.

Probably a lot. I didn't care, though. I was going to solve this.

As I walked past Lucien, he said, "By the way, your sister is fired."

Dammit.

"I had him," I muttered, looking at Alex. "It may not have looked like it, but I had—"

"I agree," Alex interrupted. "You did an excellent job infiltrating his sanctum and I appreciate that you called me in for backup."

"Wait, what?" I said, confused.

"May I ask what you found out?" Alex said, sounding completely non-ironic.

Blinking, I gave him a short rundown. "He thinks Victoria made herself into a werewolf with the gods of the forest and now they're coming after her. He was her mentor as a mage and she passed on what she learned to her drug-dealing friends, which included my brother."

"Interesting," Alex said, frowning. "And the sacrificial dagger?"

Wait, he knew about that? "He had one, but it wasn't used in the murders or any other murders I can guess. How much do you know, actually?"

"More than most, less than some," Alex said, reaching the elevator with me. "My original theory was that Victoria was a Judas Goat for Marcus O'Henry. A tool for him to break the curse on his bloodline as well as properties. I don't know if I believe a Manitou was involved, but the possibility of it possessing someone and being behind the murders is entirely possible, especially if it was summoned in a ritual gone wrong."

I stared forward. "You are really not what I expected from an FBI agent."

"Thank you," Alex said, smiling.

"Uh, is my brother in trouble for drug dealing?" I asked, worried.

"Hopefully not," Alex said, putting a comforting arm on my shoulder. It made me want to lean up and kiss him. "I'm here to solve a murder, not investigate vice. Your brother may be in danger, though, if he really has been involved in demonology."

I thought about that. "Yeah, no kidding. I need to go back to the sheriff's office and beat some answers out of him."

"Don't you mean bleat some answers out of him?"

I glared then used the keycard to summon the elevator. "Not funny. Deer puns are a sensitive subject with me."

"My apologies," Alex said.

"So, if it's not too much of an imposition, may I ask what the deal between you and Lucien is?"

"I think you already know."

"He's really your foster brother?" I asked.

The elevator opened up and the two of us stepped inside as I swiped the card to take us downstairs.

"Yes," Alex said. "The Drake family—"

Ah, Lucien was going by his mother's surname.

"Seriously?" I said, wondering why they'd take the Latin name for dragons. You know, ignoring all hypocrisy on my part. "Is it just a shifter thing?"

Alex shrugged. "I didn't name them. They were, however, the second most powerful clan of shifters in North America. Lucien's cousins still control Florida's shifters in defiance of the werewolves' control in the continent."

"But Marcus O'Henry killed all the ones in this town?" I asked, wondering how Marcus had killed all of the dragons in town without anyone noticing.

Then I realized there was only one time he could have done it. A week when every single shifter was hiding in their homes or the woods, terrified of a massive purge of their families by the government. It had been a period when there'd been riots across the country and plenty of old scores settled as the old order among supernaturals collapsed. Dad had taken me, Jeanine, and Jeremy to Grandpa Jacob's cabin while Mom had tried to prepare all the other shifters for the change in our society.

"Yes," Alex said, seeing my reaction. "A purge occurred during the Reveal. My mother, also an FBI agent, was called to investigate the murders, but discovered Lucien hiding in the woods by himself. A scared fourteen-year-old who had witnessed the slaughter of his family by human mercenaries armed with silver ammunition."

"Then why isn't he in jail?" I asked.

"The US government pardoned him and other leaders of the supernatural community as part of the bailout following the 2008 financial collapse," Alex said, disgusted. "In the end, after a car meant to drive Lucien to the airport was blown up, my mother took him into our home. He stayed with us until I went to join the FBI myself and he decided he wanted to get revenge."

I looked at him. "Wait, he's a crime boss because he wants to kill Marcus O'Henry?"

"Not just Marcus," Alex said, his voice disappointed. "He wants to take everything from the O'Henrys. I was hoping for better for him."

"But you don't think he killed Victoria?" I asked the obvious question.

"No," Alex said. "Do you?"

"No."

Neither of us said anything as the elevator moved down.

"Now you owe me some insights," Alex said, interrupting the silence.

"What?"

"Quid pro quo," Alex said, smiling. "I've shared my past and now you have to share yours."

I frowned. "I don't have anything interesting about me. Hell, you probably can learn everything about me just by looking at me. I've lived here my entire life. I attend community college. I'm really not that interesting. I mean, unless you're a weirdo who finds weredeer inherently exotic, in which case I consider you really culturally insensitive."

Alex chuckled. "Jane, you were asked to investigate the death of your worst enemy. You not only have done so, you forced the medical examiner to confess his involvement with the victim and then ran to interrogate a known drug dealer. You are many things, interesting being at the top of the list."

I blushed, flattered by his attention. "I dunno. It's not like…"

"You don't have to tell me anything, Jane." Alex turned away.

I closed my eyes. "It'll sound stupid."

"I doubt that."

I took a deep breath. "I don't want to be inconsequential. I don't want to be who I am. I want to be someone who matters. That requires being more than just a person who eats leaves three days a month."

"Uh-huh."

"You don't understand," I said, not expecting him to. "I grew up in a house where everything was judged before me. I was supposed to be a shaman like my mother. My grandfather was going to set me up with a weredeer husband to be a housewife. It was all stifling and I had plans to run away from it all."

"Still plan to?" Alex asked.

I lowered my gaze. "No. I don't. The Reveal occurred and now everyone knows shifters exist. That changed everything. I can't go anywhere. I can be shot in any state but Michigan and Vermont. I'm going to have to list the fact I'm a weredeer on any employment form and I'll be treated like I'm diseased everywhere but Bright Falls. My parents dropped the idea of forcing me into keeping the old traditions alive when Grandpa Jacob died, but now I'm more boxed in than before."

"So you've jumped into solving a murder," Alex said. "Regardless of the danger."

"Yeah, it felt…exciting," I said, ashamed of myself. "More important than anything else I've done. Did you know, last year, I asked my mom to test me to be a shaman? Something I never thought in my wildest dreams I'd ask to do, but at least it was something."

"What happened?"

"I don't have any talent with magic," I said, closing my eyes. "I can read objects and see the future, but it turns out everything else is beyond me. I don't have any talent for spirit talking. I should but…I don't. I'm more like my dad than my mom in that."

"Not the best motive to fight crime."

I grimaced. "Yeah, please don't tell Emma. I should be doing this for Victoria's sake. But, at most, I'm doing it for Emma's sake."

I had another secret. A terrible thing I did as a child, but I was over it. I'd made my peace with my actions. Honest. That really wasn't any of Agent Timmons's business, anyway.

Alex nodded. "I won't tell Emma you want to be normal but in an exceptional way because being exceptional in a magical way bores you."

"You make it sound silly," I said.

"Speaking as the wizard FBI agent," Alex paused. "It really is."

I rolled my eyes before hiding a smile. He really was entertaining. "Why do you want to know all this personal information, anyway?"

"I want to deputize you."

I blinked and turned to him. "What?"

The elevator door pinged and opened. A rush of hot air poured out and I was momentarily blinded by the crackle of flames.

Alex looked outside. "We should probably discuss this when we're not in Hell."

CHAPTER TWELVE

"Wait, hell, as in Hell-Hell?" I said, falling into the back of the elevator.

The sight that greeted me on the other side of the elevator certainly looked like Hell, though. It was the interior of the Lyon's Den, except everything was on fire while terrible flaming dogs were scattered through the room, all looking at me like I was their next meal. The heat was intense and the smell was utterly foul. Thankfully, there was no sign of the customers as I didn't think I could stand the whole 'tortured for all eternity' thing without trying to help them.

"No. Not really, but close enough," Alex said, reaching into his coat pocket and pulling out a handful of white powder he blew in front of him. It formed into a circle with a lot of strange marks on it as well as a Seal of Solomon. "There, that should buy us some time."

"Why am I here?" I asked, trying to figure out what the hell (literally!) was going on. "Breaking and entering can't be a damnation worthy offense! I don't even believe in eternal damnation."

"It's a reality wrinkle," Alex said, his voice quivering only just a bit. It was really impressive since I was terrified out of my mind.

"Assume I'm really awful at being a shaman and explain that in dumbass," I said, actually kind of jealous of Alex's displayed powers. I'd seen my mom do some equivalent things but this was one of the few times I'd seen someone actually use big, epic magic. Most of the time it worked in the form of coincidences.

This was not that kind of magic.

"You're not even close to being a dumbass, Jane. But in laymen's terms it means someone has pressed a section of the Spirit World in on this section of the material plane and we've wandered into it," Alex said, taking a deep breath. "This is some pretty impressive magic."

"You think?" I snapped. I was already starting to sweat and my makeup was starting to run. I was actually glad I wasn't wearing much in that moment, since Agent Timmons was sweating heavily as well. It had to be scorching under that trench coat and suit.

"It's also a sign the Lodge is being harnessed," Alex said, blinking. "The killer or one of their associates would need a holy spot where the veil between the worlds was weak to make this kind of summoning."

"Who cares!" I shouted, raising my hands in front of me. "Just get us out of here!"

Alex grimaced. "I actually have no idea how to do that."

"What?!"

"It's not my area of expertise!" Alex said, finally showing a fearful look. "I'm more into knowledge and defense than altering reality."

"Screw being a Jedi!" I said, closing my eyes and wishing to any god who was listening for a way out.

Much to my surprise, I heard a ripping sound and looked over to the stage where I saw an actual crack in reality about six feet in height. On the other side of the rift, I saw Lucien Lyons and Sheriff Clara. Beyond them, I saw Emma and Jeanine too. All of them looked terrified looking through the portal.

"It appears our prayers have been answered," Alex said, reaching into his coat pocket and pulling out a standard-issue Glock 23 (I learned that from the internet). It, too, had a number of symbols on the side that I believed to be Hebrew. I imagined it said, "This Machine Kills Demons." He then unexpectedly handed it to me.

"Uh," I said, taking the gun. "Alex, what are you doing?"

"Do you how to use this?" Alex asked.

"I'm a country girl from Michigan, so yes," I said, blinking. "I'm more used to using a rifle than a pistol, though. Dad often took us out hunting to scare off deer poachers."

Wow, those trips were fun. We only used rock salt, though.

Alex looked like he was going to comment on that then shook his head. "I'm going to lower the barrier I've put up and try to keep us surrounded in a spell to hold off the demons and flames. Some covering fire would be very helpful."

I suddenly regretted my desire for a more interesting life. "I've got your back, Alex. I'm your deputy...which sounds really weird and kind of sexualized. Please ignore that last part."

Alex grinned then raised his hands and started chanting something I briefly thought to be the language of magic before recognizing it as Quenya from *The Lord of the Rings*. Deer Christ on a pogo stick, this guy might actually be a bigger geek than Jeremy. His hands started to glow a blue light that surrounded us both in a nimbus. It felt like a distilled concentration of love and peace. Not a good feeling for shooting.

"Don't let the flames touch you," Alex said, his voice low. "They'll do worse than burn you."

"Right," I said, not sure how to respond to that.

The two of us then passed through the Seal of Solomon and I was almost immediately buffeted by a terrible wind that came from the walls rather than the rift. I heard the sound of Victoria's taunts echoing through the air along with my mother's frustrations about my inability to do even the slightest spell.

"You're not special because you're a deer. You're just a weirdo hipster."

"You have the Gift and a chance to build on it, Jane. I don't know why you can't do this."

I heard the sound of my cousin Jill screaming as she was pulled down into Lake Darkwater. *"Help! Help, Jane!"*

"No," I muttered, taking a deep breath. "They don't get to bring up that. It wasn't my fault. It wasn't."

That was when I saw one of the hellhounds leap for my throat and I ended up shooting it in the throat, sending it spiraling back into the flames where it detonated.

"Do not mess with me," I snapped without bravado. "Deer actually eat meat, you know! We're not herbivores! We're omnivores."

I aimed throughout the club, shooting hellhound after hellhound. I didn't always get them, but even the wounds seemed to cause the others to back off. It made me feel stronger and tougher even as I just wanted to get out of here.

We were about halfway through the nightclub when Alex stopped and once more repeated the earlier spell, looking exhausted. His elvish was garbled and he didn't finish before falling to one knee.

"Alex, you okay?" I said, wondering just how many bullets I had left.

"No," Alex said, struggling to get up. "I am most certainly not."

The sounds of my cousin's laughter filled the air as water started dripping down the sides of the nightclub, causing steam to rise. I heard the sounds of my cousin screaming for help even as I couldn't help but remember being frozen in place, unable to move.

"I'm going in," Lucien shouted from the crack.

"No!" Clara said. "Stay where you are!"

That was when I saw the image of a faceless man in a trench coat and dressed in an FBI uniform similar to Alex's standing in the middle of the nightclub. I heard the sound of a boy screaming and felt waves of nausea as well as shame.

"Alex, who is that?" I asked.

"Don't look at him," Alex said. "It's just an image of my father. Drawn from my worst fears."

The figure started advancing.

"I looked at him, Alex," I said. "How bad is that?"

"*Bad!*"

A second faceless demon appeared, this time resembling a ten-year-old little girl in a black one-piece bathing suit. Her black hair and pigtail showed her not to be my poor drowned cousin, though, but me.

Stupid, cowardly me.

"I was a kid!" I shouted, shooting at the demons repeatedly until I ran out of ammunition. "Oh hell."

"Are you scared to go in the water, Jill?" a little distorted version of my voice as a child spoke. "Don't be stupid. It's just a lake. There's no monsters here."

"Go!" Alex said, his voice rasping out. He was on both knees now. "I'll cover you."

"Get on top of me!" I shouted.

"What?" Alex said.

"Not that way, jackass!" I said, hoping this didn't get us all killed. "Just do it."

I couldn't feel the moon in this place to aid in my transformation. Instead, I focused every bit of my anger and guilt to provide the necessary fuel for the Change. It wasn't like in the movies where my body physically transformed in some excruciating body horror. Instead, it was like I changed places with a deer in some other serene place. One minute, I was Jane the Human, and the next minute I was Jane the Deer.

Jane the Deer was someone a lot more majestic than Jane the Human. I had snow-white fur and there was a power inside me that felt far stronger than anything a mere human could possess. Sometimes, I wanted to just go off into the forest and live like this. That wasn't important right now, though, and I needed to focus on getting my FBI agent to safety.

When I felt his arms wrap around me, I turned around and started jumping toward the rift in reality. A normal deer wouldn't have been able to support Alex's weight, but every shifter had not just the strength of their animal but a few more besides. The flames licked at my legs and whenever they did, I didn't feel burns but something much more painful. I remembered how I'd failed Jill, how my brother was currently rotting in prison, and a how I was probably going to die in this town having accomplished nothing in my life.

"I am going to accomplish something now!" I said, sounding just like random deer noises to anyone else.

The two demons teleported in front of the rift while I trotted through the flames. I leapt into the air, refusing to let them block my way. I didn't actually get over them so much as smash into them. I half expected to experience a hundred thousand horrible things when I did so, but instead, both demons shattered like glass before the hellish landscape around me disappeared.

I found myself running past Clara and ended up coming to a stop right in the middle of the nightclub's back lot. It was night now, the sun having just set with a light rain pouring down from the sky. The rift to

Hell behind me sealed up and I felt an end to the horrible flames and terrible guilt the place carried memories of.

It was quite the sight outside of the rift. There was Lucien, I think, looking like some kind of human-Velociraptor raptor hybrid with crocodile skin and a long, thick tail standing over the bodies of several burning dog skeletons as well as an octopus-looking thing with eyes instead of suction cups. Clara was holding a shotgun while Jeanine was standing next to Emma. I also saw Deana next to a hideous steaming stag corpse that I assumed she'd managed to put out. A closer look revealed it had a human torso and a spear for an arm. Apparently, the group had spent their time fighting demons coming through the rift in order to keep the door open for us. I wasn't sure how to thank someone for that.

"Thank you," Alex said, his voice exhausted and quivering. "I owe you my life."

"Hey, no problem," I said, still in deer form as the rain poured down on me. "It's not every day I get ridden hard and left wet."

"I can understand you, you realize that, right?" Alex said, sliding off my side.

"Oh crap!" I said. "Forget I mentioned that!"

Alex burst out laughing.

I turned back into my human form, collapsing on the ground with most of my makeup ruined and half of my press-on nails having fallen off. "Kill me now."

"Are you all right?" Lucien said, reverting back to his human form and walking over to offer his hand to me.

"Oh, yeah," I said, taking his hand. "I'm just peachy. What's a little Hell between friends?"

As my hand touched Lucien's, I found myself having a vision of us kissing passionately underneath a set of silk covers as I felt waves of pleasure pass through my body. We were in a hotel room of some kind and I wasn't that much older. My eyes practically bulged out as I contemplated this in addition to the other vision I'd had about Alex.

Oh my God, I was going to be with both. What was wrong with me? I mean, aside from the fact that if a man was doing this no one would care. Wait, dammit, don't make this a gender thing! Lucien is a drug dealer and Alex is an FBI agent. Both are incredibly inappropriate hot guys to sleep with! Okay, what was my argument again?

"Jane?" Lucien said, obviously not picking up on what I was thinking.

"Ah!" I said, staring. "Nothing!'

My visions weren't always a 100% accurate, I had to remind myself. They showed me potential futures, but it was entirely within my power to act upon them in order to guarantee they did or did not happen. Besides, I hated Lucien? Right?

Lucien looked at me sideways then helped me to my feet. "Right. Well, you owe your sister a great deal. She was the one who figured out there was a reality bubble and opened a portal to it. We've been working on this for almost six hours."

Six hours? Whoa. Turning to Jeanine, I stared at her. "You can open portals into other realities?"

Jeanine shrugged. "Mom told me how. Just because I don't like doing magic doesn't mean I don't know how."

"Where is Mom, anyway?" I asked, trying to wrap my head on the fact that a few minutes in there was hours outside.

"Traveling upstate," Clara said, frowning. "For some reason, Agent Timmons thought your brother might be in danger as long as he's in this town."

"Shocking," Alex said, coughing as he looked barely able to stand on his own two feet. "Whoever would believe there might be a party willing to use violence against those who appear to be threatening their plan?"

Clara didn't respond but just narrowed her eyes. "Well, they failed to kill you both. I think we need to put Jane under twenty-four-hour protection along with anyone else associated with this case. It's clearly much bigger than a few dead shapeshifters."

"One of which is our sister!" Emma said, sounding shocked by Clara's description of the case.

Clara looked over at Emma. "I didn't mean anything by it."

Emma's glare continued.

Alex took several breaths before stretching out his arms in a yoga-like pose and rolling his head around in circles. "I'm afraid, despite the attempt on Ms. Doe's and my life, that we cannot stop our investigation. Recent events have led me to believe the heart of this case is going to be decided in Darkwater Preserve at the Old Lodge."

"The Lodge hasn't been used in decades," Clara said, sounding more defensive than expected. "It also moves around depending on who is doing the seeking. The old shamans and witches did a lot of spells to hide it from humans. Spells that haven't been maintained."

"Nevertheless," Alex said, pulling out a flashlight. "Look we must. Jane, would you do me a favor and meet me there?"

"What?" Jeanine said. "You can't take my sister there! Darkwater Preserve is dangerous! Our cousin drowned there."

I clenched both of my hands and tried not to feel like I'd been punched in the gut. What had happened wasn't my fault. Even though I'd dared her to swim in the part of the lake that was fenced off.

Even though I'd lied after.

Not my fault.

"I'll do it," I said, my mouth dry. "No one else should die."

I had another reason to want to solve this case now.

Redemption.

Chapter Thirteen

"You want a teenage girl to help you?" Clara said, staring at Alex as she let her shotgun hang down beside her in a most non-police officer-like fashion. "Are you insane?"

Alex shrugged his shoulders. "Actually, I did spend some time in a mental institution when I was younger. That was related to my father's systemic abuse and my burgeoning magical powers, however. Medication and therapy have allowed me to live a normal life as well as harness the full capacity of my abilities, though."

Lucien chuckled at this while everyone else looked confused, myself included.

Clara blinked, obviously at a loss for how to respond. "I'm...sorry."

"Well, if I forbid her from going, what do you think she'd do?" Alex asked, pulling out a green lollipop from his pocket. It smelled like weed.

"Hey, I'm right here." I paused, gathering my thoughts. "I'd sulk an hour or two then go anyway."

"So I figured," Alex said, sucking on his lollipop. "Given that whoever is involved in this just tried to kill us both, it seemed a good idea to keep her close by instead. Though, I admit, Jane did more protecting of me than the reverse."

"All the more reason to lock her up!" Clara said, staring at us both as the rain poured down. "She's obstructed justice!"

"Hardly. We've gotten more leads from her than any other source. She is just the deer-in-the-China-shop we need," Alex said, pulling out an orange umbrella and handing it to me then pulling out another and then another to pass around the group. I suspected that was magic at work since I doubted he had a collection of umbrellas in his pocket.

"It's supposed to be a bull, not a deer." Clara shook her head, clearly bewildered. "I swear, you are either the worst FBI agent I have ever met or the best."

"Have you met any others?" Alex asked.

"No," Clara said, realizing that kind of reduced the statement's value. "You are pretty damn weird, though."

"Thank you," Alex said, pulling out a second lollipop and offering it to me. "Care for one, Jane? You've earned it."

"Uh, are those pot lollipops?"

"Entirely legal in Michigan," Alex said. "The vampires legalizing everything has some benefits."

"Worst FBI agent," Clara said, shaking her head. "Have you even solved any cases?"

"Twenty-four," Alex said. "Twenty-one multiple homicides and three kidnappings. Sexual assault was involved in—"

"Forget I asked," Clara said, taking the last umbrella and popping it over her head. It was a jet-black color with silver lining.

Lucien walked over and took the second lollipop before putting it in his mouth. "You should contact her mother instead. If the Lodge is involved, you need more than an untrained girl."

I glared at him. "Says the guy whose club recently became a Hellmouth."

Emma looked uncomfortable as she stood under a pink umbrella. "I dunno, Jane, maybe it'd be a good idea to call in the experts now. This isn't just the case of laying your hands on a body to find out the killer. I mean, you were almost killed. I'm sorry, I shouldn't have involved you."

"You're right," Jeanine said, crossing her arms and glaring at Emma. "You shouldn't have."

Jeanine was the only one without an umbrella. I wasn't too worried. Weredeer, like all shifters, were immune to catching the common cold.

"I don't think anyone expected a Hell dimension as a natural consequence of involving myself," I said, getting under Alex's blue umbrella.

"No, just serial murder," Jeanine said. "I'm taking you home, Jane. This is way too dangerous."

"You decided this *after* helping me break into Lucien's office?" I said, raising an eyebrow. "Way to stay the course, Jean."

Jeanine covered her face before pointing at Lucien. "Great, advertise it to the world, why don't you? He's *right over there.*"

"Yes, because I couldn't figure out you let her in," Lucien said, snorting. He held a red umbrella over his head while sucking on his lollipop. "I am clearly dealing with a pair of criminal masterminds."

"Be nice," Deana said, standing beside her employer. "Whitetail #1 and Whitetail #2 have won my respect. They were both willing to stand up to you, Boss."

"That's a racial slur," I said.

"Says the white American girl to the brown Indian woman," Deana said.

Oh, right. "Never mind."

Lucien surveyed the group. "This is a far larger issue than any of us. I'd like to offer my services to help you resolve it."

"No," Clara said, her voice low and threatening. "We don't need your help."

In that moment, she sounded a lot like Victoria. There was a lot of resentment there and I understood why.

"Sheriff—"

"You got my niece killed," Clara said, her voice icy. "I'd arrest you, but I don't need that kind of trouble with the undead right now."

Ah, yes, that note from Thoth in New Detroit.

Lucien didn't respond and I wasn't about to mention that Victoria had been at the heart of this herself.

"I want to help," Jeanine said, raising her voice. "I know about the Lodge. If that will keep Jane safe, then—"

Alex surprised everyone by starting to rattle off facts about it. "The Lodge is a shapeshifter sacred place built on a holy site of the Odawa people. It was a place where the veil between worlds was identified as especially weak. The Odawa villages in the area included a collection of shapeshifters who mixed with a group of similarly-gifted French fur trappers. These trappers were looking for a place to settle their families fleeing the persecution of shapeshifters begun in 1598 with the execution of werewolf Peter Strumpp. Later, these individuals would be joined by Irish and Scottish shapechangers who created the syncretic culture found here today."

I looked over at Alex. "We know our town's history, Alex."

"You've done your research," Clara said, nodding.

Alex nodded. "Yes, well, the Lodge became a place of great spiritual significance. A place administering to shapeshifters across the globe until it was suddenly abandoned in 1954 and considered cursed."

I sighed. "I can't tell you the reason why. I didn't even know the missing thirteenth clan was a bunch of dragons until today."

"Really?" Jeanine asked.

I rolled my eyes. "Yeah, well, I didn't pay much attention to my mother's stories once I found out I'd never be a shaman."

"Maybe you should have tried harder," Jeanine criticized.

"Maybe you should go back to Brad," I said, looking around. "Where is he anyway?"

Jeanine didn't meet my gaze. "He didn't stay. Apparently, he took my siding with my family against his boss poorly."

I looked at Lucien. "Nice job."

"Jeanine made her choice," Lucien said. "Albeit, Brad is a poor student of my philosophy if he thinks siding with me against the person he loves will make me respect him. Quite the opposite."

"Let's stay on topic, people," Clara said. "We still haven't even agreed we're even going to look for the Lodge. Darkwater Preserve may not be as large as Bright Falls State Park, but it's still hundreds of square miles. There's no way we can cover it all by ourselves."

"Jane's visions will help," Alex said. "I guarantee it. I believe a terrible crime was committed in the Lodge," Alex said, looking at the horizon as the rain continued to pour down over us. "One so heinous that it tainted the site and made it so it became a link to only the darkest parts of the Spirit World. I believe Victoria might have encountered that part of the Lodge and been touched by it."

"Abandoning your theory for Lucien's? Listen, I don't believe demons are responsible." I looked back at the nightclub, feeling overwhelmed by all the attention here. "Albeit, that theory has taken a hit, since I've seen they're real with my own two eyes."

"Human hands sacrificed the three victims," Alex said. "Demons do not practice religion or ritual magic. Such rites are only done by humans. That doesn't mean the clues aren't going to be found there. I need your help, Jane."

My heart started beating faster. "Oh, well, in that case, yeah, I want to do it."

"You wanted to do it before," Alex pointed out.

I admitted I did. "Why are you trusting me with all this?"

Alex smiled. "Call it intuition."

There wasn't much to say after that and the various groups broke up. I overheard some of the conversations that followed and got the general gist of Lucien not being at all happy at being let out, Clara not at all being happy with any of Alex's decisions, and Jeanine practically begging me to come with her. That last part I didn't have to overhear since it was directed at me but I didn't listen. Still, I was sorry I got her fired and would try to get her rehired by pointing out that she saved my life. That probably wouldn't work since it wasn't like Lucien and I were friends or anything. Just future lovers.

Yikes.

Really the next half-hour or so, which brought us to nearly eleven in the evening, was something of a blur. I barely registered anything as all of the events of the day came crashing down on top of me. Aside from cleaning off my goth makeup and changing my clothes so I didn't look like a goth hooker, I just went through the motions of getting ready to join the others at Darkwater Preserve. I wasn't even the one to drive the Millennium Falcon because I couldn't get the images of Jill drowning out of my head.

I wasn't bothered by the actual flames of Hell or the fact I'd nearly died there. No, I was bothered by the memories it stirred up. I'd lied to my parents about daring Jill to go in and repeated it so many times that I'd come to believe it myself. The fact that I'd been ten years old and terrified didn't mitigate what I'd done.

"Jane," Emma said, driving through the stereotypical dark and stormy night around us. The moon was a half-moon above us and I felt its power radiating down. It wasn't a full moon, but it was waxing, and the power inside me grew strong as a result.

I didn't pay attention to Emma's statement. Instead, I just stared forward, continuing to think about whether it was possible to find a way to make up for letting my cousin die. I couldn't see one but I needed to learn to live with what I'd done.

Somehow.

"Jane!" Emma said.

I almost jumped out of my seat. "Yo!"

"You've been out in space since the club," Emma said, turning off the radio. It must have been serious because it was playing Warren Zevon's "Werewolves of London", which I knew to be Emma's favorite song. I suspected she and my father must have shared a spiritual connection of some kind.

"Sorry, visiting Hell will do that," I said, unable to keep the sarcasm from my voice. "Why didn't you back me up back there?"

Emma looked confused. "What? What do you mean?"

"You told them I should go home," I said, still ticked off about that. "We've come way too far to stop now."

"You almost died, Jane!" Emma said, using more force in her voice than I ever heard. "Worse, you were almost stuck in—"

"Hell?" I said, sighing. "Yeah, I was there. It's not a nice experiencing having your least favorite parts of your religion confirmed as true."

Emma didn't respond to that. "I can't let you die."

"Yeah, yeah," I said, not paying too much attention to the anguish in her words. "I'm like a sister to you."

"No, not even close."

I blanched, realizing what I'd said. "I'm sorry, I keep forgetting your relationship with Victoria. That changes the context of what I said."

Emma sighed, clearly upset. "No, Jane, that's not what I feel at all."

Okay, now I was just confused. "Well, I'm sorry anyway."

Emma didn't say anything for a moment. "Is this really about Victoria now?"

I paused. "No, no it's not."

"I thought not," Emma said.

"It's about my brother, Victoria, Courtney, that Thomas guy, and the fact that I almost got murdered along with Agent Timmons. It's about anyone else who's going to be murdered in the upcoming weeks. This is bigger than just one person. Sorry, I don't mean to offend you."

"All right," Emma said. "I understand that."

I looked out the window into the forest beyond the highway. "I'm sorry for turning your sister's death into my own personal crusade. That's on me."

"It's all right," Emma said, mumbling under her breath. "It's why I love you."

"Hmm?" I asked.

"What?" Emma said, doing a double take. "So what do you think of that Lucien Lyons person? Wow, he is pretty."

"Yeah, I suppose," I said, trying not to agree wholeheartedly. "If you like egotistical jerks."

"Who doesn't?" Emma piped in. "Bad boys are all the rage...or so I've heard."

"I dunno," I said, thinking about my pair of visions. "The good guys aren't so bad either."

Chapter Fourteen

We had to stop on the way to Darkwater Preserve for gas because, well, the Millennium Falcon got a mile per gallon when it *wasn't* raining. I think it was every fifty feet when it was storming outside. Also, I needed snacks as I hadn't had dinner and fighting evil was hungry work. I ended up eating the majority of them in the car as we struggled to make up for lost time.

"You realize Twinkies aren't the natural food of weredeer, right?" Emma said, shaking her head.

"I hunt in the manner of my ancestors. I graze."

Emma rolled her eyes. "I'm lucky I'm a carnivore."

"Yes, we can hunt a quarter-pounder and fries for you," I said, sighing.

"I'm fine," Emma said, taking a deep breath. "Recent events haven't exactly improved my appetite."

"Yeah," I said, slurping my Root Deer. Yes, that was the name of it. Aunt Jennifer owned all of the gas stations in town.

Eventually, we came into sight of Darkwater Preserve. It was a small patchy forest around a small lake visible from the highway. There was something about the place that made my skin crawl and I didn't just mean because of the bad memories associated with the place. A weird vibe permeated the place and radiated outward. Not necessarily evil, *per se*, but otherworldly. I'd loved the feeling when I was a child but now it was just a reminder of the dark times.

"Are you okay with taking me to the Lodge?" I asked.

"Don't have much of a choice, do I?" Emma said. "You volunteered us for this mission."

"Well, I'm un-volunteering you."

"I've got your back," Emma said. "Through and through. Even though, after this, I'm totally going on vacation to Disneyworld."

"Try New Detroit instead," I said. "It's in-state and has better entertainment for adults."

"Not until you're twenty-one," Emma said, making a face. "It's also full of vampires."

"Don't be racist. Gerald seemed all right. He wasn't responsible for what happened to Victoria."

"What Victoria wanted," Emma said, her voice low. Then it cracked and I could tell she was going to ask something important. "Jane, was she evil?"

I paused. This was heavy stuff. "Victoria?"

"Yeah."

I had to think about my answer. After all, she was a rapist drug dealer involved with black magic. Evil was a pretty easy label to throw around, especially at her, but I wasn't sure that was what she needed to hear. "Evil. I don't like that word. I don't think it really exists. Everyone has a reason for what they do. Good reasons or bad. Bad wiring or not."

It was an attitude I'd stuck with since I turned sixteen and tried to reconcile what had happened with my cousin. It wasn't a very good attitude to have in a world where there were verifiable demons and monsters. Still, it was the only one I could stomach.

"I believe in evil," Emma said. "I believe there are people who do terrible things simply because it makes them feel better. It's not because they're victims themselves or because they believe it will make the world a better place. It's because they get off on it."

Wow. Where was this coming from? "You think Victoria was like that?"

"I think my whole family is like that," Emma growled, her hands tightening around the steering wheel. "I thought Clara was different, but she's been stonewalling this investigation since it began. Werewolves beat everything out of you that is good. Compassion, friendship, love, and understanding are the first to go. I hate that stupid

'Alpha' dominance thing. We'd be different if we were like real wolves."

This was perhaps too much information for one go. "I'm sure your family still loves you, Emma."

Emma didn't respond and pulled the Falcon into a parking space next to the Preserve's main entrance. The parking lot was empty except for the Sheriff's police car, a black Cadillac I assumed to be Agent Timmons's, and a third junky Ford I didn't recognize. She turned off the ignition and the car set the mood by the loud *clunk* the engine made as it ceased revving.

"Do you think it will start up again?" Emma asked, pointedly ignoring my last question.

"Alex's car is over there," I said. "If it doesn't, we're good." I hoped I sounded reassuring. I wished someone would reassure me.

"Oh, it's Alex now, is it?" Emma ribbed me, all sign of her earlier melancholy gone. I hoped it was dark enough to hide my sudden blushing.

The sign on the gate read, "DARKWATER LAKE NATURE PRESERVE. NO ADMITTANCE WITHOUT PERMISSION OF THE RANGERS' SERVICE, $10,000 FINE." It wasn't really a nature sanctuary—more of an unnatural sanctuary. They just wanted to keep people out. Well, they wanted to keep tourists out; nobody who had grown up in this town would go in there.

Except we did. My cousin's voice came and went so quickly that I wasn't sure if I had heard it, or if my guilt was just a bit clearer since having gone to Hell. Goddess, I wish I didn't have to think that and mean it literally.

There was no sign of anyone inside the cars present and that put me on edge. It was still raining and I pulled out the umbrella that Alex had given me. Standing underneath it, I checked my cellphone and managed to text one handed, "WHERE ARE YOU?"

No response.

Emma came out underneath me. "This is a little like an old horror movie."

"*Everything* in Bright Falls is a little like an old horror movie," I said, taking a deep breath. "In any case, I'm not actually going to enter the evil cursed woods without backup. I'm not an idiot."

Emma stared at me. "You entered the crime lord's office and broke into the sheriff's office."

"Once banished, twice shy," I said.

That was when a midnight-black female crow flew through the air and landed on top of the Millennium Falcon before staring at us. Then, in a thick New Jersey accent she spoke, "What's up, losers?"

I stared at the bird. "Maria?"

Maria Gonzales was the only one of my brother's friends I actually liked. The fact that she was Rudy's sister was something I didn't hold against her. However, that was before I'd found out she was a drug dealer and now intimately involved in this whole murder-sacrifice business. I was less pleased to see her as a result than I might have been. In fact, my hand went to the Taser in the back of my pocket.

"Shouldn't you say, 'Nevermore'?" Emma said, looking at the raven.

"Do I look like I'm resting on a bust of Pallas?" Maria said, still in crow form. "Also, I'm a crow, not a raven."

"There's a difference?" I asked.

"Oh no you didn't!" Maria said, jokingly. "What are you two doing here?"

"What are *you* doing here?" I asked, suspiciously.

"I asked first," she said, frowning. "If you didn't know—"

That was when my cellphone buzzed. Checking my text messages, I noticed I'd gotten one from Agent Timmons. "GONE ON INSIDE THE WOODS. PATH OPENED UP TO LOCATION. EVERYTHING SAFE."

Emma looked over my shoulder at the message. "Well, that's ominous."

I blinked. "Why is that ominous? It is the exact opposite of ominous."

"We're being reassured it's safe to go in the spooky woods!" Emma said. "Buffy would know it's a trap."

113

"Buffy isn't real!" I snapped. "In any case, Maria, you didn't answer my question."

The crow flew off the top of the Falcon (hehe) then transformed into a petite human woman about my age. Maria was an inch taller than me with dusky skin, smooth black hair, full lips, and a curvy, compact form incongruous for a werebird. She was wearing a black sweater and jeans with a piece of silver ankh jewelry that provided the tasteful goth counterpoint to my sister's sexy goth dancer's attire. She was also wearing hiking boots that had signs of mud on them.

"I am here to solve a murder," Maria said, putting her hands on her hips. "The cops are after your brother and I don't want mine getting caught up in this. Also, Victoria and Courtney were my friends."

"Doesn't that make you a suspect?" Emma asked, her voice a little more hostile than necessary.

"In the context, anyone who knew Victoria well was a suspect," Maria said, showing a remarkable lack of concern to how that looked. "Wait, Jane, you're a psychic, read my palm."

Maria stretched it out.

I stared at her. "My power doesn't work like that. Besides, we're here to solve the murders too."

"Sweet!" Maria said, showing a lot more enthusiasm than I expected. "We can be like the Hardy Sisters."

"Wouldn't that just be Nancy Drew?" I asked.

"Nancy Drew was the Hardy Boys' sister?" Maria asked. "I'll be honest, I never actually read those books. I was more into comics. *Sandman, Hellblazer, Lucifer.* All of the good stuff."

I stared at her, irritated now. "Maria, there's no way we're involving you. We need to catch up with the police and you're a person of interest so—"

"Ah, look at you, talking all police-y," Maria said, pulling out her cellphone and then presenting me with dozens of pictures of her outside various locations across the city. McDonalds, the sheriff's department, a gas station, and also a pet store.

"What is this?" I asked, looking at them.

"Evidence!" Maria said. "Check the time stamp. I wasn't anywhere near Victoria when she was killed."

I paused, checking the numbers then looking over at Emma. "Okay, that's a point in your favor. Still, it's pretty coincidental you showed up here."

"Yeah, I can't imagine why I'd show up at the site of the latest murder," Maria said. "I've been flying around here for the past few hours trying to find Rudy."

My ears perked up. "Your brother is here?"

Rudy was on my shortlist of suspects, but that was mostly because I didn't actually have any suspects. It was also just because he was a creep and a pervert. The fact that he was Maria's brother, someone I considered to be a friend, put that accusation into perspective. Also, while I might be willing to imagine someone like him could commit a murder—well, I couldn't imagine Rudy was some sort of magical genius. Whoever had attacked us back at the Lyons' Den had been packing some serious mojo. Rudy couldn't keep a job as a busboy.

"Yes," Maria said, her voice lowering a bit. "That idiot has gotten himself into something serious and I'm getting him back."

I narrowed my eyes, debating whether or not to accuse her brother right then and there. "You're part of the group being targeted."

"No kidding!" Maria said, snorting in a most un-crow-like fashion. "I hadn't noticed that when my friends started dying."

"Come with us," I said, extending my hand. "You can tell everything you know to Agent Timmons."

"No way!" Maria said. "You can't trust the Feds. They want to round us all up and put us to work in zoos. That's how they'll make money from us! Gawking tourists! Tourists who want to see us turn into things!"

I blinked. "I don't think they want to do that."

"You can trust Jane's FBI guy!" Emma said. "He went through Hell with her."

"No puns!" I snapped.

"No, that was just being accurate," Emma said, reaching over to put her hand on Maria's shoulder. "You can tell us the whole story of you, Victoria, and the others."

"Victoria said she used magic to become a shifter so she got us to join her in doing magic then we ended up selling drugs because she needed money to buy more magic from Lucien?" Maria said.

"Wow, the whole story was shorter than I thought," Emma said.

"It also involved beer, sex, and some of us turning up dead," Maria said. "Not fond of the latter."

"Victoria is my sister, remember," Emma said. "I care that something happened to her."

"You're probably the only one," Maria said. "Not to be cruel—"

"Too late," I said.

"But it's true," Maria said, sighing. "Victoria didn't give a shit about us. We were just bodies for her to work magic that couldn't be done by one person. I mean, yeah, I got what I wanted out of it, but that doesn't mean I didn't resent Victoria screwing around with me and Jeremy."

I got an ugly mental image. "By screwing around, do you mean—"

Emma interrupted. "We need to find the Lodge! It's the key to all of this."

"The Lodge finds you," Maria said, her voice low. "It's not a nice place."

"You know how to get there?" I asked, ignoring the crux of what she said. "Please."

Maria sighed. "All right, I'll go see your G-man. However, if it gets dangerous, I'm blaming it all on the one-winged raven."

I didn't get it. "Uh-huh."

"One-winged raven, one-armed man," Maria said, looking confused. "Never mind."

I pointed to the gate and sighed. "Listen, they're probably just inside. Let's just get inside. I want to hear everything you did with my brother."

Maria raised an eyebrow. "Everything? Including the sex?"

"No!" I snapped, horrified. "I meant the drug dealing and magic."

"Then specify!" Maria asked. "Are you sure we should be doing this?"

"I'm sure all the signs are pointing us this way," I said, heading to the barred iron gate in the middle of a much larger metal fence going in both directions. It circled the entire preserve from what I remembered.

"Can we do this in the morning?" Maria asked, hopefully not serious. "You two may be nocturnal, but sensible animals go around when the sun is out and you can see things."

"Agent Timmons is waiting for us, and I'm not going to just leave him," I said.

"Pity he didn't have the sense to wait here," Emma said.

I was torn between wanting to defend Alex and agreeing with her completely so I just stayed quiet.

"He went in through here," Emma said, pointing at a gap between the fence and the gate. "I can smell the crushed grass. He's not the first person to get in this way, either. It looks like this has been used regularly."

"Victoria's coven?" I asked.

"Don't call them that," Emma said.

"Why?" Maria said. "It's what we called ourselves."

Emma looked more and more irritated with every one of Maria's pithy comments.

I didn't feel like getting my clothes dragged through the bushes just yet, so I took a few steps back, got a running start, and leapt over the gate. "Super Deer Jumping Powers Activate!"

Emma and Maria shifted, with Maria flying over the gate and Emma walking through the gap in a more compact wolf form. Both shifted back quickly. On the other side, I saw a long twisted path through large foreboding pine trees with the clouds blotting out all but the barest hints of moonlight. The rain was letting up but it was still damp with the ground muddy and wet beneath our feet.

"I don't know, maybe animal form would be better here," I said.

"I don't think either form is better here," Maria said.

"If you don't want to find what happened to your brother, you can wait in the car," Emma said snappishly.

"Cool!" Maria said, about to turn around before I grabbed her by the arm.

"What's in here?" I asked, physically turning her back to the gate.

"The Old Lodge, supposedly," Maria said. "The Darkwater. The Falls, of course. A lot of pines. Ghosts. I hate ghosts."

"Spirits," I said, feeling silly after Maria had given a much more detailed answer. "Lots and lots of spirits."

"Will we see them?" Emma asked.

"Not a shaman," I said. "But I didn't..."

Damnit, I hadn't wanted to say that.

"You've been here before?" Maria asked.

"A long time ago." I walked forward down what looked like a path and called out, "Agent Timmons! Alex?"

The silence was deafening.

"Shouldn't he have heard us?"

That was when I saw a cellphone on the ground. Its screen was glowing brightly, providing some of the only illumination around us. Walking over, I picked it up and saw it had been used to send the text I'd received. It was Agent Timmons's cellphone.

Ah, hell.

CHAPTER FIFTEEN

"Okay, time for me to go!" Maria said, turning around and starting for the car again.

I grabbed her for a second time, only for her to dodge out of the way only to run face-first into Emma's chest.

"Where do you think you're going?" Emma asked, grabbing her by both shoulders.

"Away from danger!" Maria said, cheerfully. "I'm a creature of instincts and when there's something awful about to happen, the best thing to do is fly away."

"We don't know anything awful has happened," I said, my voice not exactly conveying reassurance.

"Hello! Haunted creepy woods," Maria said, gesturing about. "Cellphone on the ground. About the only thing worse right now would be you telling us we need to investigate."

"We need to investigate," I said, leaning down and picking up Alex's cellphone.

"See!" Maria said, getting away from Emma and flapping her arms about. "An even worse thing would be to tell Emma to let me go and get help."

I stared back at her. "We're not letting you go."

"Dammit, you're supposed to fall for reverse psychology!" Maria said, putting her hands on her hips. "Be more dumb."

I rolled my eyes. "We're going to find out what happened if it's the last thing we do."

"That's what I'm afraid of!" Maria piped in.

I felt a headache coming on as I tried to figure out what might have occurred. Alex was someone who could take care of himself but there wasn't much he could have done to stave off an attack like the one we'd experienced earlier. Was there? Holding the cellphone in my hands, I tried to get a sense of what had happened.

I proceeded to find myself filled with a sense of warmth and light I hadn't expected. There was a calm certainty and sense of iron-clad determination possessed by this cellphone's owner. It was something that didn't reek of self-righteousness, but someone who had experienced terrible things and didn't want to have anyone else suffer them.

I knew that feeling well.

What followed was a vision of him texting me before he was struck from behind and then grabbed in a headlock. A voice, harsh and guttural, whispered something into his ear that caused him to lose consciousness. Some kind of spell. His last thought was worrying about Emma and I. He wasn't dead, though.

"Alex has been kidnapped," I said, taking a deep breath. "We have to rescue him."

"Or call the cops!" Maria suggested.

"Cops have better things to do than get killed," I said, quoting *Big Trouble in Little China.*

"So do we!" Maria shouted.

That caused a huge flock of birds to jump out from the trees around us and sail into the air.

"See? They know what's what," Maria said, sighing.

"We can't call the cops," Emma said, frowning as she looked around. "They were already here. Did you see anything about Clara?"

I cleaned the cellphone off and put it in my pocket. "No, no I didn't."

I didn't want to bring up the fact Clara had to have been there when Alex was ambushed and should have done something. The fact that she hadn't was suspicious. As was the fact that she hadn't come with any deputies.

"I see," Emma said. "Then we have to go."

"Why does everyone keep saying that?" Maria said, throwing her hands up in the air.

"Isn't your brother out here? Don't you want to find him?" I asked, daring her to argue.

Maria instantly deflated. "You're right, he is. Rudy said he was coming out here the moment he found out Jeremy was in jail. He was already having a bit of a nervous breakdown since Courtney died."

"Was murdered," I corrected. "Was he close to Courtney?"

"She was his girlfriend, yeah," Maria said.

"Someone actually touched your brother?" Emma asked. "Willingly?"

Maria turned around and gave a nasty look to Emma.

"It's probably best if you forget I said that," Emma said, frowning. "I'm not as good as Jane at being incredibly rude during times of great emotional distress."

Maria looked over at me.

I shrugged my shoulders. "It's a fair cop."

"You need to tell us everything," I said, taking a deep breath. "Not just a short summary, but everything."

"Isn't it a bad idea to just be standing here talking when that might attract whatever kidnapped the FBI agent?" Maria said, sighing. "I'm not just following my crow instincts here. I'm pointing out some basic survival strategies."

"I have a gun," I said, thinking about the one Alex had given me. "And a Taser."

"Oh that's going to keep the Hellbeasts away," Maria muttered.

"It's a magic gun," I clarified. "Probably."

"That would have probably helped Agent Timmons," Emma said. "You know, if he hadn't given it to you."

I blanched at that.

"Which I probably should have kept to myself," Emma said, wincing. "I'm shutting up now."

"I'm also a deputized agent," I said, as if it actually meant something. "So I'm in charge."

"I'm pretty sure that's not a real thing," Maria said. "Also, you need to be twenty-three to join the FBI."

I narrowed my eyes. "Tell me *everything*."

Maria met my gaze, a fierce anger beneath her black eyes. "You want the truth? You can't handle the truth!"

Emma sighed. "Now I'm starting to understand why my ancestors ate yours."

Maria glanced between us, unhappy. "You don't know what it's like being me. Both of you are natural-born shifters. I, however, had to grow up on the wrong side of the tracks with my brother. Both of us struggling under the expectations of two human parents who hoped, desperately, that the gene would carry true."

"Both your parents are doctors," I said, unimpressed. "You have a nicer house than anyone in town but Emma, and she lives in a hotel."

"Behind the hotel!" Emma corrected. "In a mansion, admittedly. Okay, forget I said that."

"I didn't know you knew that," Maria said, looking bashful. "Everything I said about being a natural shifter was true, though. My dad was a Squib like in *Harry Potter*, though. Mom had no werecrow blood at all. She was a convert to the whole crazy nature religion your mom is the high dingy-do of. Both of them wanted shifter children and hoped Rudy would show the genes. That's unlikely when you don't have two shifter parents, though. Blame it on the fact we're not a real species."

"We are so!" I said, appalled.

"We're only able to turn into animals because millions of years ago," Maria said, dramatically increasing the timescale of how long shapeshifters had been around, "our ancestors drank some Elder God blood with the first vampires. Not exactly a heritage to be proud of. Actually, why do we act like we're all in tune with nature and stuff if we're a bunch of demon-blooded abominations?"

"Because we're awesome," I said, pointing at her. "Stay on topic."

"Right, Rudy and I wanted to be demon-blooded abominations," Maria said, deliberately baiting me.

Nothing Maria said was untrue but it still managed to get under my skin due to the fact I'd been raised by shamans. Mind you, in our religion, the difference between demons and spirits were mostly a matter of how they felt about you at the time. It was a belief that didn't feel right after my trip to Hell. I was going to have to bring that up with Mom.

"Victoria came to me last year," Maria said, her voice trailing off as if she was imagining Emma's dead sister before us. "I've always hated and loved Victoria. She had that magical thing about her that is hard to put into words. There were times when we were best friends, ya know? Hanging out in the woods? Drinking, fun, hooking up. That fun, good-time girl was the part she hid from her girl posse. The part I liked."

"You were her secret," I said, wondering about Victoria.

"One of them," Maria said, sighing. "I mean, I'm not Emma, I never hid that I swing both ways."

Emma's eyes widened.

"Pfft," I said, waving my hand. "She's not hiding it."

Emma almost choked.

"Or maybe you didn't notice she was," Maria said, looking between us. "But when Victoria became a werewolf, she changed."

"I doubt it," I said, thinking of Emma's drowning story. "Everything I've seen just reinforces she was awful."

"Don't speak ill of the dead," Maria said, looking at the trees. "Especially around here. You never know what's listening."

I didn't respond to that. "So you found out about the fact Victoria was a skinwalker?"

"Yeah," Maria said, sucking in her breath. "I was the first she shared the truth with. Jeremy was the other. We were all sort of together."

I covered my face, trying not to picture that. "I hate to say it but please go on."

"We always used to come out here because no one else would bother us," Maria said, frowning. "Jeremy was the one who suggested it because his cousin drowned out here. Err, I suppose yours did too."

I didn't respond. "Keep talking."

123

"Victoria claimed she used this place to think whenever she was about to have a meltdown about being Miss Perfect for her father and grandfather. You didn't know her like I did but she was dealing with a lot of crap. A lot of terrible things done to her."

"I know," Emma said, cutting in sharply. "She wasn't the only one. I wanted to go to Clara. To Mrs. Doe. To anyone."

Maria's face became sympathetic. "Yeah, well, Victoria turned to religion to cope."

I blinked. "Victoria? Religious?"

That was only slightly more believable than the honesty of politicians and that the internet brought us together rather than further divided us.

"Not in the churchgoing way," Maria said, rolling her eyes. "More like the 'pray on your knees when you're alone' type. Like I said, she had a lot going on in her life. One of those times, though, out here, God answered—or a god."

"The Lodge," I said.

Maria nodded. "Victoria said she'd made a promise to the spirit of the Lodge and that it would give us what it wanted if we joined in worshiping it."

"And that didn't set you off?" I asked, harsher than I expected. "Making random pacts with spirits in the woods?"

"We're not in Salem and this isn't the seventeenth century," Maria said, her voice catching in her throat. "Also, my friends are dead, so maybe I know what we did was wrong?"

I didn't respond. "I'm sorry."

"Yeah," Maria said, pulling out a pack of cigarettes and trying to light one, only to put it away before she did. "Sorry, I'm trying to quit."

"Good call," I said, hating the smell as a shapechanger. If you thought cigarette smoke was bad in a tight space, imagine if your sense of smell was ten times more powerful.

"When I say Victoria changed, I mean that literally," Maria said, a sickened look on her face. "One of the first things we started to do once we began practicing magic was channeling. Letting the Lodge spirit— we called him the Big Bad Wolf—into us."

I was stunned. "You…what now? You let a spirit inside you?"

That was like Shamanism 101. You did not do that unless you were absolutely sure they were going to leave.

"It was a rush," Maria said, sighing. "More than you could imagine. Not only were we stronger and more powerful, but the Big Bad Wolf made us feel invincible. Jeremy hated the feeling and didn't do it more than one or two times. Rudy, well, he reacted really badly to it. Rudy was kind of a self-centered dweeb before, but he became barely able to function when the Big Bad Wolf wasn't inside him."

I almost pitied him. Almost. "And Victoria?"

"Victoria loved him," Maria said, frowning. "Loved *it*. I don't think it really has a gender. Virtually the entirety of her senior year was spent running around with it inside her."

I lifted my hands in a strangling gesture. "You were letting a demon walk around a high school?"

Maria looked down. "Yeah, I guess it was a demon. We didn't pick up on that, though, until it wanted lives."

Okay, that escalated quickly. "Lives? As in people's lives."

"Not at first," Maria said, pulling out her cigarettes again and shoving one in her mouth. Unfortunately, she couldn't get her lighter to work and ended up throwing it on the ground. "It wanted animals first and other sacrifices. Whiskey, cigarettes, sex, normal stuff. You would have it possess you when you—"

"I get it," I said, sighing. "You and my brother were a full-on witch cult."

"Coven," Maria corrected. "After Courtney and I made our transformations, the Big Bad Wolf wanted five lives. It said it was repayment for past wrongs. Something that had been demanded long ago but members of Victoria's family had failed to pay on."

"What do you mean?" I asked.

"I stopped paying attention after the words human sacrifice became involved," Maria said. "That's when I bailed and so did Jeremy. Rudy—"

"What did he do?" I asked, immensely relieved my brother wasn't involved in human sacrifice.

"I don't know," Maria said, frowning. "Victoria wouldn't let it go, though. Even when we managed to put down the Big Bad Wolf and do a binding spell to keep it in the Lodge. A bit like locking it in its own house, but none of us were really thinking clearly at the time. Victoria said she needed it to protect her and her sister from her grandfather. That she'd realized what a monster he was."

I looked back at Emma. "Is she talking about—"

"Don't," Emma said, her voice icy. "Don't say a word."

I sucked in my breath, an icy chill passing over my shoulder. "Wow."

"It wasn't that kind of abuse," Emma said, softly. "Thank the Goddess."

I didn't want to ask what kind it was.

"How did dealing drugs enter this?" I said, trying to figure out if Lucien had known about this thing.

"Drugs are a good way to make money," Maria said. "Money to buy more magic as well as other things. Like drugs."

Oh, so that was a red herring. "Never mind."

"It's because of our side business that Thomas Hart ended up dead," Maria said, her voice sick with regret but also a bit of contempt and anger. "He was a lowlife drug dealer that was one of Lucien's people but one of the worst. He tried to get Victoria to pay her bills in...well, let's just say the world wasn't a worse place for him dying."

"Victoria killed him," I said, following the train of logic. "But now she's dead."

Maria looked down. "The Big Bad Wolf was using her to feed itself. It's why he hooked her up with Gerald the vampire because it wanted the pleasures of one of the undead. I think Hart was an attempt to feed it."

I stared at her. "So what, you think your brother is possessed?"

Maria didn't answer. "Someone is targeting us specifically and I can't help but think it's that monster. Rudy isn't at fault, though."

"We'll find him," I promised.

I was surprised I meant it.

CHAPTER SIXTEEN

Maria was less than impressed with my proclamation. "Oh, yeah, I'm certain my brother is as good as safe now. I have a venison waitress and a woof-woof princess as my allies against a demon god working with a serial killer."

I stared at her. "Am I this rude? Is this what I sound like?"

"Yes," Emma said. "Yes, it is."

Maria snorted then reached into her pocket and pulled out a foot-long black flashlight. "Okay, well, at least I'm prepared."

I blinked and looked at her painted on jeans then at the huge flashlight. "How did you—"

"Magic," Maria said. "Haven't you been paying attention?"

I remembered Alex doing the same thing and wondered what sort of mojo I'd have to get to conjure bricks of gold. "Right, well, we have to start tracking the victims. Every second counts."

"Every second we wasted having me tell you about me and Victoria? Those seconds?" Maria said, her voice even more sarcastic than mine.

"Yes, those seconds," I said, wishing I had a professional's training in finding kidnapped FBI agents. This was the second time I'd had to rescue Alex and I was starting to feel like Wonder Woman with Steve Trevor. "Emma, do you think you could help with this?"

Emma blinked. "What do you mean?"

I looked down at the mud splatters on the ground. "I don't know, I mean can't you—"

"Wait, you want me to act like a *bloodhound*?" Emma said, looking stunned.

"No good?" I replied.

"No, it's brilliant!" Emma said. "I mean, the rain will make it hard, but I can still do it."

Oh, cool.

"Finally, some werecrow vengeance," Maria said. "Though I'd be happier if I was the one holding the gun."

"Yeah, no chance of that." I didn't think Maria was the murderer but that was far and away from trusting her.

"What's the difference between a raven and a crow?" Emma said, looking around the muddy path for a good place to change.

"What's the difference between you and a poodle?" Maria asked.

Emma frowned. "I'll have you know dogs aren't related to wolves. Modern domesticated dogs are descended from a now-extinct sister species."

"Thank you, Ms. Science," Maria said, gesturing with her flashlight. "Now go help us find the trail. I suggest starting with the muddy footprints."

Maria gestured with her flashlight to the ground and there were a lot of muddy footprints, mostly ours, but a couple that led down the path toward the lake. Great.

Before I could start in that direction, I noticed Emma had already made her transformation into wolf form. Emma was a beautiful wolf with red-and-white fur that made her look spectacular even in the dim light of the flashlight. Wolves were not animals I was automatically inclined to like as a deer, but there was something majestic about them, at least the kind Emma became.

"What's that, Lassie? Timmy fell down a well?" Maria said. "Well, then that's Darwin at work."

"Fudge off," Emma said, growling. She was actually barking, but it was the nature of were to understand us.

"Fudge off?" Maria said, looking about ready to laugh. "Really?"

Emma looked sideways. "My parents don't like swearing."

"Yeah, well neither do I," I said, lying my ass off. "Let's get going, though."

Emma didn't hesitate to go investigating, and I couldn't help but feel uncomfortable about the fact I was leading her down this road. There was no other option; Agent Timmons and Sheriff O'Henry were in danger—that was what I kept telling myself. However, it was still putting my friend in danger because I wanted to be the hero. I was also leading her down to Darkwater Lake as we continued down the muddy road toward the place I'd lost my cousin.

I didn't want to admit it but I was also frightened. Despite the fact I was carrying a gun and a Taser. Despite the fact I was a supernatural shapeshifter with powers far beyond those of mortal women, able to leap tall fences in a single bound and outrun bicycles, I didn't go back to that lake. I didn't want to face what was out here. It would be better to get my mother, a posse, or even call on the local crime lord to save us.

But I pressed on.

Jane, are you all right? I heard Emma's voice in my head say.

"Ah!" I said, almost sliding down the muddy trail.

"What's wrong?" Maria said.

"Nothing!" I said, looking around. "Just missed a step."

"Oh yes," Maria sighed, "we are one badass crew. Fear us, mighty woods demons."

I shook my head. Then I thought at my friend, *Emma? Is that you?*

Yeah, telepathy is my Gift, Emma said in my mind as if it was the most natural thing in the world. *I've told you this before.*

You never use it, though, I thought back. *Wait, I thought you could only project thoughts. Can you read minds?*

Only when you're projecting, Emma replied quickly. *I don't like using my Gift. I have enough trouble with people thinking I'm a freak without adding the fear that I might be reading their thoughts.*

We're all freaks to the one-forms, I thought back at her.

That's not what I meant, Emma said.

I was confused. *What are you referring to, then?*

Emma's wolf form turned around to stare at me.

Wait, really? I thought back at her. *You're worried about that in 2017?*

If a wolf could show disdain, then Emma did in that moment. *Yes, Jane, I'm worried about that. Where do you think you are? Bright Falls, Michigan is not exactly a center for progressive views.*

I knew and I didn't care, I said, not sure this was the best time to have a conversation about my friend's coming out. Especially when I didn't know she was closeted.

You weren't supposed to know, Emma thought at me. *I tried very hard to keep up a front. Now it seems like it was all for nothing.*

I'm sorry, I said, thinking about what to say. Think. Project. Whatever. *Listen, if this is about that whole 'I love you' thing. Then —*

Don't worry about it, Emma said, a little too harshly. *I know you're straight as an arrow.*

Honestly, I was closer to a one on the Kinsey scale than an absolute zero. I could appreciate how beautiful the women around me were even if I was much-much-*much* more into dudes. Emma was my best friend, though, and one I could never think of in that way. I doubted that was what she wanted to hear. I'd also picked up on Emma's crush a long time ago. I'd just thought it would have disappeared by now.

Well, if you need any dating advice, then I'm here for you. When down, you can always look at me and go, 'No matter how bad it gets, I will have more luck than Jane.'

Emma mentally grumbled. *I can smell how much Alex and Lucien were both turned on by you.*

I blinked. *Wait, really? You can tell? That's awesome. My sense of smell is good but I totally can't pick up on those things. You can be my wingwolf.*

There was a growl in my mind and I realized that might be a touchy subject right now.

Sorry, I apologized.

Let's just talk about something else, Emma replied. *I'm picking up Clara and Alex's scent along with a third one. It might be Rudy's. He could be carrying them.*

Rudy is a hundred pounds soaking wet, I thought back at her. *There's no way he could be carrying two grown adults. Also, how the hell would he disable them both?*

Maybe he's a shapechanger possessed by a god now? Emma suggested.

Ask a stupid question, get a stupid answer. *Maybe.*

Do we have any Bat-God repellent? Because I'm not sure what the hell we're supposed to do when we meet him. If we meet him. I could feel Emma's fear.

It would be Deer-God repellent, I said, trying to hide my own. *For I am Deerwoman. I started as a distaff counterpart to Superstag, but took off with young girls until I eventually got my own movie with Helen Slater playing me. Now Melissa Benoist continues my legacy of Cervid-themed crime fighting.*

You have no idea, do you? Emma asked.

Actually, I did. If I saw Rudy and he came at us, I intended to shoot him. Maria present or not. I figured if Agent Timmons's gun could kill demons, then it could kill a possessed skinwalker. Instead of saying that, though, I replied, *I'll think of something.*

I was disturbed how comfortable I was with that plan. What was wrong with me?

Do you believe Maria's story? Emma thought, making a curve as we came to an old wooden staircase that led directly down to the lake shore. I could feel its presence now, pulsing with memories and pain. I couldn't tell if the feelings were magic or a product of my guilty conscience.

Possibly both.

I think it's a pretty damn elaborate lie for a girl I know to use the words 'hella', 'totes', and 'haters' unironically, I thought, still trying to wrap my head around it all. How had I missed so much of my brother's life? Had I been that wrapped up in my own thing that I completely ignored his changes? Yeah, I had. Damn. *What about you, Emma?*

Emma didn't respond for a moment, instead trotting down one step at a time. *I want to believe it's true.*

You do? I asked, surprised.

If what she says is true then Victoria didn't hate me. Didn't want to hurt me. That she was a good person underneath all of that anger and regret. Maria said that she even tried to use the Big Bad Wolf to protect me. What do you think about that?

I dunno. I…well, I don't know how to react to the fact you were abused. You never told me. I mean, I knew your parents were ass—

Emma interrupted. *It was only Marcus. Spare the rod and spoil the child. The best part of my becoming a werewolf was the fact that he didn't have to hide any bruises when I turned. Victoria had to wear long-sleeved shirts and claim to do a lot of hiking. Eventually, Grandpa just hired a private doctor.*

That made me sick. *I wish you'd told me.*

I didn't want to get you involved and it wouldn't have helped anyway. Clara tried to protect me a few times but Marcus ended up putting her in a hospital thanks to his bodyguards. He's still the Clan Lord of Clan Lords after all. Aunt Alice told me just to take it until I was an adult, like she and Clara did.

What about your parents? I asked.

Emma made a low growl. *Christopher never cared. My mother told me she couldn't do a thing about it and I had to take it.*

Maybe I should contact my mother, I started to say before realizing that was the wrong thing to say.

She knew, Jane. Emma didn't say anything else. It was just easier to turn a blind eye.

I didn't know how to respond to that.

We reached the bottom of the staircase then and I saw Darkwater Lake for the first time in almost a decade. The clouds had parted and the rain storm stopped, allowing the moonlight to shine onto it and expose the eerie location. It stretched on past two cliff sides and twisted around the preserve. There was an old wooden dock nearby and I could remember standing helplessly on it as my cousin drowned. Even the "NO SWIMMING – $5,000 FINE" sign was still there, warped and leaning right due to the climate as well as the passage of time.

Around the lake was a dirty wooden shack that looked abandoned but I remembered had been a place my grandfather had taken me several times. It was collapsed now with its roof having fallen in and the windows having been busted with rocks. I admitted some degree of guilt there, having enjoyed vandalizing the property with Jill.

"They're here," Emma said, turning back into her human form.

"What?" I said, looking around. "Who's here?"

"Them!" Emma said, looking around. "The people we're looking for. Their scent is in every direction."

I cursed. "Well, that's just great. What the hell does that mean?"

"Ooo, shiny!" Maria said, pointing her flashlight to the ground and reflecting the light on something there.

I reached down and picked it up, revealing a long silver necklace with a cross at the end over a pentacle. Silver didn't burn shapeshifters when held, contrary to some movie depictions. It only affected us when we were stabbed with it. I recognized the muddy amulet as belonging to Victoria. I'd seen her wearing it a lot in her junior year, but she'd stopped wearing it when she became a senior. That was when she'd started letting herself be possessed.

Maria made a grab for it. "Shiny! Gimme!"

"No!" I said, pulling it away from the human-shaped magpie.

"I call dibs!" Maria said. "Those laws are sacred and no shapeshifter can deny them."

"Watch me!" I said, feeling it would be blasphemous in some way. I felt that made me feel it was doubly important.

"Quiet, you two!" Emma snapped, looking nervous. "There's something here. I can feel it."

"What?" I said, turning around.

That was when I heard a ringing noise so loud and awful it caused me to grab both my ears. Emma and Maria also looked pained, with the former falling to her knees and grabbing her temples. The noise was like a siren from a 1950s air raid, but it was weird and unearthly, as if it had reverb added.

The light of the moon changed too as I saw it turn from a soothing white to blood red. Everything about me looked crimson and something nasty welled up from inside me. In that moment I hated Emma. I hated her for being whiny, clingy, and always holding me back. I hated Maria for having a weird brother and sleeping with mine. I wanted to shoot both of them and trample them with my hooves. That was when Maria charged me and I backhanded her before she turned into a giant crow woman. It was only five feet tall but it had an enormous beak, claws, and enough of a female body to make me think of the Greek harpies.

I pulled out my gun.

My gun.

Oddly, then, the weapon glowed and burned away the confusion in my mind. It was blessed to kill evil and the spell on me was nothing but.

"Wait, fight it!" I snapped.

That was when Maria grabbed me by the shoulders and started lifting me in the air. "I'm going to crack you open like an oyster!"

"Crows don't eat oysters!" I said, pistol whipping her across the face and causing her to drop me.

In Darkwater Lake something stirred, and I was briefly reminded of the scene in *The Fellowship of the Ring* where the Watcher rose and ate Bill the Pony. For those less high-fantasy inclined, I saw a series of bubbles begin to appear beyond the edge of the dock followed by slimy tentacles thrashing from within. Those filled me with a primordial terror and caused me to flash back to Jill's drowning, but this time, I remembered seeing her wrapped up in things very much like those.

No.

Had it been a monster all along? "We have to get out of here!"

Emma had returned to her wolf form and was advancing on me with murder in her eyes. "You are so mean! Mean and rude!"

Wow, she really didn't like swearing. "Stay back, Emma! This is not you!"

Emma went for my throat. That's when the red light blinded me and everything went black.

CHAPTER SEVENTEEN

I woke with a monstrous headache. I was lying down with a wet washcloth over my head and jolted up once I remembered what had happened. "Emma!"

No answer.

The sight that surrounded me was a confusing one because I was in the family cabin. Sort of. It was identical to how the cabin had been when Grandpa Jacob was alive, not redecorated like Jeremy had wanted with his posters and stuff. The place had an old rustic feel with fishing equipment, stuffed trout, and portraits of the Wild West on the walls. The floor had several hand-woven rugs done in Odawa patterns. Sunlight was streaming through the windows even as yet another rainstorm was pouring down, not diminishing the light one bit. I could see the kitchen past a load-bearing pillar, still looking like it'd been decorated in the 1950s.

Grandpa Jacob didn't own a TV and in its place was an extra stuffed couch that had been patched several times. I was sitting on the leather couch across from it, an old *Return of the Jedi* blanket over me. Beside me was a plain wooden coffee table with a steaming mug of hot chocolate inside it. The mug had a cartoon stag holding a rifle on it, along with the words, "Deer Hunting Season 2001: This time we hunt you." Oh Grandpa Jacob, father of so many weredeer traditions.

There was another quality that disconcerted me as I looked around the place. It was the fact the cabin was huge. It loomed around me not as I remembered it from the time I was an adult but like I remembered it from my earliest memories. The couch was sized for giants or me as a toddler, though I was in my regular form. I reached for my throat and thought about Emma going for it. She obviously hadn't since I wasn't dead. Was I?

"No," I muttered, shaking my head. "If I was in Heaven it would be coffee. I hate hot chocolate."

"Who hates hot chocolate?" the voice of my grandfather spoke.

Turning my head in shock, I saw the figure of Grandpa Jacob Abair. The oldest and wisest among our kind, theoretically, he was an Odawa man with weathered light-brown skin and long silver hair. Unlike the majority of the ones I'd met, he also had a thick bushy beard. He was dressed in a thick pair of slacks, a flannel shirt, and hiking boots. He had a bright smile on his face and looked not a day over sixty. I didn't know much about his past, though I understood he was originally from the Little River Band of Ottawa Indians rather than Bright Falls or the Little River Indian Reservation. Yes, that meant I was one quarter Canadian.

Rather than react in a manner similar to heroines would in a novel or movie, tearfully embracing a long lost relative. I, instead, turned around and screamed before jolting to the other side of the couch. The sound that escaped my mouth as I knocked over a lamp, jumped up, got entangled in the cord, and fell over was nothing but pure profanity.

"Oh yes," Jacob muttered. "This is going to be a great test of your worthiness."

"You're a ghost!" I said, finally getting to my feet and way more freaked out than I should have been since I handled a trip through Hell calmly.

"And you're a weredeer," Jacob said, putting his hands on his hips. "Shouldn't you be better at this?"

"I'm sorry I flunked shaman training!" I said, angry now.

"And whose fault is that?" Jacob said.

"Yours!" I snapped. "You said you were really angry to turn into a weredeer at eighteen since you'd spent your entire life trying not to be a magical Native American."

"Well I did!" Jacob said. "It was all on my French-Canadian grandfather's side that he put the magical weirdness in my bloodline. Then I ended up marrying a Caucasian weredeer girl that I swear my mother set up behind our back. You exotic white people with your mysterious connection with nature are ruining it for the rest of us."

Okay, that made me laugh. "That's really racist, Grandpa."

"I'm old, so I get a free pass."

I smiled so broadly it covered my entire face. "Is that really you?"

"I dunno. It could be. I could be a product of your imagination brought to life by this place or a spirit taking your grandfather's shape. I could also be the product of head trauma, in which case you're screwed."

I glared at him. "Not very comforting, Grandfather."

He frowned and walked over to me before picking up the mug of hot chocolate on the table and drinking it down in three gulps. "It's not supposed to be. You're up the creek without a paddle and in a real s-word sandwich. You're in frigging trouble, Jane, and I don't know how you're going to get out of it." Except he didn't say s-word or frigging. Wow, Emma was starting to rub off on me.

"Am I in the Lodge?" I asked, looking around.

"Outside of it," Jacob said. "You shifted into the Great Woods when you were about to die. Which is a good thing, since the kelpie was about to kill you."

"Kelpie," I said, blinking.

"A water horse," Jacob said. "A siren or nek. They're big ugly masses of foliage and goo possessed by demons that turn into beautiful women or stallions to lure men to their doom."

"Women or stallions?" I asked.

"Either would be very attractive to young men of my grandfather's era," Jacob paused. "Also, don't make a joke about that."

I stared at him. "How could I not? I mean, the setup is right there!"

Jacob's voice turned low. "It also drowned your cousin."

All of the enthusiasm drained from my body in an instant. "I'm sorry, Grandpa. I'm responsible. I did it. I dared her to—"

Jacob silenced with me with a light tap to my right ear.

"Ow!" I said, rubbing my ear. "Not the ears!"

"Jill knew how to swim like a selkie," Jacob said. "There was no reason to believe that water was dangerous."

"There was a sign," I said.

"Did the sign say, 'Do not enter this water or you will die?'"

"No," I said, trying to remember that day despite all the years I'd done my best to block it out. "I do, however, remember there was a family in the water. They were having fun. There were girls our age."

That was when I recalled the image of Jill, with pigtails and a Hello Kitty swimsuit, jumping in and swam out. What followed then were the screams and the cries for help. I remembered wanting to go in but being too afraid.

So she died.

I started crying.

Jacob took me into a hug and held me for a few minutes. "It wasn't your fault, girl. It was the monster's. Just one of the things attracted to this place by those damned fools leaving the door open when they abandoned the Lodge."

I sniffled a bit and pulled away, wiping away my eyes and my nose. "Why is the Lodge abandoned? Surely you have to know."

"Because I'm an old Native American spirit?"

"Because you were there when they left it," I said, frowning.

"Oh," Jacob said, sighing. "Right."

"I doubt that."

Jacob walked over to his kitchen and his old-style fridge, opening it up to reveal nothing but beer and fish. "Want a beer?"

"I'm eighteen," I said.

"So yes?" Jacob said.

I sighed. "Sure, why not."

"You're a quarter Canadian. You should be powered by this stuff."

I rolled my eyes. "Just get on with the story."

Jacob handed me a beer imported from across the border and popped the top off of his with a partially transformed hand. Hooves were useful for removing bottle caps. "How much do you know?"

"There's an evil god messing with our town?" I said, though I didn't use the word messing. I guess Emma wasn't rubbing off on me entirely.

"Not an evil god," Jacob said, frowning. "At least not originally. Spirits have to rebirth themselves regularly with the seasons if they want to stay sane. Eternity is a very long time to live and you need to live many lifetimes if you want to understand it."

"Did you learn that as a ghost?"

"No, from your mother during one of her long lectures about how weredeer religion was awesome," Jacob muttered, rolling his eyes. "Seven kids and all of them into hippie New-Age mysticism and junk."

I was ready to mention he'd almost set me up in an arranged marriage before asking, "What does that have to do with the Big Bad Wolf?"

Jacob smirked. "Is that what they're calling it?"

"What did you call it?" I said.

Jacob frowned. "The Red Wolf. It was a spirit that lived in these woods and a powerful one. A god, but a benevolent one. It took the dhampir born from the mixing of vampires and humans under its wings and taught them how to change shape. It killed many enemies that threatened his people and often possessed leaders to rule wisely."

"That's...scary."

"When you live in a world where people knew monsters were real, you often find the biggest monster you can find to protect you. It's kind of like prison."

"Why did it turn bad?"

Jacob took a long drink of his beer and stared at me.

I took a sip of mine and almost choked on it. This wasn't a Bud Lite, something all of my family agreed was terrible, but a thick, rich homebrew that probably contained way more alcohol than was allowed for a normal lager. I gagged for a full three seconds before coughing out an alcohol-fused breath.

Jacob rolled his eyes. "Lightweight."

I glared at him. "I don't drink. It's not my thing, okay!"

"It's beer!" Jacob said, sighing. "Real beer! Deer beer! Show some Canadian pride!"

"I'm American."

"Show some North American pride!"

I sighed and took a much longer drink, not even bothering to taste. That proved to be a bad idea when I gagged.

Jacob laughed. "Sucker."

I hated when he pranked me like that.

"Love," Jacob said, answering like he'd never stopped our conversation. "The Red Wolf saw the most beautiful child in all of Bright Falls and took her as a bride. He wore the skin of a man during that time and sired five children."

"I take it this story doesn't end with a happily ever after?"

Jacob frowned. "No. The bloodlines were to be kept pure back then. A weredeer and a werewolf woman was almost as much an abomination as an Odawa man and a white woman. I ended up better off than he did."

It took me a second to realize what he was saying. "They killed the Red Wolf's children."

"Yes," Jacob said, his voice low. "I wasn't there, but I knew plenty of the people who were. Called many of them friend. They torched his house with the kids inside. Some didn't know, but most did. Mob mentality. Like herd, only worse."

"It's not a good idea to anger a god."

"No, it is not."

"What happened?" I asked, trying to imagine what I would do if I had godlike power and someone killed my family. I imagined it would look like Sodom and Gomorrah.

"Bloodshed and horror," Jacob said, giving a thousand-yard stare. "There's a reason we don't talk about it. No one had known Elroy Cornstalk was a god. Who would with that name? They knew afterward, though. Human and shifter both. After the murders, the Red Wolf turned vicious and made a demand that was burned into the minds of each survivor."

"Five lives," I said, putting it together in my head. "It wanted five sacrifices from the bloodlines that killed his family."

"Yes," Jacob said. "None of us would do it, of course, though it took a lot of negotiating to make sure every other clan didn't start turning over each other's kids. Your grandmother put the Red Wolf to sleep and we agreed to abandon the Lodge. It had effects on us. Fewer children were born, the prosperity of the town was affected, and the oldest among us were always tempted to contact him. That's part of why Marcus O'Henry tried to wipe out the Dragon Clan. The Drake family had been involved and he tried to offer them up to the Red Wolf. He got four."

"Lucien," I said. "He missed him."

Jacob growled. "That idiot awakened what had been sleeping peacefully. Then Victoria walked into its grasp."

"Why her?" I tried to make sense of it. "Why didn't it just kill her?"

"The woman he loved was an O'Henry."

"Now she's a sacrifice," I said, even more confused and disgusted.

"And with him forever," Jacob said. "But the next round of sacrifices isn't done. The curse of the Red Wolf won't end until two more of the families die."

"It has to be five in a row, huh?" I felt sick.

"Yes. The Red Wolf is mad for sensation after having been a prisoner for seven decades. It was rabid for the atrocity committed against it before, but it should have been reborn a long time ago. That's the other option to deal with it. Kill it and force it to reincarnate."

"You got any god-killing weapons around here?" I asked, only half joking. We were in the Great Woods, after all.

"A true shaman can force a rabid spirit to reincarnate. Even one as powerful as the Red Wolf," Jacob frowned. "Don't ask me for more info. I hate this mumbo-jumbo."

"The Goddess couldn't have sent someone who knew what they were doing?" I asked, only half sarcastic.

My grandfather gave a half-smile. "The universe is a bit more complicated than that."

"Of course it is," I muttered under my breath. "So I need to get Mom out here to stop it."

"No," Jacob said, sighing before finishing off his beer. "Your mother won't be able to do anything against the Red Wolf."

"Why? She's the most powerful shaman in the town."

"And she'll never be any stronger," Jacob said, tossing the beer into a plastic rubbish bin from six feet away. "Your mother broke taboo during the Reveal. She violated her oaths and broke several sacred compacts. The Red Wolf would tear her to shreds."

I was confused. "What are you talking about? My mother, *your daughter*, is a saint."

Jacob didn't answer for a moment.

"Isn't she?" I asked, my voice weak.

"Remember, Marcus tried to break the curse before. That required a shaman to perform the sacrifices of the Drake family. Marcus could kill dozens of them in a single night, but he needed to perform the rites to break the curse."

I blinked then stepped back. "No, you're lying."

"The Drakes weren't a bunch of Girl Scouts," Marcus said, defensive of his daughter. "They were a vicious group of gangsters and killers. Their youngest son, Lucien, would have grown up to be every bit as bad if not for Agent Constance Timmons and young Alex. Your mother was ambitious and eager to show she could break the curse on the town. The one Marcus tried to pass off as the work of a witch he'd crossed. The truth was he was covering up for the Lodge. There's a reason only deer are allowed to learn magic. It's to keep it all under wraps and the Red Wolf asleep. Your mother couldn't kill a child in the end, though. That's why Lucien survived and was able to flee into the woods. He doesn't know about your mother's involvement, though. Otherwise, I suspect she'd be dead."

I stared at him, too horrified to respond. "My mother is a murderer."

"Yes," Jacob said. "She also did it for love."

I didn't want to know who he was referring to. "Gods above and below. This is all her fault."

"Not all," Jacob said, going to his wall of fishing equipment and pulling out a harpoon. It was a strange object for a rural fisherman to possess. "There's plenty of blame to go around from the racist jackasses who killed the Red Wolf's family to the mad beast itself. Good people do bad things."

"Then they become bad because of that," I snapped, horrified. "Jesus, I just realized, I haven't asked about Emma and Maria. Are they okay?"

"You distracted the kelpie," Jacob said, aiming the harpoon at the door before going to pick up a sheathed machete he'd hidden behind the other couch. It made him look like he was trying out for *Extreme Murder Bass Fishing*, a show that doesn't exist yet but I'm sure eventually will. "They've fled deeper into the woods. You'll be able to find them if you can get past the spirit hunting you."

"*What are you talking about?*" I shouted, having reached my breaking point. This was insane. I wanted out of the Great Woods and to get back home. If not for the fact that my friends were missing along with Agent Timmons, I'd click my heels three times and wish myself back to bed. That would work, right?

"Probably," Jacob said, tossing me the harpoon. It hit the ground at my feet. It didn't register for a second that he was responding to my thoughts.

"Please tell me what you're talking about."

"The kelpie would just go after your friends then. It's a spirit that can possess objects in the physical world to bring them to life. That means this isn't a refuge from it. My house is protected as it's a place you felt safe as a child and that is its own kind of barrier. But the moment you step out, it'll be on us."

I stared at him then at the door. "Oh no."

"Yep," Jacob said before adopting an Elmer Fudd voice. "Be vewwwy quiet. We're hunting monster."

CHAPTER EIGHTEEN

I stepped out of the cabin, hoping my grandfather would be there for me or the beauty of the Underwood. Instead, no, I was alone and back at the edge of the lake. I'd stepped out of the ruined cabin's door despite Grandfather's cabin being thirty miles away in the real world. The harpoon that had been in my hand was gone now, leaving no sign that my vision had been anything other than a pleasant dream or the hallucination of a deranged weredeer woman.

Emma and Maria were nowhere to be seen. I was grateful that they weren't corpses lying by the water. Of course, they could be in the water. I had to learn to stop thinking. Okay, I needed to examine the scene. There weren't any obvious pools of blood and...um, I should have been looking for broken twigs and bent grass or something. If there were any grass that looked particularly bent, it eluded my skills, and there were twigs in varying states of disrepair everywhere.

I probably shouldn't have quit Girl Scouts after a month. I'm sure I'd be a master tracker now if I'd stuck with it. They went into the woods, right, or was that just Boy Scouts? There was nothing left to do but look to the water.

I had not, before that moment, realized I hadn't been looking at the water, that my eyes had been avoiding the single most obvious feature of the landscape as if it were as bright as the sun and would burn my eyes. It was nothing of the sort, of course. It was as dark as its name suggested. But still, I saw no signs of them. Or anything else. The water was flat, resolutely ignoring the breeze trying to make it ripple.

Darkwater Lake wasn't large enough that I couldn't see the other side, even in the darkness, but it was large enough it would take someone quite a while to swim across. Not that I had any intention of going into the water. I'd come here with Jill, daring her to swim in the forbidden water. Nothing had changed here that I could see. They'd never found the body, so it had to still be down at the bottom of the lake. Another thing I couldn't stop myself from thinking about.

I turned away from the lake as if that would keep me from my guilt. Then, steeling myself, I turned back. "I have to find some sign here, some pointer toward where... Oh crap, I can hear the water moving."

Reluctantly, I peered back over my shoulder. Not ten feet down the bank, the water was rippling as something dark and large rose up. It was large, black, and covered in silt and stank like rotting garbage. Once the water fell off of it, I could see it was a horse. Or something shaped like a horse. A real horse didn't have glowing red eyes. It also wouldn't seem to be made of water, plants, and detritus suspended in a horse-like shape.

I remembered 'water horse' was another name for the creature in Scotland. Grandfather had called it such before. I was facing the kelpie in its true form. Even now, the vision of my grandfather was fading and I desperately wished he was beside me to fight this thing. There was no sign of his shade, if it had ever been there to begin with, and I was alone with what weapons I'd brought. I hoped my grandfather hadn't brought me here to my death, but if he did, really, then it was only justice.

Okay, I really needed to stop thinking like that. My friends needed me. *Sorry, Jill, you're going to have to wait for your pound of venison.*

"It's been a while," the kelpie said. Its voice was like a babbling brook, rushing out of its lungs like water instead of air. "But I knew you'd come back."

"I didn't," I said, wanting to back away, but the ridge around the lake made walking backwards dangerous. Besides, I wasn't going to run away as much as I wanted to. I was too terrified to. This was, literally, the creature that had haunted my nightmares for decades. Even if I had suppressed the particulars. "You must be smarter than me."

I don't think that horses can smile, but I got the impression that it was doing so anyway. "Come, Jane, we have so much to talk about."

"Aren't you supposed to look like a beautiful woman or something?" I said, speaking more in a whisper than my usual sarcastic tone. "I mean, I'd prefer for you to appear as Brad Pitt circa *Troy* or Link from *The Legend of Zelda* (don't tell anyone else about that fantasy) but I thought most spirits loved tradition."

Good, yeah, that was sarcastic. Did it help me feel less scared? Not really.

Crap.

The kelpie wasn't impressed. In fact, it looked amused, which was the worst emotion it could be expressing right now. "I can appear as a man or woman, but we have no need of illusions between us. You must tell me everything you've done."

I summoned my courage, what little I had left. "I want to know where my friends are."

The thought of Emma and Maria (though Maria was more like an acquaintance my brother had sex with—ew, bad mental image) helped me face my enemy. Turning to it, I managed to take a full half-step forward before stopping.

"Friends?" the creature asked as if it was a word from an alien language.

"The people I was here with earlier."

"The sacrifices you brought me? I gave them to Him."

I wanted to throw up. "You mean they're dead?"

No, God, Goddess, and Grandfather. Please, no. Please don't let me have done it again.

The kelpie stretched its head and shook it like a real horse. "I'm hardly the one to ask. What He demands is best surrendered to Him. Perhaps you could bring more. It's been so long."

"I'm not bringing you anything," I snapped at the creature.

"Do you want another Gift?"

My mind lurched as if trying to escape from my skull. There was something I wasn't remembering. Something I didn't want to remember. I heard myself asking, "Gift?"

Memory wasn't something humans like to acknowledge was as fickle as the weather and as substantial as a rainbow. In the 1980s, there was a satanic cult scare that involved child abuse and sexual molestation. As far as I knew, that was false despite the fact that there really were a bunch of demonic cults out there. The patients involved had created false memories through the power of suggestion by their therapists.

However, that ran into the fact human beings were *also* capable of repressing memories until adulthood about past trauma. Those evil things done behind closed doors were far more common than anyone gave them credit for. My uncle Jeffrey, a therapist, had said there was no way to tell the difference without evidence. That wasn't even getting into how magic could affect the mind. What had I forgotten?

"I helped you," The kelpie said, moving closer, its backward hooves leaving prints in the muck around the lake. "'I don't want to be like my mother,' you said. Didn't want to deal with spirits. Didn't want to see, did you? Don't tell me you've forgotten all we did for each other."

Its voice was hypnotic and made me relaxed rather than terrified. No, that wasn't right. My body relaxed but my mind was screaming. It was a dichotomy that made my present experience all the worse.

I stepped back. The more it spoke, the more I remembered, the more I wanted it to be lying. But the creature wasn't lying. I was remembering. But was I remembering right? I couldn't tell anymore. The worst part of being a shaman was losing your certainty what was true and what was real. The Spirit World made thought reality and that was a source of dreams as well as nightmares.

"I'd come into the woods," I said, quavering. "The spirits frightened me."

"But then you met me. And I offered to help."

"You said I had to bring someone else to swim in the waters."

"And you did."

"You didn't say you were going to kill her!" I said, falling into its spell. Had I given Jill up to this thing?

Yes.

No!

"You never asked. And I fulfilled our bargain and took the spirit sight from you. No more the daughter of a shaman, and I left you the Gift to see the truth of the world in your touch. So that you would learn how much hate and fear define your kind and return when you'd grown old enough. And here you are."

"No!" I screamed out loud.

"The sacrifice was well used," The kelpie continued. "I gave its soul to the old wolf spirit, made the demon strong again. Strong enough to draw those children into his circle. Once he's free, he'll pay me back with so many children to drown."

I couldn't move anymore. All of this. The coven, Victoria's death, the deaths of the others... I'd started it.

No. I hadn't!

All I came here for was swimming! To get away from Mom and Dad! I'd wanted to be a shaman as a child and hadn't started training until later.

Right?

"I can see it in your eyes that you understand now," the kelpie said. "You're one of us. I knew it as soon as we met. Welcome to the dark, Jane Doe. We're going to have so much fun."

Yes.

Everything the creature said felt true, completely true. I was evil. I was corrupt. I belonged with this forest and could stay here, becoming something powerful and dark. No more would I have to worry what anyone else thought of me.

No more jobs, no more bowing to social conventions, no more being polite when I just wanted to tell someone what I thought of them to their face. The part of me that wanted to scream no at these thoughts was getting smaller, I knew it, but it was so hard to think of why that was a bad thing with the siren blaring in my ears and... the siren. It had come up quieter this time; the shift of the moon to red had happened more slowly, escaping my attention as the kelpie spoke, trying to make me my worst self. These weren't my thoughts. Like last time, making me hate, last time, the gun! I'd touched Alex's gun and the influence had dissolved. I reached for it now, only to find it gone, pulled from me by a vine that was dragging it across the ground. I dove for it, but the kelpie's speed was fantastic. It was in my way before I even realized it had moved and I grabbed only its wet, rancid fur.

"An unfortunate choice, young Jane," the creature said, its breath fetid like a swamp. "If you won't choose to join us in life, you will have to join us in death."

"You are a liar!" I screamed.

"Maybe," the kelpie said. "Maybe not. Humans are the ones who invented truth. A tree may make a sound when it falls and no one is there to hear it, but without humans then who cares? Your lies to yourself make your life meaningful. Hope, justice, and love."

I tried to pull away, but my hand had sunk into its rotten flesh, no, not flesh, but swamp slime. I couldn't pull it back. The creature reared back with a whinny and then raced toward the Darkwater, dragging me along with it. When it reached the water it kept going, throwing itself in. I screamed once as I found myself pulled helplessly under the water.

This was my nightmare. Ever since I had watched Jill drown, ever since I'd seen this monstrosity kill her, this was the dream that kept me up at night. Being held underwater, unable to breathe, unable to even scream.

I flailed more than fought, kicking and punching, but the creature no longer had any real shape. It was made of slime, silt, sticks, and decaying pond plants. Yet, as impotent as my strikes were toward it, its mass held me under the water firmly. This was how Jill had felt. This was how she had died. Helpless to do anything but watch the daylight through the water as her need for oxygen grew and grew until…wait, that was how *she* had felt. It was night now; I was seeing her view through my power, pulling her memories from the lake itself.

For some reason, that calmed me. At least I wasn't going to die alone. I could feel the energies of the memories all around me. And there were others, so many others, who had drowned in the swamp. All that silent pain, gathering around me, glad to finally be heard at long last. My lungs were aching now, as I reached out and shared all those memories with the kelpie.

I had not, before that moment, known I could do that. The kelpie and I were both touching the water, and I could make the memories flow into it as well as myself. Made it listen to the voiceless, agonizing deaths of every person it had drowned. Made it listen to the chorus of despair that it had created.

"No!" the kelpie howled, its voice echoing through the water to my ears. "I don't want to hear it."

Tough noogies.

I shoved all of them I could into the creature. And then, lost amidst the seemingly endless march of deaths, was one other memory—the kelpie's own. Once, it was an undine, a spirit of the lake, pure and unsullied, until the forest grew dark and the spirits within it became corrupted, causing what was once clean to become foul. That memory, more than all the others, caused the kelpie to surge up over the water and release me.

For a second, I got to see the world as the spirits saw it. So much of it being wild, free, and untamed without any reason or rhyme. Humans had brought sentience to the universe with their dreams, though, or perhaps the things that had preceded humans. That had been both a blessing and a curse as they'd become capable of good and evil. Huh, maybe there was something to the Bible after all. Except man had given knowledge of it to everyone and everything. I don't remember a passage dealing with that.

I heard its voice in the water. More feelings rather than words but still clear to me. I could hear it in my soul thanks to my shaman powers. Power I hadn't been able to use for years. *So much pain. My soiled lake, toxins in my waves, chemicals in my water, carried by the rain and bubbling up from underneath. Rage from the Lord of the Forest and pain. So much pain. So much I want to give it out again.*

I erupted from the lake, breathing in huge gulps of air, not even minding that it still stunk of Darkwater Lake's fetid waters. Once I was no longer desperate for breath, I dragged myself out of the water and to the shore. There, several yards away, was the creature.

What it looked like now was hard to describe. It was still the pile of lake sludge and plants it had been in the water, but in the vague shape combining the features of the undine's female human form and the kelpie's horse-monster shape. She/it was shaking violently as its tendrils and slime kept trying to shift the whole shape into one or the other.

"Please," it gurgled. "Don't let me go back. The darkness here is too strong. Please, Jane. End this life. Let me start over."

I kept scraping what seemed like gallons of muck off my clothes as I looked for my gun and picked it up. The runes glowed and warmed me after the cold of the water. I didn't owe this creature anything. I didn't. But somehow, it felt right when I fired the gun and the bullet struck the creature's form. That was when all of the mud around it surged forth, wrapped itself around the kelpie, then glowed orange-red before collapsing into indiscriminate sludge. I didn't know what sort of spells Alex had wrapped into this thing, but it was packing a serious wallop.

Either way, the lake spirit was dead. It would eventually form a new one, but it would take years, probably, until it had anything resembling a consciousness. Even in these woods.

"Go in peace," I said, staring at it. I didn't hate it like I wanted to or feel any sense of triumph. I was just numb. Had I actually made a deal? I'd never be able to tell now that it was dead. Somehow, the fact I couldn't tell made it worse. At least if I had, I could begin the healing. Now I'd just always wonder if I was capable of something so awful. "I'm sorry, Jill."

That's when I heard Jill's voice in the wind. "It's all right, Jane, I forgive you."

I fell to my knees and broke down crying.

CHAPTER NINETEEN

I finished crying about three minutes later. Looking at the kelpie's remains, I tried to soak in what I'd done. It was not a monster anymore, just a bunch of dead weeds and decomposing rotting animals. There were bones scattered among empty beer cans, plastic rings, and worse. Once it had been a figure from my nightmares and now it was just a big floating pile of trash.

"You don't think Jill's bones are there, do you?" I asked, wiping away my tears with my sleeve. It was a somewhat questionable tactic since I was soaked from my dip in the lake. At least most of the sludge had washed off.

"No," Jacob's voice spoke. I could hear it but not see him. He'd been there with me, even if he couldn't physically help. "But even if they were, it's not her any more than this was the kelpie."

"So you're just lying and her bones are probably inside there."

"I ain't saying nothing," Jacob said.

I took a deep breath and put away Alex's gun. "I'll call someone back here to pick up her body along with everyone else's."

"Good idea," Jacob said, slowly manifestly beside me as a nimbus of white light that was slightly translucent.

"Before you continue," I said, staring at him, "you have to tell me to go to the Dagobah system."

It was easy to slip back into Jane the Jokester. It was a comfortable mask and one that felt good to wear after the horror of facing the kelpie. Besides, when else was I going to get a chance to use that kind of line?

Jacob snorted. "Your mother, Jeremy, and now you are obsessed with those movies. You should watch something educational and uplifting instead...like *Dirty Harry* or *The Outlaw Josie Wales*."

"*The Outlaw Josie Wales* was Confederate apologia," I said. "Seriously, the author of the book was a big segregationist too."

"It was still badass," Jacob said. "But I laugh at any movie where lots of cowboys get killed."

I rolled my eyes. "Grandpa, thank you for this. Sort of. I mean, yes, you put me in horrible danger and almost got me killed—"

"Those are the same thing."

"It's worth repeating!" I snapped, looking back at the dead monster. "But I feel better now."

"Liar," Jacob said.

He was right, but I wasn't going to tell him that. "I confronted some things I needed confronting."

"You didn't make a deal," Jacob said, giving me the reassurance I needed. "Spirits lie and make things up. They have the power to make you believe anything about yourself if you're afraid."

"I was," I said, ready to cry again but pushing those thoughts down. I chose to believe my grandfather's words even if I didn't miss the fact he was a spirit too. "But it doesn't matter. It was feeding on my real fears and regrets. I wanted to be normal and that's never going to happen. I have to get over that."

"Normal is overrated," Jacob said, putting his hand against my cheek as the fingers lightly passed through and left a cold oily residue. "I never wanted to be a weredeer either but I resolved to be the best warrior I could for the people who needed one. Life is a river and you never step in the same one twice. It's always shifting and changing."

I sniffed. "Where did you get that?"

"Disney's *Pocahontas*," Jacob said, chuckling. "Not exactly true to life."

I didn't want to mention I liked that movie. I had a huge crush on John Smith when I was eight. "Well, whatever the case, I'm not going to stop. I'm going to get back everyone the Big Bad Wolf has taken."

"A shaman can do that," Jacob said, pointing out a fact I didn't want to acknowledge. I'd done a shaman's duty by cleansing the kelpie's spirit. Albeit, with a bullet.

"I'm not a shaman," I said, stubbornly.

"You're whatever you want to be," Jacob said, starting to fade away. "But the power is yours if you want it. It always was."

I took a deep breath. "I guess I'm our last hope then."

There was no response.

I shouted into the air, "You're supposed to say there is another!"

But there was no other.

It was all on me.

I took a deep breath. "Okay, so now I just need to go find the eldritch location where my friends, the sheriff, and the FBI agent I think is cute are. Yeah, that shouldn't be difficult at all. There's just, what, ten thousand acres to search?"

Which, honestly, sounds like a lot, but most people can't transform into deer. Still, the clock was ticking and I needed to pick a direction for where to go. Moments later, as if answering my unspoken need, I saw the sight of a white stag standing on top of a path leading from the ruined cabin nearby. It was magnificent and reminded me of illustrations of a similar creature in a book about Arthurian myth. It was larger than any stag I'd ever seen with a huge crown that even my father would have envied. The creature stared at me for a moment then beckoned me with its head before trotting off.

"I really hope this isn't another monster trying to trap me because, wow, would egg be on my face," I said, turning into a deer and running after him.

The sense of running through the forest as a deer isn't something that I can really describe to non-shapeshifters. In human form, I'd have to keep watch on the ground and be careful to avoid tripping. As Emma would say, humans actually evolved pretty badly to walk on two legs. It's why back pain and other conditions exist.

God, Goddess, and nature had given us four-leggers many advantages over that, though. I felt free and awesome with the wind at my face even as I hoped I was coming to the Lodge. I imagined smashing myself through its front doors and banging Rudy in the face with my head.

That fantasy disappeared as I felt dread creep up the back of my spine again. I was running away from the lake, but whatever I was running to felt even worse. Not born of suppressed memories but something even more intangible. Seeing the stag's rear legs, I struggled to keep up even as I knew I was getting closer and closer to the Big Bad Wolf.

Would Emma still be alive? Alex? Maria?

Would I at the end of the night?

Forcing those thoughts away, I ran faster in order to catch up with my spirit guide and searched the darkness of the woods for some sign of my friends or the Lodge. I had no idea what it would look like but there were a thousand tiny sights all around me. The moonlight coming through the trees was no longer red, instead a pleasant silver light, but it barely provided the illumination I needed for my search. My vision was limited to being barely able to keep up with the white stag if I ran as fast as I could.

"Come on," I said, through labored breaths. "Please be close by, please be alive."

Following him through a pair of trees, I nearly ran over a pair of sheriff's deputies and Lucien. All of them jumped out of my way with Deana knocking me over with a ball of water, she conjured in the air and that hit me like a baseball bat.

"Deer!" one of the deputies shouted, aiming a rifle he was carrying.

Lucien grabbed the rifle from him and looked ready to hit him with its butt. "Idiot!"

I fell on the ground and resumed my human form, holding my hands up in the air. "Friend not food!"

It took me a second to recognize the two deputies as Harvey Chang and Dave Warren. Harvey was a goatee-wearing Chinese-American man with a spherical bald head who dressed like a cowboy while Dave was a thin African-American man with short, bushy black hair and a pair of spectacles. Both were human and people I'd had some unfortunate encounters with over the years. Apparently, some of the hunters me and my dad took rock salt shots at were less than pleased with our pranks. Harvey hated shapeshifters, which meant he was in the wrong town, and Dave liked them way too much.

"Great, Jane Doe," Harvey muttered, his voice like gravel. "This just keeps getting better and better."

"A weredeer, a sign!" Dave said, clapping his hands together. "She's meant to lead us to the missing federal agent."

Lucien did a sideways glance at Dave. "You realize magic doesn't work like that, right?"

"He really doesn't," I said, getting up. "Albeit, a white stag was leading me toward the Lodge. Did either of you see it?"

"A white stag!" Dave said, aping his earlier statement. "Magic does work like that!"

Lucien felt his face. "Don't encourage him."

I ignored Dave, who I understood to have come to Bright Falls explicitly for the purposes of being around shapeshifters so he could learn our 'enlightened spiritual ways.' My mother loved him and I did not. "What are you guys doing here?"

"Idiot thought we should come out here," Deana said, gesturing to Lucien. "Apparently he thinks his brother might be in trouble."

"He's been kidnapped by evil!" Dave said, without irony. "Alex Timmons has fallen prey to corrupted spirits! The result of man's insensitivity to the environment."

I blinked. "So you're teaming up with the local drug dealer?"

"More like local drug lord lately," Harvey said, showing not the slightest bit of concern as to what he just said. "Also, I don't care what he peddles to the tourists as long as it doesn't fall back on the locals. This has the potential of bringing in a lot of feds, though, so I'm eager to get their agent back and out of here."

"Wow, you are just the epitome of the corrupt small-town sheriff's deputy," I said, shaking my head. "I'm looking for Alex too. The Big...a bad spirit has him along with Sheriff Clara, Emma, and Maria Gonzales."

"Wow, Dave was right," Deana said, blinking. "I owe him a Coke."

"Well not about the environment thing," I muttered, thinking about the kelpie. "Oh Jesus-Stag, he really was right about that too."

Harvey grabbed his rifle back from Lucien. "Listen, little girl, we've got this under control, so why don't you run along home?"

"She's coming with us," Lucien said dryly.

"And why's that?" Harvey said.

"Because I pay your weekly kickback," Lucien said.

Harvey frowned. "Yes, now's the time to bring that up."

"It'd be wrong to abandon her in the forest all alone!" David said.

"Oh, for the Dancer's sake," Deana said, covering her face. "She's a friggin' deer! The forest is her home."

"Okay," I muttered. "Now I'm not sure who is being the most racist."

"Cervid isn't a race," Harvey said. "It's a species."

Lucien offered his hand to me, ignoring his colleagues. I took it and stood up, dusting myself off and wondering why the white stag had led me out here. I admitted, two sheriff's deputies, a water elemental, and a dragon were pretty damn helpful but none of it was going to do any good unless I could actually find the Lodge.

"I disagree," I said, taking a deep breath. "But let's put aside everything else here and focus on getting back the people who are missing. This forest is full of monsters, ghosts, demons, and has a crazy serial killer. I know something of what's going on and just killed a big-ass lake monster that has been here for decades. You also need me because there's stuff you can't see that I can."

"All right," Harvey said, surprising me. "However, you have to stay behind us. I'm not going to be held responsible for any civilian deaths. My chief priority is to get as many of you to safety as possible."

"Neighborly," I said, noting his dislike of shifters apparently didn't extend far enough to let us die. "Do you guys have any idea how to find the Lodge?"

"Lake monster?" Deana asked, looking up. "You killed it?"

"Caused it to reincarnate, killed it, redeemed it, whatever you want to call it," I said, unsure how I felt about it. I wanted to feel anger and satisfaction over its destruction but the truth was I just pitied the damn thing. It had been a slave of its nature rather than a being who chose to be what it was, and I didn't even blame it for Jill's death anymore.

Not entirely.

"Thank you," Deana said, her voice low and almost a whisper.

I blinked. "Okay."

"I've been to the Lodge twice," Lucien said, looking around. "The first time was when my family's murderers brought me there to awaken the monster within. The second time was when I wanted to find out who they were."

I thought of Grandfather's claim that my mother had been involved. "Did you?"

"No." Lucien took a deep breath. "The price was too high. Besides, Victoria had already made contact with it. It didn't have eyes for anyone but her and their little cult."

"This is on you," I said, narrowing my eyes. "As much as anyone else."

"You're right," Lucien said. "It's why I'm trying to make it right."

I was really getting annoyed with Lucien. He was difficult to stay mad at for long. He didn't come off as I thought a drug dealer and crime boss should. You know, actually sleazy and scummy. Instead, he came off more like television showed them as. I wondered if that was because he'd been raised by FBI agents. Then again, I couldn't imagine what his family thought of his lifestyle choice.

"Do you know where it is or not?" I asked, knowing the answer was ridiculous.

Lucien didn't respond.

"Great," I muttered, saying to the air. "So God, Goddess, Santa, anyone got any more miracles you can throw our way? Because I've been dealing with gods lately and I really would like some more bang for my buck. No deer puns intended."

"Faith is like a martial art, one must practice the basic forms even when you possess advanced knowledge," Alex's voice spoke behind me.

"Son of an elk," I said, turning around.

I turned around and stared at the sight of Alex, covered in leaves and missing his jacket. He looked like he'd been worked over with a bruise on his face and a cut lip. Both his knuckles were bloodied with cuts on them. His nose may have been broken as well, but I was too glad to see him to care. Then I saw the woman beside him: Emma.

Emma was soaked, with all of her clothes dripping wet and her hair hanging down over her shoulders. Her arm was wrapped around Alex's. There was a faraway stare in her eyes, not quite gazing at anything in particular.

I ran up to her and wrapped her in a hug, holding her tight. "Oh thank everyone and everything you're alive."

"You really should narrow your polytheism," Alex said, cheerfully. "Not all gods are worth worshiping."

"Hey Alex," Lucien said, holding himself in place but looking like he wished he could do like I was doing to Emma. "I guess I didn't have to rescue you."

"The thought is appreciated," Alex said, letting go of Emma. "I still owe you for your part at your den of inequity, though."

"Den of inequity, really?" I said, looking up to Alex.

Alex shrugged. "As Plutarch said, a spade is a spade."

"Hey!" Dave said. "I put up with enough of that from Deputy Chang."

"No, I mean a shovel being a shovel. It's an idiom related to calling things as they literally are since the word literally is often used to mean with emphasis," Alex said, apologizing. "My apologies if that was unclear."

"Oh," Dave said, nodding. "Sorry. I'm Sheriff O'Henry's deputy. So is Harvey here."

"Nice to meet you both," Alex said, giving a wave. "I've read much about you, Dave. You're a figure to be admired. Not so much you, Mr. Chang."

Harvey growled.

Emma, reluctantly, hugged me back. "Jane, never ever let me convince you to help me again."

I hugged her tighter. "After this, I will gladly never leave the house again."

"That sounds good," Emma said, coughing a bit.

"You were able to escape the Lodge?" Deana asked, sounding like she couldn't quite believe it.

Alex nodded. "Just barely. I'm afraid Rudy Gonzales is the killer, as he attempted to capture both myself, Sheriff O'Henry, Maria, and Emma in order to sacrifice them. He as much as admitted to being the one to have killed Victoria, but I believe his motivations aren't to achieve power but to lay the Big Bad Wolf to rest."

"The Big Bad what now?" Deputy Chang asked, looking unhappy to have had more individuals added to our makeshift posse.

"Just go with it," Lucien said. "What about the others?"

"Still there," Alex said, frowning. "I was able to get Emma away, but the others? No. We don't have much time until Rudy kills Sheriff O'Henry. He might spare his sister, but I believe the spirit of the place wants all of Victoria's cousins."

"I can't go back," Emma muttered under her breath. "I won't."

I didn't want to ask my friend to. "I understand."

"We still don't know how to get there," Deputy Chang said. "Kind of important if we're to mount a rescue."

"I don't suppose any of you found my cellphone," Alex asked.

I picked it out of my pants. It was, thankfully, still functioning despite being dunked in the water when I fought the kelpie. I made a mental note of the model for when I decided to upgrade.

Alex proceeded to type on it for several seconds. "Ah, there."

"What?" I asked.

"I'm pinging the sheriff's cellphone," Alex said, pointing to the east. "She's that way."

CHAPTER TWENTY

Well, I had a posse now.
Or maybe a herd.

Either way they had guns and that was a significant improvement over my previous situation. The discovery it was Rudy doing all of this was the non-revelation of the year and yet it made me sad. If he was possessed by the Big Bad Wolf or trying to lay to rest the monster then he wasn't really evil. Maybe my head was screwed up by my encounter with the kelpie, though, because killing people was pretty damn evil no matter what. I felt pretty damn awful for Maria, though. I mean, her brother was the murderer. Mine was just a drug-dealing black magic-using wizard. Which was better, right? Ugh. I hated finding out all this stuff about my family!

I squeezed Emma's hand. "We're going to take care of this, don't worry."

Emma pulled away, her eyes turning wolf-like. "I'm not four years old!'

I grimaced. "I'm sorry, I was just trying—"

"I know what you're trying to do, Jane! You're about to run right to the place where everything is awful."

She was right. "I'm sorry."

Emma covered her face with both hands, both of which had grown fur as she hovered in the place between wolf and human. Don't ask me how to explain it. It's not like science has many answers about magic yet. "I remember that place, Jane. It was full of whispers and memories. My grandfather and worse."

I closed my eyes. "It taunted me, too, Emma. The Lodge showed me my cousin Jill. I don't know if what it said was true or whether or not I just misremembered. This place is evil and there are evil forces here. I overcame them, though."

Alex surprised me by speaking. "My father, Elliot Blackwood, was a highly decorated FBI agent as well as a wizard himself. He was also a cruel, vicious, and unpleasant man with unnatural appetites. He could not control the latter and inflicted them upon others. My mother, Diane, for all her genius, was unable to see the evil within her own home. What my father did, though, was not as bad as what he made me feel about it. That I deserved it."

Emma looked up from where she'd started crying. "Really?"

Alex nodded. "I spent many years coming to terms with the fact the evil was within him not me. To overcome the fear and anger he tried to poison me with in order to make himself feel justified."

"What happened to him?" Emma asked.

"He died," Alex said, his voice soft. "I wished him to die every day for a year and it came true. I can't say whether I had any part in his death, as magic is slippery and strange like that. However, I have devoted myself to becoming a sin-eater as a result. I will use the pain I suffered to try to bring an end to others' suffering. I would take the agony of your experiences tonight into me if you wish me to."

I stared at him. "Excuse me?"

Emma's eyes widened. "I...don't know what to say."

"You do this for free? If so I've got some breakups I'd love to shove off on you," Harvey said, listening in on a conversation he had no business involving himself with.

"Shut up, Harvey!" Deana said, growling at him.

Dave also gave him the stink eye while Lucien kept his gaze squarely on his brother.

"I believe it is the purpose of a magician to use his powers for the betterment of all," Alex said, his voice soothing. He extended out his hand. "The word 'wizard', after all comes from the word 'wise'. I may not know anything, but I am aware of how much I don't know. One of the few things I do know, however, is that the hand of compassion is not wrong to extend even if it hurts."

Emma reached to take it then pulled it back. "No."

"No?" I said, surprised.

"No," Emma said, her face becoming like Lon Chaney's *The Wolfman* as her fingernails became claws. Apparently, Alex's speech had worked in changing her mind about returning to the Lodge. "I'm not going to pass this off on someone else. The Red Wolf deserves to pay for what it's done. I'm going to fuck its shit up."

My eyes widened at her sudden use of profanity. A second later, she turned into a red wolf again but this time a much larger and more dangerous-looking one. It was a dire wolf, only I imagined it was even bigger than the extinct canine species. Emma's present form was the size of a small pony and resembled the kind of creature Peter Jackson had orcs ride in *The Lord of the Rings* movies. There was also an angry and vicious expression on her face that made me think she was ready to rip someone in half. That Emma, my sweet and gentle friend, was capable of doing that. Emma trotted over to join the ranks of Lucien's group.

"Good doggie," I said, watching her leave.

"Vengeance is a bitter medicine," Alex said, taking a deep breath. "Though it can sometimes be achieved within justice, the ending of a threat."

I looked over at him. "You are way better at this shaman stuff than I am."

"Do you want to be a shaman?" Alex said.

"No," I said, pausing. "Yes. I dunno, maybe. I want to matter. This seems like it matters."

"You already matter, Jane," Alex said, looking over at me.

Our eyes met. His were beautiful, blue, and possessed of a power that seemed to draw me in. I hoped mine were equally fascinating.

"Remember," Alex said. "Wherever you go, there you are."

That killed the mood instantly. "Did you just quote *The Adventures of Buckaroo Banzai?*"

"Not many women your age are familiar with that movie."

"You're not that much older than me!" I said.

"Just saying!" Alex said, smiling. "Good advice is good advice!"

I shook my head and pulled out his gun before handing it back to him. "Here ya go. I imagine you'll be better at using it than I am."

"Unfortunately, I've had to use it before," Alex said dryly. "But you should keep it. I have other ways of defending myself."

I didn't know if I was comfortable gunning down Rudy after what I'd seen with the kelpie. Still, I took the weapon.

"You know your brother came out here," I said, looking over at Lucien. "To save everyone."

"My problem with Lucien is not the good in him but the evil," Alex said. "Every act he commits as a petty crime boss doesn't bring him closer to Marcus O'Henry and his conspirators but makes him more like them."

I disagreed there. "You know, I never understood why Batman didn't just kill the Joker. Everyone always talks about how if you kill a murderer you'll be just like them. That's not the case, though. One is killing evil and the other is killing innocents."

"Do you still think it's that simple?" Alex asked, surprising me. Had he picked up, somehow what had happened between me and the kelpie?

"I dunno," I said, frowning. "But if I was killing people I think I'd hope someone would put me down. Is your brother doing that?"

"Not yet," Alex said. "But I dread the day when I feel like I'd have to do him that favor. One can't wade in a lake of evil."

"Ain't that the truth," I said, trying not to remember what I'd seen. I started walking toward Emma and the others. "Let's go kill a demon."

"You can't kill a spirit," Alex said, walking beside me. "You can, however, force it to reincarnate."

"Fine by me," I said. "Let's hope its next form isn't a complete ass."

It wasn't lost on me the Red Wolf had been driven to his actions by vengeance too. The difference, though, was the fact that he was going after the children of the people who had wronged him. That was a big difference.

Would I think ill of him if he'd killed every person involved in burning down his home with his family in it? I didn't know the answer to that. Yet, if Lucien ever found out my mom was involved in killing his family, would I be willing to kill him? Probably. Damn. It made me think there was more than just a cuddly long-legged omnivore down inside of me but a little bit of a monster. I really was going to have to talk to my mother after all of this.

I thought I'd have to assume my deer form again and travel alongside Emma. Instead, it turned out the Lodge was only a couple of hundred yards away through a group of trees that concealed a nearby clearing. Except, mind you, I explored the preserve a hundred times or more before Jill drowned and I can assure you such a clearing didn't exist there before. Reality and space were like water around here, constantly shifting and flowing.

I hated water.

The clearing was a circular grassy plain surrounding a single one-story wood-and-stone house that looked like it had been sitting in the woods for decades. Despite its decay, it had electric lights powered by a buzzing generator outside but windows that were covered in drapes that only showed said lights' reflection. Hundreds of blackbirds were sitting on the roof, chimney, and a pile of logs outside like we'd stepped into Hitchcock's *The Birds*.

There was a huge black bear and group of similarly black dogs sleeping around the front of the house. They weren't natural, I could tell, but corpses carrying something vile. I knew the smell of natural animals and these smelled of death as well as sickness. The noise from earlier around the lake, that terrible alarm, was coming from within the house, but it was almost imperceptible here. Background noise.

"So the Lodge is actually a lodge," Harvey said, coming up behind us. "Cute."

"Nothing is cute about this," Lucien said, looking at the clearing. "My family had their hearts cut out here."

"I remember," Harvey said. "Like six people gave a shit."

Lucien looked ready to murder Harvey.

"No," I said, taking a deep breath. "Don't. It wants to turn us against one another. It did that to me, Emma, and Maria."

The moon turned bright red again and the alarm grew louder only for me to grab Emma and Alex's hands while concentrating really hard on trying to hold away the anger. That was when the red light dimmed and the noise abated.

"It worked," I said, smiling.

"No," Alex said, pulling out an amulet that looked a lot like the one I'd picked up off the ground near the lake. "I actually brought this to immunize the group."

"Oh," I said, reaching into my pocket and pulling out my copy before putting it on. "That probably should help."

"A bit," Alex said.

"Maybe I should learn magic before trying to use it," I said.

"A wise decision," Alex said.

None of us advanced to the clearing, all of seemingly waiting for someone else to make the first move.

Dave lifted up his rifle. It looked somewhat comical in his hands. He seemed way too nice of a guy to shoot anything. I knew plenty of decent hunters, was one some days, but we all had a killer instinct he didn't have. "Are we going to have to kill the animals to get inside?"

"They attacked me when I fled with Emma," Alex said, staring at the Lodge. "They're dangerous and part of the barriers that keep this place safe. We have to get in, though."

"Assuming Sheriff O'Henry is still inside," Harvey said.

"I'm still for letting the crazy serial killer finish her off," Deana said. "I'm not happy about any mission that begins with the premise of rescuing cops."

"Then do it for Maria," Lucien said. "Or me."

Deana didn't say more.

That was when the Lodge glowed and I saw images of translucent people carrying flashlights and lanterns as they surrounded the place. They were dressed in the attire of their professions from mechanics to police as a man resembling a younger Marcus O'Henry was leading the group alongside Mary Doe. I recognized my paternal grandmother from pictures scattered around my house. She was a beautiful woman with long, dark hair in a 1950s cut and wearing a waitress's outfit despite the fact that she was carrying a shotgun. She was far from the only woman present that refuted the idea lynch mobs were strictly a male activity.

A woman walked out of the trailer, wearing a pair of pants and a flannel shirt as she carried a shotgun, which she fired in the air. The resemblance to Victoria was tremendous, except this woman was in her thirties and looked a helluva lot tougher. Behind her were four children of various ages, all copper-skinned and looking terrified. The eldest, a boy of about eleven, concealed the others behind him.

The entire scene carried on soundlessly but I got the general gist of it. Marcus O'Henry tried to argue with his sister (?) about something, she pushed back. Mary then got up in her face and the Red Wolf's wife smacked her in the face with the butt of the rifle. That was when one of the children turned into a wolf and growled. He was trying to protect his mother. Except this mob hadn't been formed solely out of shapeshifters. It had humans, too, and one of them lit a Molotov cocktail before hurling it. That landed right at the children's feet, next to their mother, and she caught fire trying to rescue the eldest.

It was an ugly scene.

There was a lot of horror among the mob I realized hadn't all been intending violence. I didn't know the exact circumstances of what they were there for, I suspected to separate the children from their mother but a few tried to rescue the kids with her. They were held back by others as the humans in the mob actually cheered the fire on as it spread.

A nine-foot-tall wolf walked through the trees that parted for him. Its fur was blood red and its eyes glowed like embers. Marcus O'Henry turned into a wolf and fled along with several of the other shapeshifters but the rest of the mob either fell to its knees or were frozen in place by fear.

That didn't save them.

The Red Wolf stood over the bodies of some fifty human beings and a few dragon shapeshifters that day, none of them able to escape the horror beyond. Almost as an afterthought, it huffed and it puffed before blowing the fire out from its house. I understood what it was doing now. It was explaining itself.

"I understand," I said, taking a deep breath. "But the people involved are dead. Most of them. You can't avenge yourself further."

In fact, a part of me wondered why it had spared Marcus O'Henry and my grandmother. Was it because they hadn't taken direct part? Or did it just want to make sure they experienced what it had? If so, it was a lost cause. Mary Doe had been dead since before I was born and Marcus O'Henry didn't give a crap about his grandchildren. I suspected the Big Bad Wolf knew it too.

"I will have my bride and my sacrifices, Deerchilde," a voice sounding like a distorted Victoria's spoke from the Lodge. "I am still hungry."

That was when all of the animals woke up and came at us.

CHAPTER TWENTY-ONE

The chaos that followed was something I had difficulty navigating. Hundreds of monstrous black birds rushed at me and I battered them away as best I could. All around me, the much better armed people opened fire on them. It was deafening as I usually was wearing ear mufflers whenever guns went off during my dad or grandpa's hunts.

Lucien turned into a sixteen-foot-long crocodile that breathed out a cascade of fire that consumed a large number of the crows attacking us. It was accompanied by another torrent of water created by Deana, drowning many in air and exposing they were nothing more than a charge for the possessed dogs.

Emma charged forth and started mauling as well as biting everything around us. It was a furious and berserker-like attack I'd never imagined her capable of. Then again, who would have guessed I'd be taking down ancient corrupted water spirits before today?

"Forgive me, Mr. Bear!" Dave said, firing his rifle into the head of the black bear that lifted itself up to attack Emma. It promptly fell over.

"Oh no!" Dave said, horrified at hurting an animal.

"Keep shooting!" Harvey shouted, firing one shot after the other with deadly accuracy.

Then there was Alex. He just simply walked forward, carrying his amulet toward the door as the various monsters ignored him.

"How are you doing that?" I said, amazed at his use of magic. It made me regret not wanting to be a shaman. More than ever, I wanted to be able to use the power I'd seen to protect myself and people like Emma.

Corny but true.

"The Lodge spirit is distracted!" Alex said. "Come with me!"

I pulled out Victoria's amulet and held it in front of me, feeling the power inside it. I didn't believe the kelpie's story that I'd traded my cousin for freedom from my powers. However, I'd run from them for most of my life and that was a block on them.

That block was gone.

I couldn't pick up magic instantly, but I'd learned the basics from my mother and sister. Focusing on the amulet, I poured my energy through it and caused it to glow. It produced an aura twice and then three times as powerful as Alex's, creating a nimbus that incinerated possessed crows that flew into it as well as causing the Hellhounds to flee in opposite directions from it.

"Like this?" I shouted, more than a little proud of myself.

"Yes!" Alex said, knocking away one of the possessed dogs with a backhand. The creature exploded into Hellfire as a result. Damn his magic kung fu was good.

"You guys gonna be all right?" I said, aiming the amulet at the headless bear that was getting back up to attack. It caught fire and burned away to ashes.

"Yes!" Lucien said, clawing at a mountain lion slashing at him. Emma pounced on its back and tore its head clean off. "Just get it done!"

"Right," I said, not sure how the hell I was supposed to do that but realizing everyone was depending on me.

I followed Alex up to the Lodge's front door. I was scared Harvey would shoot me in the back but continued on. The lights on our amulets began to flicker as they approached the door, a terrible power sapping at everything I was summoning to fight it. My amulet eventually grew too hot to hold and fell to the ground as Alex cast his own away.

"That's not good," I muttered.

"We're almost there," Alex said, pulling out what looked like a drumstick before I realized it was an honest-to-Goddess wand. What was this, *Harry Potter*? I mean, at least use a staff when you're a wizard. "Stay behind me."

"Like hell!" I snapped. "I'm going to get this sucker!"

"You don't have horns," Alex said. "Only pregnant deer do."

"It's a figure of speech!" I snapped, embarrassed.

Alex reached for the door, only for it to open and release a gale-force wind that knocked him over and rolled him across the ground ten feet. It was like the breath of a mighty monster. The Big Bad Wolf huffing and puffing and blowing us down. I managed to stand against it, barely, by digging my feet into the ground. Inside, I saw the red light from earlier glowing brightly.

I covered my face as the wind continued to blast out. I needed to convince the monster to let me in. That meant playing to its anger, no matter how stupid that was. "It's me you want! My grandmother was one of the people who killed your family. I'm sorry but I know you don't care about that. Let me in!"

"You would sacrifice your life for your friend?" the Big Bad Wolf spoke. It had Victoria's same senior-class smugness, only with reverb. Of course, I now knew it had always been the Big Bad Wolf senior year. Seriously, who knew gods would want to attend high school? Why did it have a pressing need to be homecoming queen? The ways of the divine were mysterious indeed.

"No," I said, gritting my teeth. "I'm not sacrificing myself. However, you'll have the opportunity to kill me if I come in. I'll also have the chance to kill you, you sick, twisted *demon!*"

The wind stopped for a second. I didn't know how long its invitation would last so I turned into my deer form and ran for the inside as quickly as possible. The moment my hind legs passed through the threshold, the door shut behind me and locked. We were getting some real haunted-house stuff here. *Poltergeist* meets the *Evil Dead* movies. I still had nightmares about the television and the laughing moose head.

The interior of the cabin was completely empty with no furniture inside but scorch marks on the walls. The place smelled like burned meat and firewood, the scent of atrocities past still in the air after decades thanks to the hostile presence inside. The red light was all around us, coming from no direction in particular.

What I did see was Rudy, standing over the unconscious bodies of Clara and Maria. He was shaking as he held an identical sacrificial dagger to the one I'd seen in my vision. He didn't look possessed despite the fact his eyes were blood red, looking like he'd burst a vessel behind them. Okay, scratch that, he looked pretty damn possessed, but it was the physical features of possession versus his body language that made him look that way. He still looked like the scared uncertain boy who'd harassed me in the parking lot. If he was actually possessed by the Big Bad Wolf, I figured he'd look more confident and regal. Call me a traditionalist about these things.

I saw black soot markings on the floor, in the shape of a form with spots for five bodies. There was a sense of the Big Bad Wolf's presence throughout the Lodge but it felt concentrated there. I didn't know much about shamanism but I could identify it as an enhancer glyph. Something designed to make a location more welcoming to a spirit. The mark on the ground was pretty basic stuff, but since this had been sacred to the Big Bad Wolf for centuries, it didn't really need to be all that powerful to have big results.

I turned back into my human form. I wasn't going to persuade Rudy to stand down looking like an adorable woodland creature. "Put the knife down."

"Go ahead," Rudy said, surprising me with his answer. "I don't want to do this! I don't want to kill my sister!"

"Good," I said.

"Emma should have been the one."

"Not so good. Put the knife down!" I snapped, feeling like I was trapped in an urban fantasy novel. I pulled out Alex's gun and aimed it at him. "I will shoot you!"

"I can't!" Rudy shouted, his voice hysterical. "It's inside me! It's inside all of us! It wants revenge!"

"You're like its cultist!" I said, trying to figure out some way to appeal to him. "The Big Bad Wolf should want to protect you."

"No!" Rudy said, shaking his head. "It only wanted Victoria! We were lambs to the slaughter for it. It wants its wife and children back."

"What are you talking about!?" I asked, struggling to understand. "You killed Victoria!"

"Yes," Rudy said, confused. "No. She who is twice possessed lives. Death is not a cage for the beloved of the damned. The others moved on but Victoria didn't want to die so she let it catch her in its paw. The claws of it are sunk inside her. Even without a body, it holds her and takes her with it into new hosts. Only satisfying the curse can it be undone."

In that moment, I thought about the kelpie and how it had been warped by events. I'd never liked Rudy, but there was a hell of a lot of difference between disliking someone and wanting them dead. I decided to take a chance and put the safety on Alex's gun before laying it on the ground in front of me. He wasn't the demon. He was just possessed by one.

"I don't want to hurt you," I said, not entirely truthfully. I wasn't going to kill Maria's brother if I didn't have to, though.

"I want to stop it, to end it," Rudy said. "It's done so much evil in this town. The things I've seen. The things it's shown me. You don't know."

"I know," I said, lying. "But killing people is not going to stop it."

Actually, it just might. Lucien mentioned Victoria was looking for materials for a ritual to raise people from the dead. If this ritual was all about raising the Big Bad Wolf's dead family, it might be one of the few ways to put an end to it. I wasn't going to let it kill anyone else to do it, though.

Rudy looked at his knife and for a moment, I thought he was going to drop it to. "The Big Bad Wolf says I can kill you instead of my sister."

Ah, hell.

"Die!" Rudy shouted and charged at me.

I pulled out the Taser in my pants and then fired two electrodes into his chest. A glowing white light passed from the Taser and caused Rudy to scream. He fell to his knees, dropping the knife on the ground.

"Don't die," I said, taking a deep breath. I electrocuted him again. "Pain is okay."

Okay, that was probably sadistic.

I tasered him for a third time before walking over to the glyph and using my foot to smear it. The red light dimmed. The noise in the background also receded to almost imperceptibility. Taking down Rudy had weakened it and now the ritual sacrifice was disrupted. The Big Bad Wolf was still here, though. If I entered the Spirit World, I expected I'd have seen a nine-foot-tall wolf staring down at me. It was all the more reason not to.

"You know, I don't think you can actually do anything without people to serve as your vessels. I don't know much about shamanism, but I know they need hosts. I also think you've been throwing around your energy a lot, trying to take us down. I think you're probably spent."

No answer, which was a good sign.

I picked up Alex's gun off the ground but didn't touch the sacrificial knife. Instead, I walked over to Maria on the ground and shook her. She was soaking wet and looked as waterlogged as Emma had. I didn't know what was going on outside but hoped everyone was alright. I didn't want to stay in this creepy place a minute longer than I had to.

"Maria!" I shouted at her. "Wake up!"

"Wha?" Maria said, blinking. "What's going on?"

"It's Jane!" I shouted in her face. "You're in the Lodge."

"Why are you shouting?" Maria asked, looking away.

"Because you're..." I shouted before realizing she was awake. "Right, sorry."

I let go of her and she dropped back on the ground.

"Ow!" Maria said, climbing to her feet. "What was that for?"

"I've had a really rough day and am a naturally rude person," I said, unsure how to break the news to her. "I think it's down. Rudy is out of it."

Maria looked over at her brother twitching on the ground and the damaged symbol on the ground then felt her face. "Oh God, Rudy, what have you done?"

"It's not his fault," I said, not sure about that. "He felt forced into it."

"He killed Victoria, didn't he?" Maria asked, a look of anguish and horror on her face.

"Yes," I said, not sure what else to say. I could say he did it to stop the Big Bad Wolf but what was he doing here then? Besides, I doubted that would comfort Maria over the death of her lover at her brother's hands. That was some daytime-soap levels of awful.

"We can get him exorcised so he can spend the rest of his life in jail, right?" Maria asked, managing to make all my possible arguments for me.

"Yeah," I said, nodding. "That sounds good. Best plan I've heard all day."

I was about to go over to Sheriff O'Henry when I was cut off by a stream of fire along the floor. It zigzagged around the room, forming a pentagram around us. That was when Rudy stood up, his body covered in fire but not burning. It destroyed his clothes, though, and revealed a much better developed man than I ever imagined. The power inside Rudy had changed him and made him physically perfect even as his mind was half-dissolved.

"Oh that's not good," I said, trying to take a step back before finding myself almost burned by the fire behind me.

"You're a fire elemental?" Maria said, staring. "What?"

"You wanted to be a shapeshifter," Rudy said, his voice now so low it rivaled Darth Vader's. "I wanted to be powerful. Screw Mom and Dad's dreams. Fire is the only way to purify this place. The mob knew that even if they didn't realize it was. They'd only wanted to end the relationship because Anya O'Henry was rich and famous. But what they'd stumbled upon was a union of the divine—"

"Listen," I said, regretting electrocuting him three times. "You don't have to do this. I know I keep saying that but that's because I don't want you to kill me."

Maria elbowed me.

"Defense mechanism!" I said. "Sorry."

"It's a bad defense!" Maria said. "Really, really awful!"

"You can leave," Rudy said, causing the flames to climb up the side of the walls and hang from the ceiling in defiance of physics. "You and

Maria. I have to stay here and burn with it. Her. Two more must die to end this."

I wasn't going to let the sheriff die so Rudy could out in a weird suicide pact. "It's over, Rudy! It's beaten!"

"It's not over!" Rudy screamed. "I thought when I sacrificed her she'd be gone and I'd pay her back for Courtney but she's back! In the heads of others like suits! We can't let the children back, too, because they won't be real! Just the anger of the Red Wolf made manifest!"

What the hell was he talking about? "Rudy, stop this, please!"

Maria grabbed hold of me tightly, terrified of the flames. The fire licked at my back and caused me to suppress a scream even as the smoke was choking my lungs. A pathway opened up for us to flee, but it didn't come anywhere near Rudy or the sheriff as he walked through fire to her.

I was left with a choice, saving myself and Maria while letting the sheriff die or trying something stupid. The choice paralyzed me and in the end, I couldn't make up my mind while Maria seemed frozen with the same indecision.

Then Clara stabbed Rudy in the chest with the sacrificial dagger, despite it last being halfway across the room. Rudy stared at her, eyes wide, and tried to mouth something, but no words came out. A triumphant grin was on Clara's face and, for a moment, she looked terrifying. Then it was gone.

The flames inside the building disappeared all at once and so did the heat. My face was covered in sweat while poor Maria looked positively boiled. Clara dropped to the ground, like a puppet whose strings had been cut, leaving the place feeling empty and free. The Big Bad Wolf had departed for greener pastures, whether back to the Underwood or into a new host somewhere else.

As Green Day would say, good riddance. Maria, however, screamed and ran to her brother.

The front wall of the Lodge collapsed with a huge dinosaur-like tail smashing through the sides, followed by Lucien's hybrid form tearing its doors down. Beyond, I could see Alex and the others standing over the remains of the Big Bad Wolf's animal army. Deana and Harvey were injured and getting treated but it seemed like they'd managed to tear through everything the evil spirit had thrown at them. We'd won. Sort of.

Alex went over to the fallen form of Sheriff O'Henry first, something I felt a bit insulted by, while Emma trotted over to me. Emma was still a dire wolf and I could see several cuts on her body as well as a mangled leg. She turned into a regular human, which healed some of the cuts, but almost collapsed into my arms.

I caught her and helped her sit down, holding her in my arms. "Are you okay?"

"That's what I mean to ask you," Emma said, coughing. "Is it gone? Is it dead?"

I didn't have an answer for it as Rudy's words meant he hadn't been possessed by the Big Bad Wolf. Not completely, at least. Hell, it seemed like he was determined to die stopping it at the end. I'd say it was heroic if not for the fact I suspected it was to avoid the consequences of what he'd done.

"I don't know," I said, staring over at Maria as she cried over her brother's corpse until Lucien pulled her away. "I wish I could tell you."

"Was that vision we saw true?" Emma said, surprising me. I'd thought I was the only person who'd seen it. "Did my grandfather really start all this?"

"My grandmother was involved too. So were a lot of townspeople," I said, looking around. "This was plain old human evil at the start. It infected the spirit of these woods and turned it into a monster. Everyone else just paid the cost."

"I know that feeling."

Emma's other wounds healed a few minutes later. I helped her up and out of the Lodge before taking her to a nearby stump to tell her everything I'd learned.

And I did mean everything.

CHAPTER TWENTY-TWO

Time functioned differently in the Spirit World. By the time everyone had got back to the parking lot, it was sunrise. What followed was a bunch of park rangers, ambulance drivers, and other people becoming involved in resolving things. That included getting Rudy's body transported out of the Lodge, calling in more people to remove the bodies from the lake, and trying to get everyone's story straight for the official statements that were going to go on the public record.

I was disappointed Agent Timmons was perfectly willing to lie about the specifics. The public wasn't ready to know about the fact the town was haunted by not one but two demons, including one who had murdered Goddess knew how many swimmers over the years. Supernaturals were still too new to have their history revealed to the public. Hell, the whole murder frenzy that had started this was in part because people had a bad reaction to seeing a kid become a wolf. Still, it felt wrong.

My parents had also arrived along with the Gonzaleses, having turned around with my brother thanks to my mother having a vision of me in danger. How she'd convinced the people transporting Jeremy to come with her was probably best chalked up to "things the public didn't need to know magicians could casually do." Lord knew they'd probably lock my mother up in Guantanamo Bay until she agreed to work for the CIA if they knew she could control minds—assuming they didn't already have their own collection of mages or vampires who could do that.

It was about ten in the morning and after my sixth cup of coffee that Emma finally came to join me on top of the Millennium Falcon's hood. She looked as mentally exhausted as I did. Agent Timmons had conjured a black poncho that read "WITNESS" on the front in big yellow letters that helped keep the worst of the rain off of her. I still had my umbrella and I'd put it between the windshield wipers so I could sit underneath it like I was on the beach. It wasn't raining presently but it had been sprinkling off and on since we'd escaped the Lodge.

"This has been a spectacularly crap day," I said, offering her my thermos. It had been provided for by Lucien. Its origin explained why it tasted like it had liquor in it.

I'd been surprised to see Lucien Lyons had stayed for the press since I thought he, of all people, would be interested in keeping his role in all of this quiet. Instead, he'd done the exact opposite and somehow played himself off as a concerned citizen out to protect the community against evil. The official story was Rudy was responsible for the murders and he'd been a troubled kid suffering from drug use as well as an interest in the occult.

It made me sick.

"No kidding," Emma said, taking the thermos and pouring herself a cup in the lid. "Did I mention I never want you to help me again?"

I laughed. "You may have mentioned it."

"I'm kidding, sort of," Emma said, frowning. "Except with no humor at all. This brought a lot of stuff out into the open."

"Except for the parts being hidden," I said, frowning.

"Clara is the one who came up with the cover story," Emma said, surprising me. "Alex wanted to blame it on a ghost and clear Rudy's name. Lucien wanted to cover the whole thing up. It's my aunt who's vilifying him."

"I'm not sure he doesn't deserve to be vilified," I said, frowning. "He was completely crazy at the end."

"Maybe," Emma said, looking over at Maria as she talked with her parents. They were a well-dressed couple who looked disgusted rather than in mourning. "Did you know the mentally ill are more likely to be victims of violence than perpetrators of it?"

I thought about that. "Makes sense. The reason people kill other people is usually because of sensible but jerkish reasons like wanting their stuff, resentment, love, or hate. You aren't crazy to be a bigot, you're just an ass. If Alex is any indication, mentally ill people are more offbeat or troubled than dangerous."

I still wondered why the FBI let him in. Wouldn't he have to pass a psych evaluation to become a special agent? Oh right, he had magic. That probably got around a lot of issues. The fact he was the son of two FBI agents probably helped.

"You forgot vengeance," Emma said. "Vengeance is another reason people kill."

"Yeah. There's that. The Big Bad Wolf wants to kill the people who killed its family and Rudy kills Victoria for killing his girlfriend. I think that's what he was rambling about at least. Then Clara kills Rudy for killing Victoria."

"Also to save your life," Emma pointed out. "Do you think Maria will try to avenge her brother?"

"No," I said, thinking about how much I wanted to kill the kelpie. "Still, it's going to be a pain in the ass for her in the coming months. She's going to be known as the serial killer's sister for the rest of her life. It might be a good idea to move out of Bright Falls."

"It's always a good idea to move out of this town," Emma said, finally drinking her coffee. "It just has a way of sucking you back in."

I looked over at Maria. "Do you think I should try and help her? Be there for her?"

"I don't know," Emma said. "Would she want us around her?"

I didn't have an answer to that.

There was an oppressive silence until Emma broke it. "Have you talked with your mother yet?"

I wished Emma would give back my thermos. I needed some more liquored-up coffee. I would have been completely hammered by now if not for my weredeer metabolism. Apparently I just wasn't a beer woman. "In the literal sense of saying a few words to her whenever she asked how I was, yes. Not in the sense of talking to her about meeting my dead grandfather, discovering she was a murderer, finding out one of my grandmothers was evil, and that Jeremy may not have been a murderer but was a demon-worshiping Chaos cultist."

"I assume Slaanesh over Khorne," Emma said, showing she'd paid way more attention to Jeremy's geeky hobbies than me. Yet she hadn't watched *Twin Peaks* or *Twin Peaks: The Return*! We would have to remedy that some weekend.

"Coffee, now," I said, tired of waiting for her to pass it back.

Emma handed it over to me. "What are you going to tell her?"

"No idea," I said, closing my eyes. "But I can't work for her anymore. I can't live with her either. I need to find someplace else."

"You could come to work for my family at Pinewood," Emma said, referring to her family's hotel. "I mean, the pay is crap, but you'd be in with the management."

I blinked. "I don't know how I'd feel about working for your grandfather knowing what he did to you and Victoria."

Emma didn't react the way I expected. "Don't worry about it. If my grandfather ever tries to hurt me again, I'll kill him."

I held the thermos cup lid in my hands as I tried to figure out how to broach my next question. "Do you mean that you'll stand up to him or—"

"Rip his throat out," Emma said, lifting a fist in the air. "The Old Ways say we should have put him down years ago because he's too old to lead the pack."

"The Old Ways being the ones that hate gays and believe might makes right?" I said, not quite gently enough.

Emma gave me a death glare before sliding off the hood of my car.

"Oh come on!" I said, realizing I'd screwed up. "I didn't mean it like that."

Emma didn't respond, though.

Dammit.

Not wanting to stay on the top of my Hummer after that screw up, I slid off the side and walked over to Agent Timmons. He was wearing a waterproof poncho similar to Emma's with the words "FBI WIZARD" in bright yellow letters on both sides. He was talking to Deputy Chang and Warren with a pair of state police beside them.

Their conversation was about reports and follow-ups, so I tugged on the back of Alex's poncho.

"Yo," I said. "I need to talk with you."

Alex turned to look at me then nodded. "Absolutely. Guys, I'll get right back to you."

"You're ditching us for the teenager?" Harvey said.

"She's an adult to whom we owe our lives," Alex said, frowning. "You should remember that."

Harvey rolled his eyes. "Yeah, that's why."

"I remember!" Dave said, holding up his cellphone. "Can I get a selfie with you two after this? I need to post the truth of this awful business on my blog!"

I stared at him. "Yes, Dave. Yes, you can. Just not now."

"Aw," Dave said, looking crestfallen.

I dragged Alex off to a part of the parking lot that was slightly less full of people coming to this disaster late. "Okay, I'm really ticked off at you right now."

"I'm not exactly happy with myself," Alex said, looking over at Maria. "This case didn't turn out like I'd hoped."

"What did you want from it?" I asked.

"To save lives," Alex said, turning back. "Not to take them."

Well, that defused most of my argument. "Why are we lying about what happened here?"

"Alaska, Hawaii, and Washington state have recently overturned their *varmint laws*," Alex said, saying the last two words with pure disgust and loathing. "The Federal Supreme Court is entertaining a challenge to them all across the board. We can hope they will sign off on their unconstitutionality. However, the public is still undergoing a massive paradigm shift from disbelief to intolerance to, hopefully, acceptance regarding the supernatural."

"Oh really?" I said, looking up at him. "I hadn't noticed. You know, being one of the people who'd be shot if they ever stepped into Indiana."

Alex gave a pained smile. "I'm not questioning your awareness. I'm saying the truth of reality has to be spoon fed to those minds unprepared to accept how the universe really works. Evolution, the Big Bang, relativity, and quantum physics all changed our perception of the cosmos, but only with great difficulty. People were ready to accept vampires in part because of a century of media depicting them as more than just monsters."

"Even though most vampires are murderous bastards," I said, repeating what I'd heard from shifters who'd dealt with them.

"Not all of them," Alex said. "Better to let six guilty men go free than punish one innocent."

"What America have you been living in?" I asked.

"People can accept vampires, shapeshifters, mages, psychics, and ghosts now. Indeed, they find the latter comforting rather than terrifying. However, it would take a lot less than the existence of demons and insane gods to turn the world from slow acceptance to a new inquisition. Someday, I hope the truth to be revealed to the world so that all can partake in studying the true reality to reach a higher spiritual plane but I don't think that day is today."

"So even with vampires and weredeer out in the open, it's not all out in the open," I said.

"No," Alex said. "There's plenty of departments in Washington that would love to strap me to a stake in the middle of the National Mall and set me on fire. I shudder to think of it happening to someone like you."

Those words made me feel awkward and uncomfortable in a way entirely inappropriate to this conversation. "You mean like how the people treated the Red Wolf and his wife."

"Yes," Alex said, sighing. "America is a study in contrasts. It is a nation founded on the principles of equality and democracy but built with slavery as well as genocide. We must acknowledge both sides of our heritage to forge the future."

"One quarter Canadian Odawa here," I said, raising hand. "Also a woman. We can vote now, you know."

Alex chuckled. "Sorry, I do tend to ramble at times like this."

"Times like this?" I asked.

"When I meet someone I like," Alex said.

My face flushed. "Uh…"

Alex looked deeply into my eyes. "I'd like to help you find a teacher."

That was like a record scratching in my head. "Wait, what?"

"You have amazing potential, Jane," Alex said, putting his hand on my shoulder. "I think you should harness that potential for good."

I tried to process that. "Are you asking me out or to be a Jedi?"

"I would love to have dinner with you, but I don't think Washington will allow me to stay long," Alex said, looking disappointed. "Also, the Jedi part."

My eyes blinked rapidly. "Okay, you have to explain the Jedi part."

"Not literally, of course. What I mean is I know of an extremely powerful sorceress by the name of Kim Su who is looking for a pupil. I think you'd do well under her training if you want to continue using your powers to help the world. I also think your mother is someone you wouldn't do well to learn under."

The mention of my mother made my mouth turned dry. "Yeah, Judy and I aren't going to try studying together anymore. What's Kim Su, some kind of Asian martial arts master?"

"She's picked up a lot across the centuries," Alex said.

Centuries, huh? "She's a vampire?"

They were the only immortal supernatural I knew with the exception of spirits.

"She's something different," Alex said.

"Would I have to go to Dagobah?" I asked.

"She'd come to you."

I was actually disappointed about that. "I'll think about it."

"Thank you," Alex said, pulling his hand away. "Mankind can be a great people, Jane. They just need someone to show them the way."

"You really need to stop with these movie quotes."

"No promises."

I looked over at Lucien who was arguing with the sheriff. "You know, you should talk with your brother. He's not such a bad guy."

Alex's expression became empty. "Our mother sacrificed her career to cover up his crimes. I would have done the same were it not for the fact I know he'd just commit more of them. He killed, tortured, and stole to find out who was involved in his family's death as well as kill the mercenaries involved."

"Vengeance," I said. "But can you blame him?"

"Yes," Alex said, balling a fist at his side. "I can. I could understand if he just went into Marcus O'Henry's office and stabbed him in the chest. Instead, my brother has become a pimp and dealer in poison to savor the man's humiliation. It won't be Marcus who suffers in the end, he's an old man who has enjoyed the fruits of his crimes, but the people around him. In the end, the only results of my brother's actions are death, killing innocents, or both. Even if he takes away everything Marcus has, who is to say it will not be Emma or her cousins who comes back to kill Lucien for it in a decade's time? Victoria O'Henry's death is as much on his head as Rudy's."

"Victoria got Victoria killed," I said, once more glancing at Maria. "Well, her and the demon. Okay, Rudy too. There's a lot of blame to go around."

"Perhaps," Alex said, letting go of his fist. "I'm still angry at my brother, even if he tried to save us twice."

"All the more reason to talk."

"Talk is cheap."

"So is sex, but it's still good."

Alex looked down at me.

"I have no idea why I said that," I said, chuckling. "Ooo, it's humid out here."

"Good luck with your mother, Jane." Alex started walking toward Lucien.

I, reluctantly, started walking toward Judy Doe.

CHAPTER TWENTY-THREE

So, Mom, killed anybody in ritual sacrifice lately? No, that wasn't the attitude I wanted to take. So, Mom, how long have you been lying to me? Since early childhood or was it from birth onward? Okay, it was possible I was dealing with some suppressed anger. It was justified. Feeling betrayed was a natural consequence of betrayal after all. But I wanted to give my mom a chance to explain what I'd been told.

I walked over to Judy, John, and Jeremy who were standing next to the sheriff's car. Jeremy was looking, if anything, even more depressed than Maria. I wanted to grab him, throw him on the ground, and trample him. The only thing that stopped me, aside from not being a murderer, was the fact he had just lost his girlfriend and best friend too. Still, I needed to talk to him, too. We could have maybe stopped this if he'd just cooperated. We? Who was I kidding? I was bussing tables twenty-four hours ago and now I was Jane the Demon Slayer.

Finally I reached my family and tried to figure out what to say.

Dad spoke first. "Jane, you're grounded for the rest of your life. What the hell were you thinking doing all of this?"

"Jane had my permission," Judy said, coming to my defense.

"What?" John said, turning to her. "Are you crazy?"

"I met with Grandpa Jacob's ghost. I killed a monster. I've been to Hell. I'm totally shaman-ed up," I said, closing my eyes.

John opened his mouth as if to argue then slumped his shoulders before hugging me. "I am so sorry, honey. I'm happy for you, too, but I never actually wanted you to become a shaman. It's a terrible life full of danger and threats."

"Yeah, no kidding," I said, not returning my father's hug. "There are some things I need to tell you. Lies I told in the past. I'm sorry about them too, but first I need to speak with Mom."

"Anything you can say to me, you can say to your father," Judy said, frowning. Apparently she'd picked up on my 'I am royally ticked off at you' tone.

"I really don't think that's the case," I said dryly. "This is personal."

"Female stuff?" John asked, cheerfully.

Lord, my father was dumb as a bag of hammers sometimes.

"Yeah, Dad, sure," I said, not wanting to get into it but still sarcastic. "That's exactly what it is."

Judy frowned. I suspected this wasn't what she'd seen in her vision. "All right, Jane, I'll speak to you alone."

"Is Maria all right?" Jeremy said, having a traumatized look on his face. He was drinking his own cup of coffee from a Styrofoam cup.

"What do you think?" I said, harsher than intended.

Jeremy looked down at the ground, realizing it was a stupid question. It was the first thinking he'd done all day in my opinion. I wanted to comfort my brother, but I was too angry at everyone in my family, myself included, to do so. This event had exposed a lot of family secrets and killing the kelpie hadn't made me feel better about my actions eight years ago. I still hated myself for not rescuing Jill. I could move past it now, maybe, but I'd told myself that before.

I handed Jeremy my thermos of spiked coffee. "I think this magically refills itself. You're going to need it."

Jeremy took it. "Thanks. Listen, I didn't—"

"I know everything," I said, staring at him. "Way, way more than I ever wanted to know about what you've been doing out in the woods."

"I can explain—" Jeremy started to say.

"Oh, you'll talk to your sister but not your father?" John said, his voice cold. "God Almighty, if my mother were alive today."

"She'd probably burn him alive," I muttered.

"What?" John said.

I gestured away from the sheriff's police cruiser. "Let's go where no large Cervid ears can hear."

"Our ears are not large, everyone else's are small," John said, still trying to be the cheerful source of humor in our relationship.

I was going to miss that.

Knowing just how effective the ears of my family were, I didn't stop until we were on the other side of the parking lot next to the freeway. The extra sounds would help drown out what we were saying. I didn't want anyone picking up on this conversation. Hell, I didn't want to have this conversation, but that wasn't an option anymore.

I mean, what did you say when you found out your saintly mother was a multiple murderer? Oh and the local crime lord who saved your life twice in one night was probably out to kill her? That was another reason why I didn't want anyone else nearby. I probably should have waited until we were home but I wasn't exactly thinking clearly after a night of almost being killed repeatedly.

Hindsight.

"All right," Judy said, crossing her arms. "What is it?"

I stared at her. "The Drake family, the Red Wolf, demons, you, and Marcus O'Henry."

My mother didn't respond for a moment. "Dad was talkative, wasn't he?"

"He tried to get me to drink beer," I said, disgusted. "It was awful."

"Where is your Michigan pride?" My mother said, staring. "It's even more offensive given your Canadian heritage."

I paused. "You know, I want to make a joke but I can't. Nothing seems particularly funny right now."

"I understand," Judy said, not saying anything else.

"That's it?" I asked. "You're not going to deny it?"

"I'm not going to lie to you," Judy said, looking over at Lucien. "I killed Mr. Drake's parents and his older sister. I didn't know about the murders of the other Dragon Clan members in the town but there were never that many to begin with. I thought I could put an end to the curse on the town and placate the spirit of the Big Bad Wolf."

Even she referred to it that way. "You know he's looking for the person who killed them."

"Yes," Judy said, turning back to me. "I knew that was a danger when I let him go at the last minute. He was a fourteen-year-old boy and we were in the Lodge—"

"Stop," I said, staring at her. "This isn't you."

"No," Judy said, closing her eyes. "It was who I was. I did a lot of things as a shaman for the Cervid clan back before the Reveal that I'm not proud of. I clouded memories, covered up homicides, and laid curses. Without the protections of human law, it fell to me to protect the clans and that included lots of black magic. If you want to know my body count—"

I lifted my hands as if to strangle her and then covered my ears. "Jesus Christ, you bake cookies on Sundays and still go to church as well as teach people about Wicca! You're not Glinda, you're...you're...a bad witch!"

Okay, not my finest moment, but I hadn't slept in over twenty-four hours. Plus the whole day that included visiting hell and witnessing a homicide.

"Do you want me to turn myself over to Agent Timmons?" my mother asked. "My earlier crimes were pardoned along with the rest of the shapeshifters grandfathered in under the bailout treaties, but I can waive that right."

"No," I said, surprised at my own vehemence. "I just don't want you to be the person who did that."

Judy looked down. "People are rarely one thing, Jane, and that's something you'll find if you do decide to become a shaman. When I was your age, I wanted nothing more than to be powerful and terrifying. Magic was like a drug and I ignored the higher spiritual implications for the allure of power. I got involved with a lot of bad people."

"The O'Henrys?"

"And vampires," Judy said. "I was the witch in the story Marcus O'Henry used to explain why his line and this town were cursed. The difference was, I never betrayed him and helped him do a lot of terrible things."

A disgusting image was in my head and I wanted it gone. "Grandpa Jacob said you also did it for love. Who was it?"

"Christopher O'Henry," Judy said. "The two of us had an on-again, off-again affair."

What was it about my family? "Does Dad know?"

"Yes," Judy said. "Your father and I weren't married because we wanted to be. We married because it was expected of us and our society. Therianthropy is a gene that doesn't pass down perfectly because it's a magical trait rather than a dominant gene. It's why we try to make sure shapeshifters marry other shapeshifters, or did until the modern era. Eventually we fell in love, but that took a very long time."

I was afraid to ask my next question. "Is...is Dad...John...my father?"

"Yes, you and Jeremy are both John's."

The implications of that stuck with me. "But not Jeanine. Holy shit. What, *she's dating her own brother*?"

"Actually, they're not blood related at all."

"This is some Appalachian D.S!" The D, obviously, stood for deer.

"Don't insult the Appalachians," Judy said. "That's where my family is originally from."

"Obviously."

"It's your family too, dear."

I covered my face. "I'm not a Baratheon, I'm a Lannister."

"I should probably not mention John has been asked to go out and fertilize other Cervid women over the years to make sure they gave birth to shapeshifter children."

I stared at her through the creases in my fingers. "Stop talking. Please."

My mother, helpfully, stopped.

"Does Jeanine know?" I asked, realizing there was a reason she looked almost nothing like us. Suddenly, the fact she was buxom and beautiful like the O'Henry women while my brother and I were lithe as well as small took on a sinister new shade.

"No," Judy said. "I'd appreciate if you didn't tell her."

I had no idea how to respond to that. "Would you have told her before she married Brad? Or was that some kind of twisted way to make sure Christopher's grandkids inherited his and his wife's money?"

"Be polite, Jane. You did a great service for our community and you saved your brother from imprisonment. I also have heard from the others you killed the kelpie in Darkwater Lake. I've spent years trying to punish it."

"You knew about that too, huh?"

"You were too young to know," Judy said. "I wish I'd told you about it."

"Yeah, well, you kept a lot of things from me and now I'm stuck keeping your secrets." I shook my head then walked away.

"Jane!" my mother called after me.

I ignored her.

I ended up tromping off into the woods, ignoring the fact those haunted woods were a veritable hellhole of evil energy. Again, not exactly thinking clearly. The woods felt different, anyway, with the aura of magical power diffused and weakened. It was still haunted, I could tell, but the Big Bad Wolf was gone.

Gone but not forgotten.

Finding a tuft of grass, I considered turning into a deer and just running away. Instead, I just sat down and tried to make sense of it all. I'd always liked to think the shapeshifters were different from the vampires and other hidden races. That we were somehow more "normal" and decent than the others who killed, brainwashed, or tortured to keep themselves safe. Apparently, that wasn't true. We were all the O'Henry family. That was a crappy way to think of my best friend's family now that I thought about.

Hell, it was my family now.

Kinda, sorta.

"Boo," Jeremy said, coming up from behind me.

"Be gone, foul spirit, leave the living in peace," I said, not bothering to turn around and waving my hand. "Something-something hinder you, if I may."

"Does thou not knowest the prophecy?" Jeremy said, making a fake booming voice. It was from the cartoon *Return of the King* versus the book or Peter Jackson movie. "No man may hinder me."

"I forget the rest of Eowyn's lines," I said, chuckling. "But I assume the Witch King was really annoyed at the wordplay cheating."

"According to my literature professor, Tolkien was annoyed at Macbeth being killed by a cesarean baby instead of the more obvious prophecy twist."

I shrugged. "For me, I think prophecies should be straightforward and true. It makes it more interesting. Fate shouldn't have to cheat you."

Except for the visions I'd had about me, Lucien, and Alex. That had been awkward before I'd found out they were brothers.

"Like Mom did when she saw you save the day?" Jeremy asked. He took a seat by me on the grass, putting his left arm over my shoulder. "Because you did save the day. You saved the day for the entire town."

"Did I?" I asked, looking at him. "Your girlfriend is dead. Hell, most of your friends are, period."

"You saved Maria and you saved me," Jeremy said, frowning. "I can never repay you for that."

I closed my eyes. "Jeremy, I'm honestly not in the mood right now. I found out Jeanine isn't Dad's, one of our grandmothers was a KKK nut, and Mom was totally the villain from *The Craft*."

Jeremy didn't respond. For a second, I hoped it was because he was stunned into silence. Then I saw the uncomfortable look on his face.

"You knew!" I said, pulling away. "How the hell am I the only person who doesn't know these things?"

"Just lucky, I guess," Jeremy replied. "I learned a lot of uncomfortable things when I was trying to be a wizard. Also, our mother is Fairuza Balk?"

"Why didn't you tell me?" I was genuinely hurt. "You used to tell me everything."

"You always wanted to get out of the supernatural and into the quote-unquote real world. I always wanted to get into it but never could."

Damn, that felt awful now. "What about now?"

Jeremy looked down at the grass. "Now, my girlfriend is dead. My best friend is her killer. There's also Courtney. I liked her but she was more Maria's friend than mine. For what? So a sixty-year-old wrong could be avenged."

"And it wasn't," I said. "The Big Bad Wolf killed a lot of innocent people at its Lodge. It also wanted to kill you and me because we're descendants of the people involved. I feel like a *Star Wars* quote is appropriate here but don't have the energy to say it."

"Once you start down the dark path, forever will it dominate your destiny."

"That's the one."

"Yeah."

The heavy silence was oppressive.

"You need to look after Maria," I said, sighing. "She's going to need someone to be there for her and I don't think her parents are going to be much help. Call it a vibe."

"You mean how they went on television to blame the music and video games he enjoyed for why he went psycho?"

"Yeah," I said, grimacing. "Maria is going to need someone like you."

"If she ever wants to see me again."

"Yeah."

The two of us stayed together for another couple of hours until we were allowed to go home.

Wherever that was.

CHAPTER TWENTY-FOUR

Home turned out to be Pinehold, working fort of the O'Henrys. Emma wasn't speaking with me but she'd sent me a text to show up for work at seven a.m. on Monday, which I proceeded to do, and it was now Wednesday. I got a room at the hotel that was nicer digs than any apartment I could afford. I spent mornings in the kitchen, afternoons at college, and evenings cleaning. It wasn't leaving me much in the way of free time, but I was grateful for that as well. More than anything, I didn't want to think about what was going on in my life and work was a good distraction from that.

I finished my third round of "Carry On my Wayward Son" by Kansas around nine in the morning while washing dishes. I was wearing an apron over a pair of blue jeans and a Christmas shirt that showed a reindeer posse hunting Santa along with the line, "End slavery. Overthrow your oppressors." I hadn't slept well the night before and was haunted by nightmares showing the Big Bad Wolf and Victoria threatening Jeremy. I would have gone to therapy about it but I couldn't afford it.

Pinehold actually wasn't that bad of a place to work. The place was massive with its own casino, spa, hot springs, wilderness retreats, mini-mansion cabins, three pools, and golf course. It catered to everyone from high rollers to locals passing through. The place was a kind of weird "rustic chic" that made it feel very much like a shapeshifter's residence while also having all the luxuries of civilization.

The place had also had a massive spike in business since the Big Bad Wolf had been banished. It was too soon to tell, but the place used to have trouble filling half its rooms and it had been jam-packed since my arrival. While there were simpler explanations for why this happened than the curse being lifted, like a convention was being hosted here or two, I couldn't help but think there was more to it than that.

My phone made a deer bleat, which told me someone was texting me. Putting my next tray of dishes into the steam washer, I picked it up and looked at it. I half expected it would be another entreaty from my parents to come home. Instead, it was Lucien. "HOW WOULD YOU LIKE TO HAVE DINNER TONIGHT?"

I texted him back. "CAN'T. WORKING."

"THERE WILL BE CHERRY PIE."

I paused, debating whether I should turn him down for all the various reasons that ranged from him being a drug dealer to him being a big ol' drug dealer. I made a mental note that we were not going to have sex. Probably. Dammit, I did not think that last part! Sighing, I texted him back. "MAYBE."

His response was, "DEER CANNOT RESIST CHERRY PIE."

I smirked then texted him back. "THAT IS A STEREOTYPE. ALSO TRUE."

He sent me an emoji of a dragon breathing fire.

"You going out with Lucien?" Emma asked behind me.

I jumped and almost dropped my cellphone. "Gah! Stop with your ninja-wolf moves."

Emma giggled behind me. It was a welcome release after a weekend of worrying about her hating me. "Aren't you possessed of super-hearing?"

"I will buy a dog whistle to torment you," I said, turning around.

Emma was dressed in a beige Pinehold maid's outfit with a green vest and white apron. A little nametag was on her lapel. "You are too cruel."

I wanted to hug her but felt yucky and gross after working for the past three hours. "How…how are you?"

Emma hugged me anyway. "I've been working hard. Sorry, I haven't been able to see anyone. It's been cleaning, college, and back to cleaning."

"They have you working as a housekeeper?" I asked, surprised to see my super-rich friend doing the labor of us poor working class shapeshifters.

"All of my credit cards have been cut up," Emma said, not sounding the slightest bit upset. "Grandfather Marcus didn't react well to my refusal to get married to a nice werewolf boy from Utah."

"How did you react?" I asked.

"I bit his hand," Emma said, smiling. "Alice gave me the job at three times the normal salary, though. She said she always wanted to do that."

I frowned at her. "My sympathy is less than it could be with that revelation."

"Says the lady getting a free room," Emma said.

"Point taken," I said. "I still have to pay for my meals, though."

"Oh you poor thing!" Emma said. "Besides, three times a housekeeper's normal salary is still crap."

I snorted at that. "But yes, it must be a tough time for you."

"It is," Emma said, frowning. "They still haven't gotten around to doing Victoria's funeral. That's not happening until Friday. Christopher is back, but he's been spending a lot of time in his study. He even met with Agent Timmons a few times."

"Alex is still here?" I asked, surprised.

"You didn't know?" Emma said, equally surprised.

I frowned and pulled out the dishes to start stacking them. "No, Alex and I went on a date but it was super awkward when he got interrupted three times to talk about dead bodies. His boss at the FBI is a real battle ax."

"Damn, I'm sorry," Emma said.

"It was still nice," I said, thinking about how he'd been a perfect gentleman.

Which sucked.

"So you are going to date Lucien despite the fact he wants to kill your—" Emma started to say.

"Let's put that fact in a box," I said, putting my hands up in front of her mouth. "A box we bury in the backyard with all your bones and squeaky toys."

"That's racist...and funny."

"I'm sorry for what I said."

"It's okay," Emma said, before biting her lip. "I just don't like being weak anymore. I want to be strong and stand up to the people who hurt me. You and Victoria inspired me to be better."

I tried to rationalize how in the world Victoria's crazy demon worship cult plan was anything to be admired before just nodding my head. "If you want to change, then I will support you in this. We're best friends forever, Emma. Through thick and thin, rain or sleet, as well as the occasional journey through Hell."

"Yeah, let's not do that again."

"Oh, you didn't even go through there! You just got kidnapped by evil."

"Let's not do that either."

I was about to talk more about events when Alice O'Henry walked into the room. It was easy to tell when she did because it was like a light going off in the room. Remember how I said most shapeshifter women were ridiculously beautiful? Yeah, when Alice was the one whom the other O'Henry women called "the pretty one." You can start by imagining a buxom Nicole Kidman in an Italian business suit dress and you'd be off to a good start.

Uncomfortable, in a dress only slightly less fashionable and very clearly a knock-off of Alice's, was my sister. She had her hair in a ponytail and was wearing window glasses (shapeshifters didn't need corrective lenses) while holding an iPad.

"What in the world," I said, looking at my sister.

Alice walked over to us with my sister following along.

"Good evening, Ms. Doe," Alice said. "Emma."

"Uh, hey," I said.

"Hi Alice," Emma said, blinking, "I see you got your new assistant."

"Ms. Doe." Alice blinked as if trying to figure out how to differentiate us. "Jeanine is working out to my satisfaction. Thank you for recommending her."

"Wow, you rock, Emma," I said, turning to my friend.

"Thanks," Emma said, smiling.

"Does this mean you're back with Brad?" I asked.

Jeanine gave me a withering stare. "No, he made his own choice. However, Mrs. O'Henry-Ford knows talent when she sees it."

I had to wonder about that since my sister hadn't attended college and had been a grade-C student. It wasn't that Jeanine wasn't smart, she was my mother's heir after all, it was just she didn't give a crap. Then again, I imagined a magic-using assistant who could open or close portals to hell was always in high demand.

"Congratulations," I said, wondering if Alice cared what that would do to her nephew. I'd seen Brad once since my stay at Pinehold when he'd wandered past the kitchen, completely loaded, and looking miserable.

Alice reached over and put her hand underneath my chin. "Your work here, Ms. Doe, has also been adequate. You know, there's ways you can make a lot more money here than just cleaning dishes and rooms."

Emma growled.

Alice smiled at Emma like she was being cute. "I meant working the blackjack tables. It's always best to put someone small and adorable there."

Way to reverse a compliment there. "Don't I have to be twenty-one for that?"

"Only if you gamble," Alice said, chuckling. "Think on it."

"I will," I said, wondering why Emma was giving her sister the stink eye. Even Jeanine looked uncomfortable with that.

"Oh, that reminds me," Alice said, reaching into her pocket and pulling out a magnetic card room key. "The man staying in the presidential suite asked for you by name. Please go attend to him."

I was about to ask who, but didn't know that many people who could afford that. Was Lucien trying to surprise me? If so, that was uncalled for. Albeit, if he had cherry pie waiting for me then all was forgiven.

Alice looked at Emma. "I'm very proud of you, Emma. You've done an amazing job stepping up. You could have a very bright future in the family business."

"You're not my mother, Alice," Emma said.

"Neither is your mother," Alice said, leaning over and giving Emma an unwelcome kiss on the cheek before departing.

I watched her depart with a sexy sway of her hips. My sister followed close behind, like Marcie did Peppermint Patty.

"Okay, what the hell was that all about?" I asked, looking over at Emma.

"You mean your sister being my aunt's Smithers or the offer?" Emma asked.

"Either. Both."

Emma shrugged. "Alice wants to be Clan Lord of the werewolves when Grandpa is gone. She's got the money for it. Her own money too. Enough to bribe most of the elders in other states to overlook the fact she's a woman. However, she's afraid of being taken out by a witch. Having one beside her in permanent employ works for her, especially after Victoria's death."

"Plus," I paused, not sure how to bring this up, "she's kind of your sister."

"Heavy on the kind-of," Emma said, revealing she knew. "Jeremy told me."

"Wait, what?" I asked. "When did he tell you?"

Emma paused. "When I was buying Sparkle from him."

I felt my head and cursed my brother to several different hells. "Nobody in this town learns a damned thing."

"It helps me study!" Emma grimaced. "Besides, Jeremy promised he was getting out of it! He just, you know, wanted to know if I wanted it."

"Where did you meet him?"

"The Lyons Pit," Emma said, uncomfortable. "Sunday. Before I started working here. I was trying to see if I could get a date with a girl."

"Did you?" I asked, not wanting to condemn my friend.

Emma beamed.

"You dog," I said, chuckling. "Well, I'm not happy about you still being into that or my brother still dealing drugs. I hope Lucien kicks Jeremy and Maria to the curb about that. They don't need that kind of trouble."

Emma muttered something about my being an afterschool special.

"What was that?" I said, holding out my ear with a hand cupped around it. "Deer ears pick up something."

"Nothing," Emma said, blinking. "Oh, you should take your break now."

I nodded and went to the punch clock before calling over to Chef Robert the Omnipotent (he was apparently a cooking-show chef for like a minute) that I was doing an errand for Alice. I got a string of profanity in return that I took as his acceptance.

"What was the other thing about?" I said, going into the side room to change into my housekeeper uniform, closing the door between us.

Emma didn't answer until I came out, looking almost identical to her except for a couple of cup sizes.

"Don't ever take Alice's offer for extra work," Emma said, looking me up and down appreciatively.

"Why's that?" I asked, putting my hands my hips.

Emma grimaced. "Errr, let's just say Alice runs a number of specialized services for the guests."

My eyes widened. "Your sister is a *madam*?"

"I'm sure she'd say otherwise," Emma said. "She'd be shocked, shocked to find drugs and prostitution going on at Pinehold. However, let's just say Lucien and she have a relationship far more comfortable than one should exist when he's trying to destroy my family."

"I think he's only trying to destroy Marcus."

"He should get in line," Emma said, gesturing for me to take the lead. "But in a way you should be flattered. I mean, she totally thinks men (and women) would pay to have sex with you."

"Yeah, I'll pass," I said, listening to Taylor Swift's "Out of the Woods" as we exited the kitchen into the grand wooden halls of Pinehold. The floor had a fine green carpet and the air smelled incredibly fresh. That was due to them pumping oxygen into the casino so people were more likely to stay up and gamble. "Lucien being a pimp in addition to dealing drugs is another reason why I'm totally going to text him I don't want to date him. After my cherry pie, of course."

"You fiend!" Emma said, feigning shock. "But you really should consider him. He's got a lot of great qualities."

"What are you, his agent?" I asked.

"Well, it's just I was seeing Deana that night and—"

"Oh sweet White Stag Jesus figure," I muttered, rubbing my temples.

"What?" Emma said. "She's awesome!"

Thankfully, it wasn't a far walk to the presidential suite. Knocking on the door, I said, "Housekeeping. It is, I, Jane the Magnificent."

No answer.

I slid my key into the door handle and saw the light flash green. That allowed me to open it. A man's hand reached around the door, grabbed me by the arm, and pulled me in. *Dammit, it never ends!*

CHAPTER TWENTY-FIVE

Despite being a hundred pounds soaking wet, I was a weredeer and that meant I throw around humans three times my size. I was about ready to do so when I smelled Agent Timmons's cologne and blinked. It was a brand that smelled a bit like a forest and immediately caused me to stop struggling. That was when Emma pushed her way in and grabbed my attacker's arm then bit down hard onto it.

"Emma, what are you doing?" Alex said, looking down on her. He was wearing a blood-splattered white button-down dress shirt over black slacks. It was half-open and covered in sweat from what I assumed to be a recent struggle.

Emma looked up from where she was holding his arm with her teeth to no reaction. She let go by opening her mouth wide and stepping back. "I'm rescuing Jane."

Alex let go of me and dusted off his hand. "I don't think that will be necessary. I apologize for pulling you in but I didn't want to be seen."

I smelled blood in the air then looked over at Emma who did the same. Someone was injured in this room, though it didn't seem to be Alex. I wanted to look at the bed but couldn't see past Alex from this angle.

"Okay," Emma said, closing the door behind her. "Uh, why didn't I take off your arm?"

"Were you trying to?" Alex asked Emma.

"Yea," Emma said. "Doggy death shake."

"Please don't," Alex said.

"But how —"

"Magic," Alex said.

"Ask a stupid question," Emma muttered.

I managed to get around Alex and headed to the bedroom of the presidential suite, getting a good look at the source of the blood smell. Much to my surprise, I found a makeshift hospital where Maria was lying on the blood-soaked silk sheets with the breakfast table covered in everything from bandages to sterilization equipment. She looked like she'd been stabbed, but as a shapeshifter, she should have been fine. Except if the weapon had been silver or magical. Then I saw the sacrificial dagger on the table behind a roll of bandages.

Oh crap.

"Hi Jane," Maria said, flapping an arm in my direction. "Could you move out of the way? I'm watching *The Bachelor* on Hulu."

I stared in horror. "What the hell happened to you? Was it the Big Bad Wolf?"

"Yep!" Maria said, continuing to gesture for me to move. "Just when you think you're out, it keeps pulling us back in."

I felt my head and stared at the ground. "Oh hell."

"Move!" Maria said.

I stepped three feet to my right.

"Thank you!" Maria said. "Rose ceremony!"

Emma popped her way past Alex as well, staring at the sight. "What happened?"

"I decided to stay for a few more days to make sure things were worked out," Alex said, turning around. "I also wasn't sure the Big Bad Wolf was defeated. I turned out to be right, as it made another play for the survivors."

I immediately thought about my brother. "Is Jeremy all right?"

"I don't know," Alex said, closing his eyes regretfully. "I contacted your mother to make sure he was warned, but I moved Maria here to treat her after driving off the demon's host."

"Who?" I asked, wondering whom we'd missed.

Alex opened his mouth to make a dramatic pronouncement.

"Emma's goddamn brother-murdering aunt, that's who!" Maria said, looking away from the television. "I'm so mad, I can't even appreciate the fact Chris has been kicked off the show!"

"What, really?" I turned to look at the screen before realizing Emma needed me. I'd planned to binge watch it this weekend.

"Clara?" Emma said, covering her mouth. "No, that's not possible."

"I'm afraid so," Alex said, closing his eyes. "Worse, she's possessed not just by the Big Bad Wolf but Victoria's specter. It's why it's able to do it despite her not being involved in the coven. Clara is a blood relation. It's loophole abuse of the laws of magic."

Maria nodded and sipped a Coca Cola she took from the nightstand. "It sucks because Alex went to all the trouble of purifying us of our witch's marks too. That should have been the end of it."

"You are way too cheery for being stabbed," I said.

"Did you know healing spells make you high as a kite?" Maria asked.

"Uh, no," I said, blinking.

"They totes do!" Maria said, smiling. "The warm love and benevolence of a non-evil deity's blessing! It's like pot, only better!"

"You know healing magic?" I asked, still turning over the fact the sheriff was possessed and this disaster wasn't over. Healing magic was one of the rarest Gifts because it took a special kind of person to do it. My mother was absolute crap at it despite excelling in nearly all other disciplines.

"A little," Alex said, regretful. "I can only do the basics. To be a true healer requires a genuinely good soul. I have taken human life before and will do so again. That leaves me unable to learn the higher mysteries. Impure."

"So you're more paladin than cleric?" Emma asked cheerfully.

Alex's expression was pained. "Not even close."

I raised my hand. "Okay, no, we're not getting into any more weird mystical mumbo jumbo. We're going to figure out how to find the Big Bad Wolf and kill it for good."

I felt like such an idiot. Rudy had been trying to tell me about the twice-possessed. It was just the guy was so stressed he had babbled nonsense rather than coherently stating, 'Oh, hey, Victoria and the Big Bad Wolf are possessing Clara. Don't trust her.'

"Can we actually kill gods?" Emma asked.

"Gods are just spirits," I said, shrugging. "I don't know about killing them, though. I killed the kelpie but that was with your gun."

"The Merlin Gun," Alex said.

"The what?" I asked.

"It's a gun made by Merlin. It's a pretty self-explanatory," Alex said, shrugging.

"There is nothing self-explanatory about your gun being made by a fictitious wizard." That, of course, reminded me he practiced martial arts taught to him by a British science-fiction show. Personally, I'd never been a big fan of *Doctor Who*. I only watched the David Tenant episodes and that wasn't for the plot.

"It kills evil beings as long as the cause of the wielder is just," Alex explained. "Even gods."

I opened my mouth and looked sideways. That was a princely gift. It wasn't a blessed weapon, it was an artifact and those were considerably rarer. "Why did you give me this?"

"You needed it more."

I stared at him. "Do you like anything normal?"

"Burger King Whoppers with just mayo."

"Fascinating," I said, meaning it. I liked those too! Except he didn't mention cheese and a Whopper without cheese was like a bowling ball without a liquid center. "So all we need to do is get me close to Clara and shoot her? The monster is dead?"

"We are not shooting my aunt!" Emma snapped, staring at me. "That is the opposite of just!"

"I know," I said, feeling my temples. "I'm just trying to work this out in my head. Does anyone else know you're here?"

"No," Alex said, putting his hands in his pockets. "After rescuing Maria from Clara and her deputies, I brought her here under the principle of hiding in plain sight. I have a very good talent at being ignored whenever I need to be."

"Her deputies are helping her?" I asked, stunned. "They're in on this?"

"I don't think so," Alex said. "I think Victoria, for lack of a better term, has them under her spell."

"Can't you call in the authorities?" I asked.

If this was the movies then there'd be some elaborate reason why we couldn't get their help, but Alex was an FBI agent and this was a serious threat to the public.

"No," Alex said, confirming I lived in a world that operated by bad-movie logic.

"The FBI wouldn't want to deal with a possessed shapeshifter?"

Alex shook his head. "Oh no, Director Hague would be all over it. He hates the supernatural and would send in the National Guard and use it as an excuse to find reasons to detain every shifter he could."

I grimaced. "Great."

"Exorcise her!" Maria said, changing the channel from *The Bachelor* to a show about Vikings.

"What?" I said, turning around.

"Exorcise Clara," Maria said, finishing her Coke. "If you don't want to kill her, drive out the spirit from her body then shoot it. Can we get some room service?"

"No," Alex said.

"Can we exorcise her?" I asked. "I mean, the Big Bad Wolf tore a hole in reality last time we fought."

"It's not got its former coven mates to possess and Victoria is its link to Clara," Alex said, considering it. "It might be possible due to the fact we don't have to break the demon's connection to Clara but Victoria. It's piggy-backing on her."

"Is there any way we can save my sister?" Emma asked, looking between us. "I mean, she's not the one actually doing all this. She's possessed and she possesses others while possessed. I mean, twice-possessed, which I didn't know was possible."

"For gods, anything is possible," Alex said. "The same for humanity."

I, meanwhile, looked at Emma with a sense of sympathy. I didn't want to mince words around her. "Your sister is dead, Emma. She's a ghost now that's being used by a monster. The only way to free her is destroy it."

Emma balled her hands into fists and didn't say anything for almost half a minute. "I want to be the one that kills this thing."

"I'll get the Merlin Gun from my car," I said, having hidden it under the driver's seat.

Yeah, I was a real smuggling mastermind, wasn't I?

My cellphone rang. I checked its ID and it read, UNKNOWN.

"An ominous sense of dread fills me," I said, hitting ACCEPT and putting it to my ear. "Hello?"

"Hello?" I asked, my throat suddenly dry.

"Good morning, Jane," Victoria's voice sounded on the other end of the line. It caused the phone reception to crackle and pained my ear.

"Shouldn't you be in Hell?" I asked. "You tried to send me there, but I think you'd like it much more."

Emma glared at me.

"Oh," I added. "Emma is glaring at me because she's the only person in the world who gives a crap that you died."

Emma's mouth widened in horror.

"I care!" Maria said, calling out. "Give me the phone!"

"No!" I snapped at her.

"Aww," Maria said, looking ready to pass out.

"Are you with Agent Timmons?" Victoria said. "Do you have my sacrifice?"

"She's not your sacrifice!" I snapped. "She loves you."

"Love is a strong word," Maria said, accidentally knocking her Coke off the nightstand.

Emma displayed what sort of person she was by immediately going to clean it up.

"You are going to bring Maria to me and the knife," Victoria said, her voice sounding distant and absent.

More like the Big Bad Wolf.

"And why the hell would I do that?" I growled.

"Don't taunt her, Jane."

"Why?" I said, glaring at him. "What is the dead bitch, and I mean that in the female dog sense, gonna do? Her demon lost its special place."

"I have your family," Victoria said, laughing. It was a weird, almost comical witch's cackle, as if she was going through the motions of being evil.

I narrowed my eyes. "You know, I was going to maybe lead you to the light or whatever after I dealt with your demon but I am going to find a way to kill your soul. Like, full-on oblivion. What people think happens after you die but doesn't."

"Maybe I should take the phone." Alex reached out his arm and I slapped it away.

Anger was replacing my fear.

"I have your brother, your sister, your mother, and your father," Victoria said, acting like my threat didn't matter. "They're all tied up with me. Judy made a game effort to drive me out but your mother made a sacrifice in my name. She was marked by her offering and could no more harm me than fire could harm the sun."

"Am I talking to the Big Bad Wolf or Victoria?"

The laughter was a combination of both. "I am the will, she is the vessel."

"Uh-huh," I said, having no idea what that meant. "So you want me to trade Maria for my family."

"What?" Maria asked.

"Only one more must die to complete the ritual," Victoria said, her voice hoarse. "That doesn't have to be your brother."

"The ritual to resurrect your family," I said.

"Yes," the Big Bad Wolf responded, no longer sounding like it was a woman at all. "I will have my children restored and my bride."

"How does Victoria feel about you trading her for another woman?"

"I will give her a new body in the sheriff's. She, too, will join my pack."

"Male wolves," I said, rolling my eyes. "Never satisfied with just one spouse."

"Polygamy is actually perfectly natural in nature," Emma said, getting up off the floor. "Especially for—"

I put my hand over my cellphone. "Emma, I love you, but shut up."

"Right, sorry," Emma said, looking down.

"People die," I said, trying to control my fear as I debated what to do. "Your family will eventually grow up and pass on. That's how it works."

"I will use the vampire to make them immortal," the Big Bad Wolf said. "That is why I shared Victoria's blood and body with him. To seal my control. When he changes my children, I will punish him for defiling her."

I couldn't hide my disgust. If this was the way it treated the people he supposedly loved then screw it and the Lodge it manifested in. "Your children are, well, children."

"It doesn't matter," the Big Bad Wolf said. "All that matters is they will be mine forever."

No use arguing with the corrupted nature spirit. "What if I could offer you another body that's been marked? One that hasn't been cleansed by Alex. It really doesn't matter who is killed, does it?"

"They must be descendants of those who murdered my family," the Big Bad Wolf said. "That is the ritual's basis. Hate and rage for the wrongs committed against me are what allow me to reach beyond the veil of worlds to bring back those I care for."

I wondered what its dead wife and child thought about this plan. It had been decades since they'd died and I liked to think you didn't just stay static after death. Grandpa Jacob certainly looked like he'd been enjoying himself in the meantime. Would he just shove their adult ghosts into their remains or had he picked out new bodies for them? I was pretty sure resurrection came with a steep cost beyond needing to kill someone to do it because otherwise everyone would be doing it. The fact I suspected its wife would be horrified by the plan to rip her and the boys out of Heaven to turn them into vampires wasn't something I could sell to the Big Bad Wolf, though. It'd taken the train to Crazytown—correction: Eviltown—and there was no return trip.

"What about Lucien Lyons?" I said.

"Jane, what are you doing?" Alex asked.

"He would be acceptable," the Big Bad Wolf said. "So would Marcus O'Henry. Victoria was going to trade her grandfather for your brother. If the others had not betrayed her, like Courtney going to the police, Victoria would have just given me evildoers. You wouldn't have had to lose so many associates."

"Yeah, blame the victim," I said. "Okay, maybe you have a deal."

"Agree."

"I said *maybe*. I know the danger of agreeing to a pact upfront. Tell me where and when you want the goods."

"Midnight at the lumber mill," the Big Bad Wolf said. "I will bring you your family alive and unspoiled. Do not test me."

"I'm sorry, Jane," Victoria's voice added after.

Both hung up.

"Jane, what are you planning?" Alex asked.

"A double cross, obviously," I said, looking up to Alex. "Uh, do you think your brother will be willing to help?"

"Maybe," Alex said. "But I think we're going to need some extra supplies."

Maria looked at us. "By the way, I'm staying here. Just letting you know."

"No, we need you to help," I said, a plan forming. Maria would be essential to getting my family out if, who was I kidding, when things went pear shaped. "So get yourself un-high and ready to help."

"That sucks," Maria said, sliding out of bed and revealing a decently done bit of makeshift surgery. "Can I get one more hit of Cure Light Wounds before I go?"

Alex sighed. "Sure. Jane, I want you to know I trust you but I wished you'd consulted with me before making this plan."

"Yeah, well, I'm making this up as I go along. Do you normally listen to eighteen-year-old girls?"

Alex smirked. "Oh, Jane, no one could ever mistake you for anything but a woman."

"Bow chicka wow wow!" Maria said, pointing finger guns at us.

I looked back at her. "Okay, no more magic for you."

CHAPTER TWENTY-SIX

We ended up sneaking out the side of Pinehold with the aid of Alex's magic and a bit of old fashioned, "look like you're supposed to be here." I was probably going to get fired for this but it was a small price to pay for my family. I will say, though, I was less than pleased with Alex's choice of escape vehicle.

"Seriously?" I said, sitting in the passenger's seat, looking out through the Falcon's windows into the dark clouds beyond. "We have an entire fleet of cars to choose from, all the O'Henry family's, and you choose mine?"

The four of us were packed into my car and we were driving through the worst storm I'd seen hit Bright Falls since, well, at least a decade. The rain was pouring down so hard it was hard to see a foot beyond the windshield. It was almost noon but it might as well have been early evening for visibility.

Emma had changed out of her housekeeper's uniform into a pair of jeans and a gray hoodie with the Bright Falls Wolves logo on the front. We'd managed to get Maria out of bed into some of Emma's clothes that she presently wasn't bleeding into. She was suffering from magic withdrawal, though, which manifested in wearing black sunglasses while complaining of a massive headache.

I'd changed into a pair of Capri slacks and a white blouse I'd very much like to have saved for an occasion other than this. It was the clothes I'd been planning to wear for a meeting with my literature professor today to explain why I hadn't done any work on my last assignment.

"Your 2001 Hummer is a very formidable vehicle," Alex said, his voice calm despite the fact he'd just spent the past few hours patching up Maria and was now heading out to prepare for a rescue attempt of four hostages. "Fuel efficient? No. Formidable? Yes. The latter may be more important now."

I felt my face. "I am surrounded by Hummerdinger fans."

"Seriously, we could get trampled by a herd of buffalo and be fine," Emma said, bouncing in the back.

Maria, meanwhile, banged her head lightly against the left rear door window. "Magic…magic…my kingdom for some magic."

"Sorry," Alex said, shaking his head. "All tapped out. Besides, you're almost healed."

Maria snorted. "Almost is not completely, Harry Potter."

I was grateful, in a way, to have a distraction like this. It kept me from thinking about the fact my family was tied up and held prisoner by a murderous werewolf possessed by two spirits. One who had the full authority of the law behind her, so there was no chance of calling the police on her.

"May I ask where we're going?" I asked, having realized I hadn't asked beforehand. "I know we have our work cut out for us in convincing your brother to be our hostage, but I'm sure with him as backup—"

"We're not going to Lucien's," Alex said, squeezing the steering wheel hard.

"We're not?" Emma asked. "But they totally helped us last time."

"We can," Alex said, correcting himself. "But I want to take us somewhere else first."

"Disneyland?" I asked, unsure where my favorite FBI agent could want us to go. He'd already said we couldn't get ourselves reinforcements.

"My master, Kim Su."

"The lady who was supposed to teach me magic but never called?"

"It's been a weekend, Jane. It's not like she's going to e-mail you a response."

"Why not?" I said. "Archmages can use the internet."

"I sent her a message," Alex said, sighing. "However, while she's sent me a response, it requires a bit more to get her to come to a new location."

"Can we can the mysteriousness of mysteriousness? What do you mean?"

"I want to physically summon her tower to this state and town so we can talk to her. If she can help directly, that'd be great, if not then I'd love for her to give us an item or spell to exorcise Clara O'Henry so we don't have to kill her."

I blinked, processing that. "Okay, maybe there's a reason wizards talk cryptically. Summon her tower? Like Isengard?"

"That would be awesome!" Emma said, grabbing the headrest of Alex's seat. "Will it have a flaming eye?"

"No," Alex said. "It takes whatever appearance would be appropriate for a location."

"Boring!" Emma said, falling back into her seat.

"Can you please stop talking?" Maria said, feeling her head. "I need an ice compact and maybe a hundred Bloody Marys."

"I'm pretty sure you're faking now," I said, glancing at her in the rearview mirror.

"Who was stabbed by the magic knife of stabiness?" Maria asked. "The one that killed my brother?"

There wasn't much you could say to that. "You were."

"Damn right," Maria said. "So let's go find this old wizard lady and kill Emma's sister."

"We are not killing my sister!" Emma snapped.

"We're killing one of them but it doesn't count because she's dead!" Maria said, turning to her. "That's fine by me."

Alex smiled and laughed, which I did not think to be an appropriate reaction. "Like road trips with my sister."

"You have a sister?" I asked, surprised by this revelation.

Alex paused. "No."

There was a finality to it which put me in mind of Maria.

"She died?" I asked.

"Yes," Alex said. "I killed her."

Suddenly six eyes were staring at Alex.

"Not willingly," Alex said, his voice low. "I've been party to your tragedies so I feel it only right you know some of mine. I tried to save her from my father once. He was beating her badly and perhaps worse would have happened. That was when my powers first manifested. I willed him to die. Samantha...she died too."

"Jesus Christ on a pogo stick. That is messed up," I said, before realizing that wasn't exactly a sympathetic response.

Alex made a turn down a road that I knew led nowhere. "Yes. It left me traumatized and hearing voices which, combined with the fact I'm neuroatypical, led them to misdiagnose me with something much worse. I spent a year in a mental institution as I mentioned. I eventually returned to my mother's home but it was never the same between us. In fact, I believe that's part of the reason she adopted Lucien. It was her chance to have a do-over with a child she hadn't utterly failed or hated."

Yikes. "I'm sorry, Alex. That's...terrible."

"It is what it is," Alex said. "After I finished high school, my mother and I parted ways. I sought out a mentor for sorcery and ended up studying under Kim Su after a particularly grueling series of tests. I completed my degree in psychology simultaneously with finishing my final test to become a master of spirit magic. Given my family history, nobody wanted me joining up. I managed to just squeak by, though."

"Because you were a wizard?" Emma asked.

"I speak fluent Spanish and know a little about forensic accounting," Alex said. "That put me over the edge with the other magical candidates."

I saw there was more to the story. In my head, I saw a vampire rapist being stabbed with a wooden dagger in a sorority house by a trench-coat-and-hat-wearing Alex, a pair of police officers behind him. The idea of Alex being a vigilante fighting evil in the post-Reveal world amused me before I remembered "hunters" had always existed and tended to target people like me.

That explained how he'd managed to get in the FBI. It was just an irony that he was probably a guy who was more liberal than most in supernatural law enforcement. A part of me envied him. How could it not since I was ready to track down and murder my second evil god of the week.

"Wait, if you're a master of spirit magic, then why can't we just use you to exorcise the Red Wolf?"

"I don't have the juice for it. Not a spirit as powerful as it."

Huh, well, that was honest. "So if we don't get Kim Su's help we're—"

"Yeah," Alex said.

Well, we had the Merlin Gun. I wasn't going to let my family stay endangered. I just hoped Emma would be able to forgive me, though I doubted she would. I really hoped Alex's Yoda would come through for us.

The car pulled to a stop in the middle of an empty trailer park which was set for demolition. It had been taped off with signs built around it. The O'Henrys had plans to turn Bright Falls into a resort town like New Detroit, but so far, they'd only managed to make one enormous hotel which had never been more than half full until this week. The fact they were planning on building another hotel here by the look of the signs said they sometimes had more money than sense.

"What are we doing here?" I asked.

"The summoning," Alex said.

"Ooo, Grandpa isn't going to like that," Emma said. "Do it!"

"It's going to take a lot out of me," Alex said, raising his hands. "I'm also going to need everyone else to do something."

"What?" I asked. "Chant? Hold hands? Pray?"

"Close your eyes."

"Okay," I did so.

"Everyone," Alex said. "That means you, Maria."

"Aww!"

A second passed.

Alex said, "Okay, you can open them now."

"What?" I said, opening my eyes. "You can't have…what the holy hell?"

A strip mall had appeared out of nowhere in the middle of the woods, displacing the deserted trailer park and surrounding us with a road to town. Even the weather was different as the rain had suddenly let up even though I could hear it just a few hundred yards away. A patch had emerged in the clouds above us.

The strip mall wasn't particularly impressive with a Dollar Store, Big Buy, an IHOP, a beauty salon, a game store, and a few other strip mall sort of places. All of the businesses seemed open and there were people in the parking lot we'd suddenly found ourselves in. I also noticed, at the end of the half-square of stores was a small store called "KIM SU'S THE TOWER - FOR ALL YOUR OCCULT AND SCENTED CANDLE NEEDS."

I did a double take between it and Alex. "Are you frigging serious?"

"I'm afraid so," Alex said.

"You conjured this?" I asked, stunned. "Just how powerful are you?"

"Not as much as you'd think," Alex said. "Kim Su keeps an extra-dimensional pocket of time and space around her so she can move around at will without discomfort. I didn't create this, just called it to Bright Falls. It exists in other places simultaneously at her will and time. However, for the purposes of Bright Falls, you could go down to the mayor's office and find it's always been there."

"Wow," I said, shaking my head. "What do they sell in the stores here? Mogwai?"

"Mostly toilet paper and liquor," Alex said. "When you get to be as old as Kim Su, you want access to all of the stuff you like without difficulty."

"It is wrong I find this both awesome and incredibly lame?" I asked, trying to take it all in.

"I was hoping for a real tower," Emma said.

Maria stepped out of the car. "If anyone needs me, I'm going to be buying liquor."

"That's probably not good given your condition," I said, watching her leave.

"It's antiseptic!" Maria called back.

I watched her depart into the liquor store by the Big Buy.

"I like her!" Alex said, smiling.

I rolled my eyes. "Is it safe to let her go wandering about with evil gods in the woods? Which I'm really upset isn't a euphemism."

"This is probably the only place in Bright Falls which is one hundred percent safe from the Red Wolf," Alex said,

"Call it the Big Bad Wolf," Emma said, her voice low. "It hasn't been the Red Wolf in a very long time."

I looked over at the Tower store. "Does your master know we're coming?"

"Now she does," Alex said, frowning. "Mind you, it may be on the other side of the line between polite and incredibly presumptuous to summon her home to this place. We didn't exactly leave on the best of terms."

I felt my head. "Now you tell me. What did you do?"

"I kinda-sorta stole the Merlin Gun," Alex said. "I wanted to hunt evil with it."

"You are not nearly as nice and law abiding as an FBI agent should be," Emma said, frowning.

"You're right about that," Alex said, unbuckling his seatbelt. "But I try."

I reached under the passenger's seat and pulled out the Merlin Gun before making sure the safety was on and hiding it in my purse. I didn't normally carry one, but I was dressed up for today's meeting. Thankfully, I'd brought my work shoes so I wasn't stuck wearing high heels trying to save my family. "Yeah, giving me your gun feels a whole lot less cool now that I know it's hot. Also, was asking her to teach me an apology?"

"No," Alex said. "I believe you have a talent which should be nurtured."

"What was yours?"

Alex paused. "I thought it was to bring justice. Now I think it's more to be a defender of humanity in all of its forms."

"Isn't that the same thing?" Emma said.

"Sometimes," Alex said.

I tried not to gag at the righteousness on display. Then again, I didn't blame Alex for wanting to go out in the world and slay monsters. If I'd had his childhood, I'd try to make up for what had happened to me too. I couldn't imagine being responsible for the death of…oh wait, yeah I could. Huh, maybe the FBI agent and I had more in common than we thought.

The three of us headed through the glass door of the Tower shop and I was immediately overwhelmed with the auras within. The Tower looked like a combination of knick-knack shop and one of the post-Reveal occult stores which had popped up in recent years. There were a variety of knives, swords, and axes on the wall but no guns.

I saw dozens of ordinary objects on tables, marked with little cards and tags ranging from teddy bears to expensive jewelry under glass. Bookshelves were filled with spiral notebooks next to expensive medieval-looking volumes and those were next to regular shelves of the store's titular scented candles. I also saw a comic book rack with *Action Comics* #1 and *Detective Comics* #1 that didn't look like reprints but were next to more recent comics (also a few *Playboys*).

And everything inside this place was magic.

Having the ability to sniff out magic, I found my attention going in every direction around me, trying to trying take in all of the auras about me. I accidentally bumped into a table that caused a baseball to roll against me and I was filled with an image of it being used to win the World Series. The item had since been enchanted to bring general good luck and success to any contest one engaged in. My hand also waved over a key that I found out had been carried by a thief for decades as a good luck charm that could increase one's ability to not be seen. Another item was a lucky rabbit's foot which, ugh, made a person able to have sex for hours. I paused, thinking about that, then checked the price. Really? Ten bucks? I needed a shopping cart.

No, Jane, focus!

"I think Stephen King wrote about this store," Emma said, looking around. "Except this is a lot trashier."

"If we can't get Master Kim's help in defeating the Big Bad Wolf, then maybe we can find aid in the objects here. Everything has a price."

"Our souls?" Emma said.

"No," Alex said, pulling out his credit card. "Something much costlier."

That was when I heard a deeply annoyed young woman's voice with a...Southern accent? "A werewolf, a wizard, and a weredeer walk into my shop. It sounds like a joke but I'm not laughing."

That was when I heard a shotgun cock.

CHAPTER TWENTY-SEVEN

I turned to see a girl who looked about my age with long raven hair, copper skin, and Asian features I was inclined to say were Chinese but that covered a lot of groups. She was wearing a pair of shorts, a blue robe that was open in the front, and a shirt with floral patterns. I also saw a pair of unicorn slippers on her feet. It was the ultimate in 'I don't give a crap' wear. Except, I also noticed she was carrying a shotgun too. It was covered in the same sort of sigils as the Merlin Gun. In a room full of powerful objects, it stood out as the strongest.

"Master," Alex said.

"Dumbass," Kim Su said. "Deer lady, Wolf lady."

"Hi!" Emma said, cheerfully.

"You look like a teenager," I said, trying to avoid drawing attention to the fact she was pointing a gun at us.

"You look like an adult," Kim Su said, lowering her shotgun. "When I was young, you probably would have five or six kids and then die at thirty in childbirth so your husband could remarry."

I grimaced. "How old are you?"

Kim Su paused. "Actually, I'm not too sure. Things get a little hazy after the last three thousand years, but it was after the Elder Gods ruled the universe. I recall it still being a novel idea that the Earthmother and Sun had convinced the vampires as well as werewolves to turn against their masters. Most of the New Gods were still new back then."

"I don't recall this from my *Bulfinch's Mythology*," I said.

"You wouldn't." Kim Su shrugged. "Humanity still has trouble with the idea it's a fundamentally uninteresting species to the rest of the universe."

"We are not!" Emma said, indignant.

"I don't think you're included in that," Alex said, correcting her. "Kim Su is of the old school that thinks of humans, mages, shapeshifters, and the undead as all different species."

"And what are you?" I asked, not really disagreeing with her. Humanity couldn't get along with itself so why should it be a big happy family? Strong fences made good neighbors and wow, that was racist again. I blamed my mother and dad now.

Kim Su stretched her arms out over her head, shotgun in one hand. "I am Kim Su, First of the Magi (as far as you can prove)! Holder of the Akashic Record and Master of So Many Disciplines Even I Don't Remember Them all! That's an official title by the way. Grandmistress of the Order of the Sun and former High Priestess of Mia!"

"Mia?" I asked.

"That's what I call the Earthmother," Kim Su said. "I like to change her name every few decades after my latest favorite actress. I think her next name will be Snookie."

Wow, she was already behind the times. "I take it you're from the ham-and-cheese school of sorcery?"

"I am a wizard, so I can do or say whatever I want," Kim Su said. "It's really awesome and you should try it. Being obnoxious and not getting stoned for it is a privilege modern women should not take for granted."

"Believe me, I'm very appreciative of it but I need your help," I said, deciding I liked Alex's mentor.

"Yeah, and yet you came with Alex," Kim Su said, glancing at him as she rested her shotgun's barrel on her right shoulder. "My greatest disappointment."

Alex lowered his head. "I'm sorry."

I started to defend him. "Alex is—"

"Working for the government!" Kim Su interrupted, her mouth open in mock outrage. "I mean, did you retain nothing of what I taught you? You could have been a drug dealer like your brother, head of a cult, a mass murderer, or a supervillain and it'd make me think more of you. At least tell me you're having sex with models while using your powers for personal gain."

Alex did his best to maintain his composure but I could tell he was furious in the way adult children got in the presence of parents. "This is important, Master."

"You graduated, so it's Kim Su or Sexy Lady to you," Kim said. "You stopped being my apprentice when you decided to go out on your own. There was no more I could teach you anyway."

"Really," Alex said.

"Oh hell no, I could have taught you new tricks every day until you died but you wouldn't get to actually use any of them," Kim Su said. "Besides, some of the stuff you do is impossible, like creating new gods out of TV shows and altering reality. You should stop that as we follow the laws of physics in this store—at least as I define them."

"My family has been kidnapped," I said, taking a deep breath.

"Well that sucks," Kim Su said, walking to the counter and stepping behind it. She plopped her shotgun on the top. "What do you want me to do about it?"

I blinked. "I dunno, help?"

"Sorry, but I don't get out of bed in the morning unless it's an Elder God being awakened from its slumber. That's why I have minions."

"Minions?" Emma asked, looking at some of the goods in the store. I saw her pick up a handheld shopping basket and start browsing while I talked with Alex's master.

"It sounds better than apprentices," Kim Su said.

"It really doesn't," Alex said, walking up to her. He looked like he was trying to stay calm but it was clear Kim Su was getting to him. "Master, I beseech you, it was you who taught me to use my powers for good and the benefit of mankind."

Kim Su furrowed her brow. "That doesn't sound like me. You must be thinking of some other kickass archmage."

Alex looked like he was ready to throttle her but managed to keep a straight face. "Jane is the woman I told you about. Her potential is immense and she could be a force for good in the world if she had your assistance. That's not going to happen, though, if the local demon brings her family to harm."

"The local demon has kidnapped them, that's already bringing them to harm," I corrected, walking up to her. "I can return the Merlin Gun to you if you do."

Kim sat down in a stool that made her stand face-to-face with Alex. "You mean, return my stolen property to me in exchange for a reward even though you received it from the guy who stole it?"

"Yeah?" I suggested.

"Keep it," Kim said, patting her shotgun. "I've got like three. The weapons crave violence and sending souls to Hell. It's what you get when you make them out of angelic metal and summon an Ophanim into one."

I recognized that as a Christian angel type, that caused me to blink a bit. My gun had an angel inside it? That was a little unsettling. "Uh-huh. Well, what would make you want to help me?"

Kim Su paused and conjured a pair of glasses before leaning over the counter to look at me intently. "You claim to be a weredeer, right?"

"Claim?" I asked.

"Yeah, they're shamans lately," Kim Su said. "That's new. I want you to prove it."

"Okay," I said, ready to turn into a deer. "Just point to where you want me to transform."

"No, no, that can be faked by magic. I need you to do something more substantial."

"Like what?" I asked.

"Make a pun," Kim Su said. "A good one."

"What?" I said, angry she was joking around like this when my family was endangered.

"Oh Lord," Alex said, covering his face.

"We don't have time for this," I said, balling my fists. "People have died."

Kim Su sighed. "My dear, I have born witness to more murder, genocide, and raping than you could possibly imagine. I drove a spike into a Persian king's head to save the Jewish people, gave Arthaeus a sword that could cut through steel, and managed to sneak in Nazi Germany to make sure Hitler's plan to sacrifice all of Berlin to become a god failed. The Merlin Gun made it look like a suicide since I shot him right against the side of his head after forcing cyanide down his throat. His vampire lover too. Believe me, I'm aware people have died. They always died but if my ways sound strange, it's because I know what I'm doing."

My eyes widened. "You did all of that?"

"Maybe," Kim Su said, straightening her back. "I could also be saying complete deershit but you'll never know."

I pinched the bridge of my nose to ward off a migraine. "And if I do this, you'll help?"

"Maybe," Kim Su said, crossing her arms.

I took a deep breath. "Okay, I was going out one day wearing a slinky dress with a purse full of mushrooms when my mother came out and said, 'You can't go out like that.' I asked, 'Why?' Then my mother said, 'Because you don't want people to think you're a deer of loose morels.'"

Kim Su stared at me.

"Because deer eat a fungus called morels," I said.

Kim Su raised an eyebrow.

"All weredeer are not good at puns!" I snapped at her.

"Why is the purse full of mushrooms?" Emma asked, calling from a table containing a stack of autographed Farrah Fawcett photos. No idea why those were there.

"It's a joke, it doesn't have to make sense," I said.

"So the cents are in your purse?" Emma asked.

"Who is the weredeer here?" Kim Su asked.

I frowned. "Lady, I do not appreciate your pressuring me to conform. Being a weredeer is hard! Not only do I have to put up with the puns, every other woman in my race has long legs and can walk in stiletto heels without difficulty. Every guy constantly wants to butt heads with each other. Also, things are never salty enough. That includes salt."

"Now I believe you." Kim Su grinned and pulled out a sheet of white paper from a '90s-style printer behind her then picked up a Sharpie to write on it.

"You didn't before?" I asked, exasperated.

"No, I did," Kim Su said, shrugging. "I just have so few amusements in my old age. Also, I regenerate any wound so don't talk to me about shoes. I'm incapable of building callouses on my feet, so they're permanently tender."

"Ouch," I said. "Emma doesn't wear heels because her feet are permanently padded."

"They are not!" Emma shouted as she picked up a Bionic Woman action figure.

Alex looked like he could barely suppress laughing aloud.

Kim chuckled. "Have a look around and see if you find anything you'd think would help. I'll also write you a spell that will allow you to banish a god."

"Alex said he didn't have the juice to do it," I said, blinking. I was trying to figure out exactly what was needed to save my family and didn't need to be distracted by Kim Su's desire to make us put on a show. "Juice?"

"Magic is like building up a muscle. A lot of it is hard work but some of it is genetics. Alex punches like Bruce Lee, but that doesn't mean much compared to some of what is out there."

"Who do you punch like?" I asked.

"Albert Einstein," Kim Su said, scribbling something on the paper. "It took me three hundred years to gather enough magic to make this device. Unlike most of our kind, I refuse to engage in pacts with spirits or feed off a cult. I have more knowledge than most any other mage alive, but I'm not the most powerful magic user in the world, not by a long shot."

"What about me?" I asked.

"You're a shapeshifter of a lineage that has cultivated magic within itself for a few millennia, so you should be fine. It's really the question of how much you're willing to sacrifice to the magic that will determine how powerful you can become."

I made a *whoosh* gesture over my head.

Kim Su smiled. "Magic isn't like science. It doesn't continue to exist independent of you and regardless of your feelings. You use magic to change the world, it changes you back."

"That's not always a bad thing," Alex said.

"Spirits love you," Kim Su said, folding up the piece of paper and sliding it across the counter. "Good ones and some bad. You're also devoted to a cause. I prefer to own my soul free and clear."

"Maybe that's why I had to leave," Alex said.

"You're not just here because you like it," I said, looking around the room. "You're here because you're hiding."

"When you try and make the world a better place, you make enemies." Kim Su sighed. "Azazel, Aleister Crowley, the Ultralogists, the Cult of Transcendent Ones, and more than a few vampire Old Ones. Being one of the few genuinely immortal beings out there, I can usually just take a few decades off every century or so to let them die off or get themselves killed fighting each other. I made a mistake in the eighties and if I leave my home then I'm likely to get found by people who would make a fight with me look like Bambi versus Godzilla. No offense."

"I like Godzilla," I said.

"He reminds me too much of Lucien," Alex said.

I snorted and opened the envelope. It read "GET OUT" in big black letters. "Wait a minute, what the hell is this?"

"The spell for exorcising Clara O'Henry," Kim Su said. "That will be five ninety-nine."

"'GET OUT'?" I said, no longer finding her antics amusing.

"You can say it in Latin if you want to," Kim Su said.

Alex felt his head. "Kim?"

"The magic is in her not any chants or books," Kim said, sighing. "You know that better than anyone, Alex. The charts, words, and astrology help. You can even borrow magic from spirits when you're a regular human to make rituals work if you know the right names but at the end of the day, magic is will plus belief plus lineage times juice equals niftiness."

"Thanks," I said, growling. Unfortunately, being a deer, it didn't really work for me and I sounded adorable rather than threatening.

Kim sighed and gestured for me. "Come here."

I reluctantly leaned over the counter.

Kim put her finger to my forehead. "Understand."

The next thing I knew, I was on the ground foaming at the mouth and shaking. Alex and Emma were by my side.

"Ugh!" I said, choking and spitting to one side.

Kim was sitting behind her counter still, now reading an Italian copy of *Glamour*. "You're welcome."

"What the hell?" Emma shouted, calling to her.

"Ask her," Kim Su said.

I climbed on my feet and almost launched myself over the counter before pausing in mid-step. "Huh, I know how to exorcise people."

Kind of. I understood vaguely how the process worked in the same way I knew how to breathe without thinking about it. I could summon my will and inner strength to do it but it would be without any subtlety or form. Just raw power. It was like she'd added a third Gift to my visions and psychometry.

Wow.

"Yes, I have taught you one spell," Kim Su said, giving a mischievous smile. "The Keanu Reeves way. I don't recommend doing it again. I mean, it only has a small chance of liquefying your brain every time but those odds are not ones I'd like to test."

"No kidding," I said, needing to catch myself on the countertop.

"Oh don't be a baby, you didn't even wet yourself," Kim Su said. "I could tell you about some of my apprentices who—"

Alex pulled out a ten-dollar bill from his wallet and handed it over. "Thank you, Kim. I don't think we'll need anything else."

Kim rung it up and handed him over the change. "A word of caution, Alex. The Red Wolf isn't just a small-time spirit. It is the manifested spirit of Bright Falls and a child of both the Earth as well as sky. You can kill it and probably should but there will be consequences to it. All the defenses it has placed around this town will be pulled away and there will be a rush to replace them. Nature abhors a vacuum."

"I'll take my chances," Alex said, placing his hand over his heart. "Better to fight evil than leave it to continue harming the innocent."

"Because that attitude has never gotten America in trouble before," Kim said.

She had a point there.

Emma looked torn between saying something and accepting the spell Kim Su had worked on me was for my own good. Instead, she lifted her hand basket full of scented candles and handed over her debit card.

I gave her a sideways look. "Really?"

"What?" Emma said. "She has sandalwood and cherry."

I rolled my eyes.

CHAPTER TWENTY-EIGHT

The three of us moved to depart Kim Su's store after making our purchases, Emma carrying a brown grocery bag full of knick-knacks she'd picked up. Alex had bought himself a silver lighter, though my nose told me he hadn't even been around second-hand smoke recently. I'd bought a copy of Fox Mulder's "I want to believe" poster. The original owner had been so fanatically devoted to *The X-Files*, it had allowed the poster to become a holy relic that would increase the natural protection of any home against evil. I wasn't sure if I believed that but the poster would make a kickass addition to my room (or a "Glad you're not dead" present for Jeremy).

Thoughts of my family temporarily exited my head when I saw, standing just outside the door we'd walked out of were three familiar faces pointing guns at our heads. It was Deana wearing tactical combat armor and holding an M16 (or possibly some other big assault rifle-looking gun, I'm not an expert on these things), Gerald Pasteur holding a Beretta aimed only vaguely in our direction, and Lucien holding a Desert Eagle in each hand like he was in a John Woo film.

"We need to talk," Lucien said, his voice full of accusation and fury.

"Obviously," Alex said, cocking his head sideways. "You do realize there's no actual benefit to using two pistols at the same time, right? It destroys your accuracy and if you want to fire multiple times, you should just use a machine gun. That's why they were created."

"Maybe they're magic guns," Emma suggested. "Maybe the spirit of Chow Yun Fat taught him gun-fu."

"Possible," Alex said, furrowing his brow. Clearly, he was taking her suggestion seriously. "But unlikely. Besides, he could just enchant a machine gun."

"Quit helping, guys, please," I said, closing my eyes and wondering if I'd infected them with my sarcasm or like had attracted like.

"Shut up!" Lucien said, putting away one of his guns and waving the other between us. "You lied to me! Both of you."

"There's three of us here," I pointed out. "But I'm going to assume you mean me and Alex."

Emma grumbled. "Thanks for including me, Jane. I appreciate that."

"You're welcome," I said.

Emma glared at me. "I was being sarcastic. I can do that too, you know."

"Really? I had no idea."

"Right." Emma looked at Deana as she put down her grocery bag. "You can forget about a second date."

"Eh." Deana shrugged, nonplussed. "It happens."

"You cannot frighten me, brother," Alex said, puffing up his chest and crossing his arms. "Death is but a doorway. Some souls are obliterated by the light beyond and others made part of it. For me, it is but a transformation, but for you, it is end."

"Did you literally just say if you strike me down I shall become more powerful than you can possibly imagine?" I asked, looking at him.

"Not *literally*," Alex said, embarrassed.

"Yeah, well speak for yourself," I said. "I'm not ready to join my grandfather in the Great Meadow in, well, not the Darkwater Preserve. It turned out Belinda Carlyle was right. Heaven is a place on Earth."

Lucien fired his gun in the air. It caused everyone in the parking lot to drop their groceries and flee for safety. "Quit the banter."

"I'm not sure that's possible," I said, looking at him and realizing he wasn't going to shoot us. I'd seen him kill the animals in the forest and come at the Lodge. Lucien just wanted to scare us. At least, that's what I hoped was going on. "It's ingrained in my DNA like the ability to become a deer and love of mushrooms."

"Your mother killed my parents and brother," Lucien hissed, his mouth glowing orange and red as fire flicked out from his mouth.

I blanched as I closed my eyes. I was really hoping that would never come out. "I'm sorry."

Even Alex deflated.

"I'm sure she had a good reason!" Emma said, defending the indefensible.

"Don't help, Emma," I said, sucking in my breath.

"You knew," Lucien's voice carried an immense amount of betrayal. "Both of you."

It should have surprised me Alex had figured out my mother's involvement but it didn't. Despite the fact he was one of the few people not related to the disaster at the Lodge, he seemed to be far more on the ball than anyone else involved in this. Then again, maybe it wasn't that big of a leap to make the person involved in ritually killing the thirteenth clan's leaders would be the local person in charge of rituals. No wonder we'd never talked about the Dragon Clan's destruction in the Doe household.

"I deduced," Alex said, sounding appalled but sympathetic. I'd wanted him to talk to his brother but not about this. Crap. He didn't stop there, either. "Now, what are you going to do? Murder Jane? Murder me? Have you lost yourself so much to hate that you will commit the same sin as your family? The woods are full of Drake and O'Henry corpses as well as those caught between them in their feud. I had thought you better than this."

I closed my eyes, half expecting Alex's words to get us killed. When I opened them, I was surprised by Lucien putting his gun away. Gerald and Deana reluctantly did the same, Deana putting her rifle over her shoulder.

"No," Lucien said. "I am going to kill Judy Doe, though."

"Like hell you are," I said, taking a step forward.

Deana stepped forward herself. She conjured yet another ball of water but this one turned into a sword made of ice that hovered in the air. Huh. That was actually pretty cool. A lot more intimidating than her usual water-balloon attacks.

"You're not going to kill Mrs. Doe," Emma said, looking between us.

"Thanks, Emma," I said, glad to have her backing me up.

"You're being manipulated," Alex said, looking between them. "The Big Bad Wolf is almost certainly the party who informed you of this fact. It wants to disrupt our attempts to rescue Jane's family. By making you our enemy, we'll be more inclined to turn you over."

I tried to understand the logic behind that but failed. Then again, I wasn't a vengeance obsessed demonic spirit out to resurrect his family. It did point to the Big Bad Wolf knowing we were planning on a double cross, though. I just prayed it didn't fall upon my family. I loved all of them despite the lies.

"Stand in my way and I'll kill you," Lucien said, walking up his brother. "I've grown more powerful than you…"

I stared at him. "Can possibly imagine?"

Lucien stopped mid-sentence. "Dammit, you've got me doing it."

"I'm not going to let you hurt my mother," I said.

"Like you could stop me," Lucien said, his face returning to normal. "Come on, Alex, take your best shot. You're only human and playing in the game of gods."

Seconds later, Lucien was flying through the air and landing on top of the Millennium Falcon's hood. I hadn't even seen Alex move but knew he'd given him a punch that would have put Mike Tyson to shame. Deana and Gerald went for their guns again. Clearly, that little display of bravado hadn't gone the way they'd expected it to.

I pulled out the Merlin Gun that glowed in their presence. I moved the gun between the two. I saw Gerald waking up as a vampire and slaughtering his parents as well as being unable to control himself during several feedings while his creator exalted in the former doctor's pain. I saw Deana committing war crimes on behalf of the government, gunning down villagers and burning fields until she'd discovered her bosses weren't the US government but a corporation wrapping itself in

233

the flag. "This gun thinks both of you deserve to die. It hungers for your deaths."

Emma had already changed into her dire wolf form and was growling at the pair. "I will kill you both! No one hurts Jane and lives!"

Aww, that was sweet of her, also creepy.

I made the mistake of trying to read the gun and that almost caused me to drop it. Drop it and scream. My mind was overloaded with images of battlefields where winged humans were impaled on adamantine spikes, epic monsters battling it out in Eden-like fields, and spirits being stripped of their forms before being cast in a great darkness. A great darkness they filled with the nightmares of souls so they'd have something to occupy themselves with. The Merlin Gun kept me from dropping it, forcing me to tighten my grip but it removed any doubt that this gun was inhabited by an angel. An angel who thirsted for blood. Which made me wonder which side it was on in the Great Rebellion I'd seen a glimpse of.

THE RIGHT SIDE, the words spoken in a conversational tone which, nevertheless, boomed in my skull. *NEVER DOUBT IT.*

"Dial it down," I whispered to the gun. "No one has to die here."

BUT THEY SHOULD.

"Less talking," I said to the gun. "More threatening."

Emma and Alex both cast me a sideways glance.

Gerald surprised me by putting his gun on the ground while Deana hesitated to go for her weapon.

"The gun is right," Gerald said, his voice filled with remorse and self-loathing. "To be a vampire is damned. I merely wish company and friendship until the Angel of Death claims me."

"Shut up," Deana said, almost hissing. "Everything I did was justified. I did what I had to do."

LIES, the gun whispered.

I was suddenly less confident about wielding this weapon.

Gerald looked at her with pity in his eyes. "I used to tell myself that too. It helped for a time."

Lucien climbed off the top of my car and walked twenty feet back to us. I really hoped he hadn't damaged anything permanent, because it was going to be hell getting it fixed on my salary. "Okay, that was a lucky shot."

"Don't make me do anything you'd regret," I said, really wishing I trusted the others enough to put my gun away. "This thing has a mind of its own. I'm not kidding."

Deana stared. "I could fill your lungs with water before you even tried."

"Then my brother would kill you or Emma or both," Lucien said. "Or I would. No one dies without permission. Now put down your weapon."

Deana finally put her gun on the ground. "This is a bad idea."

I had a vision, perhaps sparked by the Merlin Gun's previous revelation, of Deana being recruited by Lucien. He'd gone after the mercenaries who'd killed his clan and torn them apart like Liam Neeson in *Taken*. At the end of the vision, Deana had been ready to die only for Lucien to spare her. That gave me hope this could be resolved peacefully. I didn't want to hurt Lucien, let alone kill him to protect my mother from the consequences of her actions.

"It is a bad idea," Lucien said, trusting us about as much as we trusted him. "But I want answers, not corpses."

"Like why we didn't tell you?" I asked. "I dunno, maybe because *she's my mother*."

Lucien's eyes turned a reptilian yellow as he glared at me. "Your mother is a murderer."

"Yes, so are you, Smaug," I said, not aiming the Merlin Gun at him.

"What about you, Alex?" Lucien said. "My own kin by spirit if not blood."

"I had my reasons," Alex said, not flinching as he stared into his eyes. "But I've never been obligated to help you avenge your family. To spill more blood and taint yourself further. I would have helped you bring them in, but you've already killed too many."

"Not until they're all dead!" Lucien growled, flame shooting from his mouth that almost reached Alex's face.

Strangely, the gun didn't feel any compulsion to aim itself at Lucien. I got the impression that the spirit within didn't feel like any of the murders he'd committed were unjustified. That bothered me as I realized it wouldn't help me protect my mother. As far as the Merlin Gun was concerned, killing her would be justice. Maybe it would be but that didn't matter. She was my family and I'd do anything to protect her.

"If the Big Bad Wolf kills Judy Doe then you will never get your revenge," Alex said, surprising me with his next words. "You also have an obligation to meet. The Red Wolf killed Victoria O'Henry, Courtney Waters, Rudy Gonzales, and others in your service. You've always claimed you looked out for your people. Well, now is the chance to prove it. Which is more important, avenging your dead family, or the people who pledged themselves to you? One of who is still alive."

I was pretty sure, in my case, the answer would be avenging my family. It sounded like a pretty stupid argument to me, unless I was talking to Ned Stark. I mean, seriously, gang members were not the kind of people who took oaths of loyalty seriously. Organized crime was a pyramid scheme where obligation went up, not down.

Strangely, though, Lucien stopped talking and frowned. It looked like he was seriously considering Alex's words. "Dragons are defined by their oaths. Our word is binding in a way humans cannot understand."

"I doubt that," Alex said. "Dragons are human. However, I know you hold your word to mean more than other humans'."

"I vowed to avenge my family," Lucien said, seemingly cutting off further negotiation. "However, when Jeremy Doe vowed to work for my organization, he came under my protection. So did the others, and I failed them. I will help you liberate him and destroy the Big Bad Wolf then I'm going to go after Judy."

"Oh hell no," I said, glaring at him. "You touch my mother and you're dead."

"So be it," Lucien said, not looking at me. "It would be your right."

I was about to yell at him when I heard a shout in the air followed by seeing two glowing bolts of energy fly through the air. "Feather attack!"

The glowing bolts, which I saw to be feathers, slammed into Lucien's back and he was staggered by the attack before another two bolts sailed into Deana, causing her to fall to one knee. That was when she went for her M16.

Gerald, instead, moved faster than anyone I'd ever seen and appeared behind Maria, who was standing behind Lucien's group. There was a brown bag full of liquor bottles at her feet. Gerald grabbed Maria with a headlock and said, "Do not struggle."

Deana looked ready to fire anyway before Lucien pushed her gun down to the ground.

"No killing!" Lucien shouted, his face turning green and scaly as claws grew from his fingers. "Not unless I say so."

Deana said something in a language I didn't recognize but I suspected was telling him to do an anatomically impossible action.

"Maria!" I said, ready to shoot Gerald in the face and anyone else who stood in my way of rescuing her.

"I saw you were in trouble so I tried to rescue you!" Maria said, faking cheer. "Yeah, I'm not doing that again."

"Smart move," I said, wondering if this was going to end up as a bloodbath regardless.

"Join us in freeing Jane's mother and let us duel afterward," Alex said, his voice calm and composed.

Duel? Was he serious?

"If I win?" Lucien said.

"Then I'll be dead," Alex said. "If I win, you'll leave Judy Doe and her family alone for the rest of their lives and beyond."

Lucien stared at him then looked away. "Very well. We have an accord. Gerald, let her go."

Gerald did so. "I only took her hostage to keep Deana from killing her."

Maria felt her throat and coughed. "This is why crows don't try to be heroes. It never works out well."

"We are now allies," Alex said, offering his hand.

Lucien shook it then turned to me.

I, reluctantly, did so. "Our date is off."

"So I gathered," Lucien said. "A shame."

Emma turned to me and cocked her wolf's head to one side before speaking in her inappropriately cute voice, "Is it just me or did we step into *Game of Thrones* when I wasn't looking?"

"Apparently," I said. "Man, Jeremy is going to kick himself for not being involved."

Maria snorted. "He would have attacked and gotten us all killed."

"Like you?" I asked.

"Hush, you."

"People have a real problem with me killing people today," Deana said, hanging her gun on her back with its strap. "I don't like it."

"Nor should you," Lucien said, turning back to us. "However, we should save our anger for the Big Bad Wolf."

Yeah.

Alex pulled out his cellphone. "Apparently, the Big Bad Wolf had another method of weakening us before the final fight than sending you to attack us."

I did a double take. "What do you mean?"

Alex pointed out to the sky as the clouds had parted, only to reveal the night sky rather than daytime. "It's eleven thirty at night. We have less than half an hour to get to the lumber mill before they're sacrificed. Knife or no knife."

Damn frigging demons!

CHAPTER TWENTY-NINE

Thankfully, the old lumber mill was only about ten minutes away by Millennium Falcon and the customized red Hummer-looking vehicle Lucien drove (of course he would drive something like that—it was practically the successful drug dealer's vehicle of choice).

Unfortunately, the road was washed out, so the last mile of our journey had to be done on foot. I didn't have difficulty because I had a pair of hiking boots in my car while Emma took her dire wolf form again. Maria assumed the form of a crow that fluttered from treetop to treetop.

Alex and Lucien walked up behind me even as I wondered if I should turn into a deer to get there faster. I wasn't about to abandon them, though, due to the fact I needed serious backup. Even so, every minute felt like an eternity.

"Why would the Big Bad Wolf affect our time?" I asked, finally sick of just trudging along in silence. "How the hell does it even do that?"

"It may be no longer entirely in control of its mind, if it ever was," Alex suggested. "It's merged into a gestalt with Victoria with Clara as their mutual puppet. Part of it may want us to bring the sacrificial knife in order to bring back its children while another might wish us to fail so they don't lose their special place in the Big Bad Wolf's heart."

"No points for guessing which is which," Lucien said.

"It's just a theory," Alex suggested.

"Back to the whole idea it might reverse time if it wins and kill us problem," I said, deciding to stay on track.

"The Spirit World exists outside time but block time is objectively correct so while it can move our perception of time forward or slow it down, it can't actually reverse time. It can also superimpose the Spirit World's physical reality on certain locations to make reality more mutable. It's basically the same things humans do with magic but with more oomph," Alex explained.

Or tried to.

"Did anyone get that?" I asked, completely confused by what he just said.

Emma nodded. "Yeah, he said it can't reverse time and it can make things weird."

"Thank you!" I said, glad I had Emma as my science coach. I could kick the crap out of her at math, though.

"Vampires have a similar thing but we can only affect our own personal auras," Gerald said. "It's why we appear so fast."

"Weredeer just are really quick," I said, simplifying things. "No need for magic."

"Except you turn into deer and have no use for biology," Alex said. "Spirit imposing itself on flesh and then back again. The laws of reality proving bendable."

"Uh-huh."

"Reality works like *The Matrix*," Maria said, fluttering down on top of Emma's wolf head. "There is no spoon."

"Get off of me," Emma said.

"But we'd make such a great team," Maria said, flapping her wings. "You can stand in front of me when dangerous things are occurring and I could not die!"

"As long as the sequels aren't involved in this explanation, I've got you," I said, lying. I was clearly going to have to re-orientate my worldview if I wanted to make a go at being a shaman.

Unlearn! Unlearn!

"I'm just glad I don't have to worry about what you guys do," Deana said, saying the first nice thing I've heard from her since meeting the elemental. "Creating water and controlling it is as natural to me as breathing."

"Water tribe!" Emma said, still sporting Maria's raven form on her head.

"I have no idea what that means," Deana said.

"So why are you involved in all this, Gerald? I would have thought you wouldn't want anything to do with this business," I said, calculating we only had a few hundred yards until we reached the mill. Which was good since we were rapidly running out of time.

"Sheriff Clara is my friend," Gerald said, surprising me. "I may have lost my position at the sheriff's department regardless but I will see her restored. I'm still an exile to the vampires in New Detroit, so I also require a patron to survive out here. I am not so powerful a vampire to be able to live without protection."

"Really, I thought all of you guys were super-strong badasses," I said. "Except for the sunlight, stake through the heart, crosses—"

Gerald snorted. "That's the problem right there. Everyone knows the weaknesses of vampires. The Old Ones of our kind hate the young and fear being displaced since only another Old One or an exceptionally powerful mage or shifter can destroy them. Thus they have a vested interest in destroying us while we're weak. New ones are still constantly made but few reach old age. Most die long before they would have died as humans."

"And Lucien is your boss now?" I asked.

"Yes," Gerald said. "I have promised him fealty in exchange for protection. I also am going to be able to work in the free clinic he's set up in the Outlands. It will be a chance to save lives rather than take them."

I didn't know if my next question would be taken as rude but I had to ask it anyway. "Is it safe to be a vampire doctor in a clinic?"

"Sometimes," Gerald said, ominously. "I have enslaved my will to the dragon, though. It's as close to a guarantee I will not kill unless he orders me to."

"People are sheep," Deana said, shaking her head. "A few less won't make any difference."

"Real bunch of winners you've got here Lucien," Maria said, flying to my shoulder. "Totally not a bunch of vicious killers."

"Revenge requires a special skill set," Lucien said. "So does victory."

Honestly, I couldn't imagine it would be that difficult for Lucien to just march up to Pinehold, turn into a dragon, and eat Marcus O'Henry. He was an old wolf now and Alex had kicked his ass earlier so it couldn't be that difficult. Of course, Alex had kicked Lucien's ass today too, but that wasn't in full dragon form either. Still, I wondered what he was waiting for? Was he really interested in some sort of crazy *Count of Monte Cristo* plot? Because if that was the case Emma's livelihood was at stake.

I wasn't able to say anything more because I'd misjudged the distance to the Drake Lumber Mill and we passed through a set of trees to something that looked like it was off the set of a big budget horror movie. The Drake Lumber Mill was a five-story-tall concrete building with rusted metal roofs and hundreds of broken windows. It was massive, stretching across the horizon with five-foot-tall weeds and grass blocking out all entrances.

The horror movie element was the fact every single one of those windows was pulsating with the same red light which had glowed within the Lodge, except it was much darker here now. The light seemed to pulsate like a heartbeat and with the color of blood. The siren was present too, but fading in and out in a way I had to strain to hear. That would have been something I could take as a positive sign except for all the flesh monsters.

Yes, I said flesh monsters.

They were hideous to look upon with bodies that were grafted out of multiple corpses both animal as well as human. They were naked and sexless, crawling on all fours (or sixes or eights) up and down the side of the building like spiders. Many of them had tails like Lucien did in his dragon form while others sported wolf heads or those of stags. I saw at least one grab a bird out of the air with an eight-foot-long tongue that was impossible for its size.

"What *the hell* are those?" I asked, cocking my head to one side. "When did we wander into *Resident Evil*?"

"The Damned," Alex said, closing his eyes. "The Red Wolf does not trust our presence so it has summoned the tortured spirits from its realm into physical reality. Those bodies are things it's made of animal, human, and other flesh."

"Where the hell did he get the bodies?" I asked, my mind violently rejecting the possibility my family would be among them.

"The purge of my clan," Lucien said, staring down. "Those are spirits he's trapped and tortured."

"You don't know that," Alex said, his voice not sounding entirely certain. "He'd have to have expended most of what the sacrifices offered to him have given him. Even then, he'd have given up even more of his old self. To become almost completely a creature of Hell."

"I don't care," Lucien said, becoming the gigantic crocodile he had earlier except even larger. It was the kind of thing people might look at and think, instantly, *dragon* rather than a scary-ass swamp-dwelling predator. That was when Lucien shouted to the air with an accompanying blast of flame, "Demon, I come for my people!"

"Your people?" I asked, looking at him sideways.

The Big Bad Wolf responded by laughing with Victoria's voice and it echoing in my mind. "I did not come here to listen to you, sacrifice. You, Lucien of the Drake family, are coinage that is no longer currency. Did you never think your movements were directed by a higher power? I felt your need for vengeance and whispered to you with your parents' voices when you returned to Bright Falls. You built your empire out of hate, but it was not to your ends but mine. To give me access to the materials I needed."

"Lies!" Lucien roared, his voice becoming feral and animal-like, which didn't normally happen when shapeshifters transformed.

"Are they?" the Big Bad Wolf spoke. "Why, then, have you hesitated claiming your revenge? Your will was weak and you were disgusted by the murders you committed against Deana's unit. You spared her not because you wanted her help finding your family's killers but because you hated what you'd done. Why else do you think you went to Jane and your brother? When I told you of Judy's involvement, you could have gone to her house and massacred her family. A fitting revenge. You, instead, wanted to be talked out of it."

Lucien's eyes burned every bit as much as the fire in his stomach.

I hadn't thought of that. Pulling out the Merlin Gun from my back pocket, I fired it in the air and immediately regretted wasting the bullet. "Listen here, Beelzewolf, I've just had enough about you screwing with my life. If what you say is true, compassion isn't a weakness. It's a strength. You were the one broken by your family's death! You were the weak one who couldn't move on! Almost everyone involved is dead and you're cowardly going after their children and grandchildren!"

"Jane, don't taunt the monster," Maria said, having gone completely rigid on my shoulder. "It's a really bad idea."

I didn't stop, though. "Most of those people weren't there to hurt your family, either! It wasn't a lynch mob. Yeah, they were racist jackasses, but there was only one person who attacked your family and he died that night! You avenged your family but you couldn't let go of your hate so you've ruined this town and its spirits. Hell, you ruined Victoria and you claim to love her. You may be a god but you are the most pathetic, infantile, murderous piece-of-crap gods I have ever heard of! Oh and you let the kelpie kill children, so screw you for that too!"

The siren disappeared and the red light went out in the lumber mill. All of the flesh monsters proceeded to climb through windows and holes in the roof, disappearing from sight. That was when the entire area started shaking and trees started falling over. An earthquake registering at least a few points on the Richter scale was occurring all around us.

"I think it's safe to say you've offended it," Alex said, looking around before picking up a stick and drawing a circle around us in the mud. It wasn't large enough to accommodate all of Lucien's form as his tail and mouth went over it.

"Good," I said, before realization I might have condemned my parents to a horrible death washed over me.

Oh, why couldn't I keep my big mouth shut!

The entire forest was then bathed in the brightest red light I'd seen yet. Like the vision of the past, I saw my family sitting down tied up in the center of the lumber mill next to a bunch of old saw blades. They were covered in sweat, their clothes dirty, and there was a nasty silver burn on the side of my father's face. Jeanine's clothes had been torn so her bra was still visible and she looked like she'd thrown up on herself before she was gagged.

My mother had an inverted pentacle drawn on her forehead in blood. I suspected it was designed to keep her from using her powers. Jeremy, by contrast, was just staring forward with a dead look in his eyes. Harvey Chang was standing over them with a silver chain wrapped around his right fist. I could smell the verbena it had been soaked in, something which worked on shapeshifters like acid even as the silver prevented it from healing properly.

"Now they will die," Victoria said, her voice echoing in my mind. "Your fault."

"No," I whispered.

That was when Dave walked up toward them, as if in a trance, and lifted up a hunting rifle to Jeanine's head. Except he stopped in mid-step and didn't pull the trigger. I blinked and heard the entire forest had gone quiet. The vision seemed frozen in place but so did everything else.

"What the?" I asked, turning to my side and seeing my group looked every bit as confused as I did.

Except for Alex. Alex was holding up the lighter he'd bought at Kim Su's. "This was used to give a dying soldier one last cigarette by his lover in the platoon during Vietnam. It contains a minute of time. Go."

"Can't the Big Bad Wolf affect time?" Emma asked, looking up.

"Yes," Alex said, trembling. "I am putting everything I have into holding it into place."

"Let me help," Lucien growled. "Please."

"You're needed," Alex said. "Because the monsters will come soon. I have seen it. I may die, I may not. My foresight is crap. Go Jane, save your family. The others will cover you."

I felt an overwhelming sense of gratitude as well as relief. I shouldn't have, since it was very possible this would get Alex killed. I wouldn't let that happen. I would make sure everybody lived. Somehow.

"You really are a miracle worker, Alex." I focused on transforming into the biggest, toughest-looking doe imaginable. That result wasn't that intimidating, but I would take it over my normal deer form.

"Not even close," Alex whispered under his breath.

I took off as fast as I could for the lumber mill, making it impossible for him to hear the next part of my statement. It was possibly the last words I'd ever exchange with the beautiful FBI agent. Even so, just about everyone else followed and while they didn't move as quickly, I knew they were coming to fight with me.

We were going to slay the monster.

Or die trying.

CHAPTER THIRTY

I smashed through a wooden door by kicking it open with hooves that had the strength of several men before lowering my head and walking into the lumber mill. The sights and smells that greeted me on the other side assaulted my senses, making me nauseous.

The Big Bad Wolf's spirit realm and physical reality had merged here, even more so than in the Lodge. The walls bled profusely from every crack and tear in the concrete while I felt the sides exhale like lungs before breathing in fetid air from an invisible swamp. Apparently, Alex wasn't strong enough to stop everything from moving and I prayed to God and Goddess both that that still applied to my family.

The machinery was twisted and deformed like a Rube Goldberg device (or *Mouse Trap* if you remember the board game). The saw blades hung from string all around like wind-chimes while conveyor belts moved up and down in twisting patterns. Some hung from the ceiling while others led nowhere.

"So..." I said, frantically searching for my family. "*Silent Hill* rather than *Resident Evil*."

The flesh monsters were frozen in place all about, staring in every direction with no sign of awareness. On the second floor, overlooking the blood and sawdust soaked floor was a beautiful woman in a slit black evening dress. It took me a second to recognize Sheriff O'Henry dressed up in Victoria's homecoming dress. She had her hair up, was wearing jewelry, and had makeup on too. I had to reevaluate my opinion about her looks since she was quite fetching dressed up, even if Alice still blew her away.

The Big Bad Wolf turned to me. "You should have brought me the knife, little girl."

"Who said I didn't?" I said, having put it in my back pocket. "I'm just not going to let you have it."

The Big Bad Wolf screamed and I was blanketed by a chilling cold. I would have found it hilarious, the Big Bad Wolf actually able to huff and puff to blow people's houses down, but it didn't seem terribly funny right now.

Ignoring the breath even as it caused frost to appear on my flank, I jumped on top of one of the conveyor belts before jumping to another in a game of leap frog before getting around them to see where my parents were held. The image was identical to the one the Big Bad Wolf had projected into my mind. Dave was aiming his gun at a terrified-looking Jeanine while Harvey stood over them, ready to beat them some more with silver. I charged toward them, only to see time resume its progression.

Dave aimed at Jeanine's head. "Goodbye, pretty deer lady!"

"No!" I screamed.

"FEATHER ATTACK!" Maria cried out again, flying over my head and hitting Dave in the face with two of her glowing feathers.

The crow's magic caused Dave to fall backward before Harvey pulled out a .45 caliber Magnum, aiming it at my father's head. I slammed into him, head first, and sent the deputy flying through the air and against the wall. I didn't know if I'd killed the man, but didn't particularly care in that moment.

Back at the front of the lumber mill, I could hear the rest of my group arrive and the most grisly of sounds echoed. The flesh monsters were attacking with both Lucien as well as Emma engaged in battle with them. I also heard the sound of gunfire. That told me Deana and Gerald were fighting too. A part of me was terrified that Emma was going to get herself killed. She wasn't a trained fighter and was doing this all for me. I had to suck it up and focus on getting my family to safety. Transforming back to human form, I ran to Judy and cut her bonds first. I ended up using the sacrificial knife, which felt like a terrible idea, but I didn't have much choice.

"I am so angry at you right now," I said, shaking my head before pulling her gag out. "Are you okay?"

"Destroy the seal!" Judy shouted.

I was about to rub off the blood off her forehead when another gust of wind struck us. It sent me flying through the air along with my siblings and parents. The ice cold air blasted my face and arms before we landed with a *thud* against the wall behind us. I was terrified of them having been impaled on a saw blade or piece of jagged metal but saw everyone was alright, though Jeanine was screaming something at me from behind her gag. I cut her bonds then handed her the knife before stepping over their bodies and going to face the monster that had attacked us.

I saw her.

Or, more precisely, it.

The Big Bad Wolf had manifested fully and appeared as a giant nine-foot-tall glowing-eyed monster. It didn't actually look like a wolf that much anymore. Instead, it was a kind of horrific sallow-skinned, tumor-ridden, thing that just so happened to be vaguely canine. Alex was right using all of its magic to warp its surroundings had mangled the god badly. It reminded me of—and I couldn't believe I was thinking of this right now—Tolkien's description of Morgoth. The Valar had expended so much of its essence to corrupt the land that it was no longer remotely what it once was. What it was, though, was still damned intimidating.

I lifted up the Merlin Gun. "Go ahead, make my day."

WITH OUR COMBINED STRENGTH, WE SHALL DESTROY IT. The Merlin Gun's thoughts filled my head and they were all of bloodshed as well as destruction. I also felt it gathering energy; that meant the Merlin Gun probably wasn't capable of killing it outright.

"I'd slit the throats of every one of you," Victoria's voice spoke, except it sounded like she had a mouthful of gravel. "I shall not stop after you are dead. I will sacrifice the descendants of every single person involved in the massacre of my beloved. I shall become more than I ever was and lift my children to godhood."

Emma bolted past one of the conveyor belts beside it and came up beside me, still in wolf form. "Victoria, no! You don't want to do this!"

"I think we're a little past that," I said, only now remembering we were supposed to take the Big Bad Wolf down without killing Clara.

SHE IS A NECESSARY CASUALTY OF WAR.

Shut up, Gabriel.

I AM NOT EVEN CLOSE TO HIS POWER.

The Big Bad Wolf stared down at Emma and took a step forward. "You betrayed me! You have led my enemies here to kill me!"

"We're not your enemies!" Emma howled.

That was a lie, but one I wasn't going to correct her on.

"Jeremy loves you!" Emma said. "Jeanine loves our brother even though he's being a dick. You're possessing Clara and making her into a monster! Don't you see this thing is every bit as bad as Grandpa?"

There was a flicker of hesitation as the Big Bad Wolf seemed to stumble for a moment and I blinked, surprised Victoria had that much control. I was also surprised that Emma's words had managed to reach her.

"I don't hate you!" Emma said, capitalizing on her advantage. "I know what you did for me now! Clara can help you! We can help you!"

The Big Bad Wolf put an enormous paw over its snout as if struggling with something inside it. Then its eyes lifted up and they were glowing red with hatred.

"Uh-oh," I said, the Merlin Gun screaming at me to fire but I couldn't.

Wouldn't.

That was when the Big Bad Wolf brought its enormous paw around and knocked us into the air. I think Victoria and Clara were fighting back, since otherwise we would have been crushed underneath it.

"I am the Earth and the North Wind's own child!" the Big Bad Wolf shouted. "The ground beneath me is my flesh and the trees my fur!"

I stood up despite the fact that I felt like my leg was broken and would need another minute or two to heal. I clenched my teeth due to the pain but stared at the monster anyway. "Yeah, well, right now you have a face only a mother could love. How does she feel about you being a murderous piece of garbage?"

The Big Bad Wolf roared and would have charged me, except that Lucien smashed through the conveyor belts behind me and latched his enormous gator jaws around the demon's neck. The dragon breathed flames all across it, clawing and mauling its side. The fact that it was technically Clara in there didn't make me feel bad about it.

KILL IT, the Merlin Gun commanded.

"Can you help me drive it out?" I said, wishing to God I had some magical support here. I'd been hoping to get Judy's help. "We can save Clara and kill this thing. Maybe even free Victoria's soul. There has to be something not skanky-evil about her if my brother liked her. Probably."

My leg's bones popped back into place.

Goddess and God dammit!

I DO NOT PROTECT, I ONLY PUNISH.

"Great," I said, growling. "No wonder Alex left you."

The gun grew very hot in my hand and I briefly wondered if it was going to reject me. The gun started to cool, which made me think snark didn't rank very highly on its list of sins. Unfortunately, as I debated what to do next, Lucien was thrown from the Big Bad Wolf's back and knocked away by an enormous paw. He landed right beside my mother, who was free and now carrying the sacrificial knife.

Oh no.

"If I give you this son of the Drake family, will you let my family go and trouble this land no more?" Judy said, lifting up the knife underneath Lucien's throat.

Lucien turned back into a human in response, only for her to grab him in a headlock and hold the knife steady.

The Big Bad Wolf looked over at her. "Yes. We have an accord. I have no wish to see you or your insolent offspring ever again."

"No!" I screamed.

"It's for the greater good, honey!" Judy called over.

I lifted up the Merlin Gun and aimed it at her. It glowed bright and hot and I knew it recognized her for what she was. "He came here to save Jeremy and Jeanine! Shamans are supposed to protect people!"

Judy stared at me then looked at Lucien, who was keeping his eyes closed and his throat exposed, then dropped the dagger before stepping away.

"I'm sorry, Jane. I..."

"Shut up," I said, having lost virtually all respect I had for my mother in an instant. "Grandpa Jacob would be so disappointed in you."

I wish I hadn't said that but it was true. The Merlin Gun stopped wanting to kill her, though.

"Pity," The Big Bad Wolf said. "The dagger is mine, though."

I threw down the Merlin Gun and stared at him before shouting, "Get out!"

The Big Bad Wolf's form shimmered a second and some of the tumors on its body disappeared. "You are not strong enough. You will be less strong once I have frozen you solid and shattered your remains."

"Get out!" Jeanine shouted, having managed to get herself free.

"Get out!" Emma shouted, having no magic except what she was born with, but joining her power to ours anyway.

"I also say get out," Maria said, standing in raven form on top of one of the rafters. "By the way, I'm converting from your worship. You suck as a god, like Jane said. I'm thinking of trying Unitarianism."

"Get out," Judy said, whispering. "You have ruined enough lives."

The Big Bad Wolf gradually became something much more wolf-like until it was a beautiful shining red-and-black lupus that shrank to the size of Emma's form. It was visibly in pain and I saw its eyes continue to glow. The Big Bad Wolf was still inside her.

I picked up the Merlin Gun and walked toward the demon-possessed wolf. "Victoria, I know we've never been friends. Hell, I didn't like you before you were possessed, but you are stronger than this thing. Protect your sister one last time."

The much-smaller wolf spirit was pulled from Clara's body by a ragged-looking translucent-white Victoria dressed in the homecoming gown I'd seen their host in earlier. Her mascara was smeared and there were red claw marks all across what I could only assume was her soul. The Big Bad Wolf was fighting her, but reacting more like a cat that didn't want to be put in a crate than a god.

I aimed the Merlin Gun at the monster. "I'm sorry, Vicky."

"Just shoot it," Victoria said.

I pulled the trigger and the glowing bullet passed into the Big Bad Wolf's side as Victoria's ghost faded away into a bright light. There was a look of profound relief on her face and I hoped Heaven worked like *Return of the Jedi* with last-minute repentance being a way in.

NOT MY DEPARTMENT, the Merlin Gun said.

The Big Bad Wolf didn't die immediately, hissing and thrashing on the ground while the wound glowed a brilliant orange hue. I lifted the Merlin Gun and fired again into the side of its head. Because it was a spirit, a headshot didn't do any more damage than a shot elsewhere would have, but it caused the monster to scream out. No great gusts of wind or frozen air came out this time, just a small cloud of ice. I walked over and pressed the gun right between the monster's eyes. The third bullet did it. A good thing, because I only had two left. The lumber mill shook and all of the gravity-defying weirdness around us vanished, transforming the place into just another junked-up abandoned building. The air lost its foul stench and a great spiritual weight I hadn't even realized was there vanished.

"Ding dong, the wolf is dead," I said, not exactly feeling like celebrating.

JUSTICE IS SATISFIED, the Merlin gun spoke. AWAKEN ME AGAIN ONLY WHEN THERE IS SOMETHING WORTHY OF DESTROYING.

"You got it, chief," I said, intending to put it in a box and bury it in the woods with hopes of never seeing it again.

"Jane—" Judy started to say.

I raised my hand. "I think it's best you communicate through Dad for the next, I dunno, awhile."

Lucien climbed to his feet and walked past me. "Everyone is all right. I'm linked to my people. Gerald and Deana are wounded but will heal."

"And Alex?" I asked, terrified that my beautiful FBI agent was dead.

"Fine," Lucien said, not bothering to look at Judy. "You should take him out for cherry pie."

I didn't comment on the fact he was a lot more of an honorable person than my mother had proven to be. That made me more inclined to overlook the fact he was a drug dealer. "What about Judy?"

Lucien looked back at my siblings staring at Judy in confused horror. "We've done enough."

EPILOGUE

Marcus O'Henry's office was nice enough that if it wasn't inhabited by a complete monster, I might have dragged a sleeping bag into it and lived there. It was larger than many apartments, with enormous bookshelves along the wall, lush green carpet, and a huge antique oak desk covered in paperwork. The crowning part of it, though, was it had a gorgeous glass window view of the town's titular shining white falls. My ears were capable of hearing their rush down from the cliff face Pinehold was built over even though the window was designed to be soundproof.

The Old Wolf himself was sitting behind his desk with a pen and writing on a yellow pad. He was wearing a white button-down shirt, suspenders, and a pair of glasses which told me the Gordon Gecko look was deliberate. I supposed that made him a literal Wolf of Wall Street. Marcus didn't seem particularly troubled by the week's events and didn't acknowledge me when I opened the door to walk in.

I was wearing a pair of jeans and a pink t-shirt with a white stag on the front. Beneath it, it said, "Got Deer?", which I assumed was a bad joke about the stag being horny (ouch, I didn't mean to make that pun). I wasn't dressed up for work and my future at Pinehold washing dishes was uncertain despite the fact I was even gladder to be out of my parents' house. I'd left behind the Merlin Gun even if I hadn't yet gone through with my plan to bury it.

"Shouldn't security be escorting you out?" Marcus finally said.

"Amazing what you can get past when you're best friends with the boss's granddaughter and claiming you're delivering a sympathy card."

Marcus reached over to the phone. "Well, I'm going to tell them you delivered it and to escort you from the premises. I'm also pleased to tell you that your services are no longer—"

"I know," I said, my voice low and cold.

Marcus paused. "Know what?"

I scrunched up my brow. "You know, I've been thinking a lot about what happened. So much that it kept me up at night. Victoria, the Big Bad Wolf, the sacrifices, and all that. I couldn't quite figure out how to make it all fit."

"Life is funny that way," Marcus said, his canines exaggerating as his eyes became predatory and doglike.

"The big question for me was why was Victoria in the woods to begin with? I knew Vicki before she turned into the mean girl she became her senior year and while we were never friends, I knew she'd never take her stilettos out into the woods voluntarily. Certainly not the Darkwater Preserve when she had all of this nice hotel land to run around."

"What are you implying?"

"You sent her to the Big Bad Wolf," I said, my voice dripping with disdain. "You weren't able to deliver Lucien and his family to the demon ten years ago. I don't know what you were offered in exchange for it, maybe it was just ending the curse on the town, but the fact you tried it meant you had some sort of deal set up. Then I thought about the resurrection plan which it mentioned. Nature spirits don't think about that sort of thing, even when they're being corrupted. Someone would have had to put that in its head."

"Black magic is very dangerous but not uncommon if you know the right people," Marcus said, giving a half-smile. "The children probably would have risen as some sort of undead creatures, but I suspected it was past the point of caring."

"That's another reason why you persecuted all but the Cervid magicians in town," I said, nodding. "You're a shaman too."

He laughed. "Wizard. I don't pray to any god but myself."

"You are willing to make deals with them, though," I said. "You screwed up your end of the bargain and didn't want to risk its wrath by going back. You reconsidered when you saw Victoria grow up and start to look like your sister. You sent her into the woods as an offering. Your own flesh and blood."

"My brother's flesh and blood," Marcus corrected. "Victoria is my great-great grandniece, the same as her sister and brother. Enough that I'm willing to let them wander around the hotel, but not so much that they aren't expendable to my dynasty. I'd claim your sister as my true offspring but she, sadly, showed her mother's traits."

Wow, he was a real piece of work. "The demon claimed your daughter, though, and tried to enact the same plan as before. You couched Victoria through all of this in exchange for not hurting Emma anymore."

"A small price to pay." Marcus leaned back in his chair and removed his glasses. "I even managed to convince her to get vampire blood to provide me with a bit of a boost in my old age. Enough that I don't have to worry about any challenges from younger wolves when I attend the Moonmoots. The rest of the drugs she sold allowed me to maintain plausible deniability that I wasn't paying for all of the magical paraphernalia she needed to try the ritual for a second time."

"Did you tell her to go after my brother?" I asked.

Marcus smirked. "It would have served your mother right, but no. I only encouraged the Red Wolf to go after the others when they balked at sacrificing others I'd picked out. Killing Lucien off in the present day was part of the plan, of course. The Dragons have oppressed the werewolves and prevented our ascension to rulership for centuries. With the Red Wolf's blessings, we might have overthrown the vampires eventually. Its death, though, at least means we don't have to deal with its temper tantrums anymore. So, in a way, you have my thanks."

Any disbelief I'd had about there being a curse on the town was dispelled by the fact every business in town was flourishing. It turned out people must have been deliberately avoiding the town until this point since it was on a straight shot to New Detroit and within traveling distance to enjoy a beautiful countryside vacation. The fact that business had been somewhat improved since the Reveal meant either the Big Bad Wolf's power hadn't been enough to ruin the entire town or his sacrifice of the Dragon Clan had bought him some reprieve—I didn't care which.

I shook my head in disbelief. "Do you know how many people have died because of your plan?"

"Apparently, I need to kill one more," Marcus said, leaping across his desk and turning into a dire wolf in one easy motion.

That was when he was sprayed in the face with verbena-spiked mace, causing him to scream. He'd forgotten I was faster than him even in human form. I'd also been prepared for him to pull something like that.

"Argh!" Marcus shouted, turning around even as I proceeded to electrocute him.

The immense dire wolf howled before I gave him three jolts, just like Rudy, before giving him a fourth for good measure.

"Security!" Marcus howled, literally, before turning back into an old man.

The doors burst open, but it wasn't his security guards who waited for him; it was Agent Timmons with a group of armed FBI agents behind him. Alex pointed his wand at the man on the ground before a flaming blade shot forth from the top, stopping just short of the agent's neck.

"Marcus O'Henry, you are under arrest for a variety of crimes ranging from attempted murder to trafficking in forbidden magic. Your Miranda rights will be read to you before interrogation, I assure you," Alex said as he dropped a pair of silver handcuffs on the floor in front of him. "Do not attempt to resist."

"You can't arrest me!" Marcus said, staring at them as he sweated from the close proximity of the pseudo-flaming sword in front of him. "I am the leader of all werewolves!"

"A title not recognized by the US government or most of the other werewolf clans in the country," I said, pulling out my cellphone. "By the way, this is much better than a wire for recording conversations. What are you, a Bond villain?"

Alice O'Henry, Clara, and Christopher O'Henry were at the door behind the FBI. I also saw Emma hanging behind them, staring down at the figure before them.

"Kill these idiots!" Marcus shouted.

Alice looked down at her father. "I suggest you refrain from those kind of threats now, Father. It won't be possible to extirpate you from this problem. They have some very special witnesses against you."

My mom, Lucien, and others. Lucien had turned over everything he'd accumulated on the O'Henrys after a lengthy shouting match with his brother about going to Pinehold to kill Marcus. The only reason he'd chosen not to, it turned out, was that the other witnesses were their own kind of vengeance. My dad wasn't happy with my mother being "forced" to testify, but it was the first step in her winning back enough of my trust that I'd ever speak to her again. I knew Jeremy and Jeanine weren't returning her calls either. Strange how isolating being a mass murderer and evil sorceress could be.

"I have immunity," Marcus said, looking between them. "All supernaturals do for the crimes of the past."

"Not for trying to kill fourteen-year-old Lucien after the purge of the Dragon Clan or for any of the other crimes you've committed since," Alex said. "Your family has been willing to cooperate with me in exchange for leaving their assets untouched and their own immunity to prosecution. That includes several federal crimes."

"You'll never make it stick."

Alex shook his head. "The federal government is considering creating more legal protection zones than New Detroit and other vampire cities. Bright Falls is earmarked for being one for shapeshifters and the removal of you will expedite that process. Both sides want you taken down. The people who view you as an enemy of their agenda and the people to whom you are now an embarrassment."

That had been the reason Alex had stayed behind in Bright Falls and talked with Victoria's father. The others too. A gift for his brother. I was glad I could be a part of it.

Even if just in a small way.

"A reservation, you mean." Marcus spat on the ground at Alex's feet. "I will burn this family to the ground before I let it be taken from me. Do you think any of you are without sin? I can get them to throw out any deal with you. They want us all dead."

"Perhaps," Alice said, her voice icy cold. "However, you have neglected your business too much. I have made many contacts with the Brotherhood of Fenris and other gangs that have members imprisoned in South Dakota's so-called Super-Pen. People you were unwilling to sully yourself by dealing with. Many have family on the outside. Husbands, wives, and children that could be well taken care of, should their loved ones do me a favor. Your stay in prison can be comfortable, Father, or it can be *short*."

Marcus growled at her. "You wouldn't dare."

Then he looked down, now looking uncertain.

"I remember the beatings and worse." Alice's eyes narrowed. A lifetime of pain, shame, and regret echoing through her next words. "I am the Alpha wolf now."

Marcus turned to Alex. "Did you hear that? She threatened me."

"I didn't hear anything," Alex said, looking to his associates. "Did you hear anything?"

"Hmm?" I said. "I turned off my cellphone's recording a while back."

Marcus, very reluctantly, put on the handcuffs then visibly deflated. That allowed the other FBI agents to examine him before leading him out of the room. The way Christopher and Clara watched him go, I couldn't help but think they were every bit as happy to see him arrested as I was.

"You can put away your lightsaber now," Alice said, going to a nearby bookshelf and pulling a bottle of bourbon out from a hidden compartment within.

"Flaming sword," Alex said, disigniting his wand and putting it back into his interior jacket pocket. "Completely different."

I smirked. "Come on, it even hums."

"I won't mess with Disney's copyright lawyers," Alex said cheerfully. His expression turned serious. "I appreciate everyone's cooperation in this."

Alice poured herself a drink in one of her father's glasses. "Don't congratulate yourself too much, G-man. The only reason you're leaving this place alive is because we owe you for avenging Victoria as well as ending the family curse. That applies to you, too, Jane."

I now regretted turning off my cellphone's recording. "How nice of you."

Alex didn't respond.

Alice took a drink of bourbon. "Getting rid of Father is also convenient, since ingesting vampire blood meant he could have been around for another fifty to sixty years. I'm not going to wait that long to be the first ruler of all shapeshifters. Don't think for a second I've forgotten that you're the enemy."

"I am only an enemy to those who hurt others," Alex said softly. "You might take this as an opportunity to reevaluate the legacy you're leaving for your family."

Alice snorted. "You're part of the federal government. The only thing keeping them from herding us all to our deaths, no deer puns intended, is money and fear. Secrecy was our best ally against the humans and eventually that's not going to be an option. Then the world will be divided up along species lines."

"I hope you're wrong," Alex said, looking at the others. "Do you believe this."

"No," Clara said. "I'm glad you did what you did. I owe you my life."

Alice shot her sister a nasty glare, apparently having expected family unity on this point.

"I don't care," Christopher said, taking Alice's bourbon away from her and taking his own drink. He was a handsome man who looked like an older version of Brad, which was kind of weird since they didn't have a close blood relationship. "My father's greed took away the one thing that mattered in my life."

"You have other children, Chris," Alice said, looking sympathetic to her brother.

"Do I?" Chris said, walking past Emma.

Emma looked devastated.

"So I guess this means I'm fired?" I said, looking over at Alice.

"No," Emma answered for her. "With Marcus gone, I have part of the hotel too. You can be the house detective."

I snorted.

"Tour guide?" Emma suggested.

Alice gave both me and Alex a withering look. "Stay out of O'Henry business, both of you. All the senators my grandfather owned are owned by me now and I have a lot of information on Washington's finest. I also have connections with the vampires. Ones my father stupidly let atrophy. Someday you will be taking orders from me and we can end this farce."

Alice O'Henry turned around, leaving only Clara and Emma. Clara looked like she hadn't slept in a week, and I couldn't blame her. I bet she would have nightmares about this event for the rest of her life. Still, seeing the way she had her arm wrapped around Emma, I couldn't help but think she was one of the good O'Henrys. That was relieving because it was clear Emma wasn't getting much support from her actual parents.

"She has got a bug up her ass about humans," I said, saying what everyone else was thinking. I looked at Alex. "Can't you arrest her for threatening a federal officer?"

"Not without damaging the case against Marcus," Alex said. "She's also right that the government isn't a friend of supernaturals. Yet. As bad as I think the criminal activity of the O'Henry family may be, I think it may be the lesser of two evils than shutting it down completely."

"Do you believe that?" I asked.

"No," Alex said softly. "However, it'll keep my brother out of trouble too. He and Alice are already talking about ways to pool their resources in making Bright Falls the Reno to New Detroit's Las Vegas.

If other people come after them, though, I won't protect them. Lucien has made his choice."

I was disappointed by that but not surprised. "So we've solved the mystery and unmasked the Big Bad. What now?"

Alex smiled and clasped his hands together. "Cherry pie and coffee, anyone?"

Jane Doe Will Return in:

AN AMERICAN WEREDEER IN MICHIGAN
Book Two of The Bright Falls Mysteries

About the Authors

C. T. Phipps is a lifelong student of horror, science fiction, and fantasy. An avid tabletop gamer, he discovered this passion led him to write and turned him into a lifelong geek. He is a regular blogger and also a reviewer for The Bookie Monster.

Bibliography

<u>Novels</u>
The Rules of Supervillainy (Supervillainy Saga #1)
The Games of Supervillainy (Supervillainy Saga #2)
The Secrets of Supervillainy (Supervillainy Saga #3)
The Kingdom of Supervillainy (Supervillainy Saga #4)
The Tournament of Supervillainy (Supervillainy Saga #5)
The Future of Supervillainy (Supervillainy Saga #6)
The Horror of Supervillainy (Supervillainy Saga #7)
Tales of Supervillainy: Cindy's Seven (Supervillainy Saga #7)

I Was a Teenage Weredeer (The Bright Falls Mysteries, Book 1)
An American Weredeer in Michigan (The Bright Falls Mysteries, Book 2)

A Nightmare on Elk Street (The Bright Falls Mysteries, Book 3)

Esoterrorism (Red Room, Vol. 1)
Eldritch Ops (Red Room, Vol. 2)
The Fall of the House (Red Room, Vol. 3)

Agent G: Infiltrator (Agent G, Vol. 1)
Agent G: Saboteur (Agent G, Vol. 2)
Agent G: Assassin (Agent G, Vol. 3)

Cthulhu Armageddon (Cthulhu Armageddon, Vol. 1)
The Tower of Zhaal (Cthulhu Armageddon, Vol. 2)

Lucifer's Star (Lucifer's Star, Vol. 1)
Lucifer's Nebula (Lucifer's Star, Vol. 2)

Straight Outta Fangton (Straight Outta Fangton, Vol. 1)
100 Miles and Vampin' (Straight Outta Fangton, Vol. 2)
Vampiraz4Life (Straight Outta Fangton, Vol. 3)

Wraith Knight (Wraith Knight, Vol. 1)
Wraith Lord (Wraith Knight, Vol. 2)
Wraith King (Wraith Knight, Vol. 3)

Dark Destiny (Dark Destiny, Vol. 1)
Destiny's Paradox (Dark Destiny, Vol. 2)

Brightblade (The Morgan Detective Agency, Book 1)

Space Academy Dropouts (The Space Academy Series, Book 1)
Space Academy Rejects (The Space Academy Series, Book 2)
Space Academy Washouts (The Space Academy Series, Book 3)

Psycho Killers in Love

Anthologies (as editor)

Blackest Knights
Blackest Spells
Tales of Capes and Cowls
Tales of the Al-Azif
Tales of Yog-Sothoth

Michael Suttkus, II, lives in Leesburg, Florida, with three cats, one of which actually likes him, and his family, with whom he fares better. When not working at a game store, he's playing games, reading science books, or otherwise being incredibly nerdy. Also writing! Because he has to feed cats whether they like him or not.

Bibliography

I Was a Teenage Weredeer (The Bright Falls Mysteries, Book 1)
An American Weredeer in Michigan (The Bright Falls Mysteries, Book 2)
A Nightmare on Elk Street (The Bright Falls Mysteries, Book 3)

Lucifer's Star (Lucifer's Star #1)
Lucifer's Nebula (Lucifer's Star #2)

Brightblade (The Morgan Detective Agency, Book 1)

Daughter of the Cyber Dragons (The Cyber Dragons Series, Book 1)
Revenge of the Cyber Dragons (The Cyber Dragons Series, Book 2)

Space Academy Dropouts (The Space Academy Series, Book 1)
Space Academy Rejects (The Space Academy Series, Book 2)
Space Academy Washouts (The Space Academy Series, Book 3)

Curious about other Crossroad Press books? Stop by our website:
http://crossroadpress.com
We offer quality writing
in digital, audio, and print formats.

Subscribe to our newsletter on the website homepage and receive a
free eBook.

www.ingramcontent.com/pod-product-compliance
Lightning Source LLC
Chambersburg PA
CBHW030119180626
46812CB00002B/476